The Darkest Place

The Darkest Place

Helen Walters

To order additional copies of this book, contact:
Xlibris
1-800-455-039
www.Xlibris.com.au
Orders@Xlibris.com.au
766976

Chapter 1

As she opened her eyes, the pain seared through her face, the light burned her eyes, and the thumping in her head shook her whole body. She lifted her head and was dizzy; the room began spinning. She lay back down again and closed her eyes. A minute passed, and she opened her eyes again. She had trouble focusing on her surroundings; she rubbed the sleep from her eyes and slowly lifted her whole body from the bed and stumbled her way to the bathroom. She leaned on the basin for support and looked in the mirror at her reflection. Her left eye was slightly blackened, her lip swollen and bloody, and her cheekbone bruised. She lowered her head and slowly took a long, deep breath. Thoughts started rushing through her head. Why was she here, and what had she done so wrong that she was being punished this way? She just didn't understand. She believed she was a good person. So why?

She pushed back off the basin and turned to the shower. The sound of the water rushing from the showerhead provided instant relief. She stepped into the shower and let the perfectly warm water wash away the sins of the night before; the smell of shampoo for a minute eased her pain. The suds ran down her body, and the water soothed the aches. This was her alone time, and she cherished every moment. When she was done, she turned off the faucet, stepped out of the shower, and wrapped herself in a paper-thin towel and dried herself. Every stroke hurt; she found that every bruise and every sharp pain reminded her how her life had turned out.

After getting dressed and attempting to hide her face with make-up, she wandered into the kitchen. It was a mess—dirty dishes on the sink, empty bottles on the bench and table, and a broken glass that hadn't been cleaned up properly on the floor. The pantry door was ajar and had something smeared on the edge. She looked closer; it was blood. Her blood? she wondered. She knew it was hers. She put her hand to her face and held her breath. She couldn't let herself cry, not here and not now. She walked slowly into the lounge room and surveyed the area. Bodies were sleeping all over, not so much asleep but passed-out from the previous night's entertainment. But it was the smell that was the worst part. The stench was foul—stale beer mixed with body odour mixed with pizza and cigarettes. She went to the balcony doors and opened them both; the fresh air rushed in and smelled beautiful, and instantly, the bad smell dissipated. She quietly made her way back through the lounge, picked up glasses and plates along the way, and added them to the pile sitting on the kitchen sink.

As she was cleaning up, images of the night started coming back. She remembered arguing with her husband over something not worth the effort; and as he left the kitchen, he shoved past her, which was when she stumbled and hit her face on the open pantry door. She remembered he stopped for a moment and came over to her, but she pushed him away and ran to the bedroom, slamming the door behind her and collapsing in tears on to the bed. This was where she spent the rest of the night. She could hear the laughing and carrying on from the lounge but didn't want any part of it.

Touching her face again and feeling the pain, she took some painkillers from her purse and got ready to leave for the market. Her only concern now was to get more food and have lunch ready for when he awoke. She shuddered at the thought of the argument that would follow if she failed to do what was expected of her. She promised a long time ago to be there, for the good times and the bad, in sickness and in health till death do them part. Till death. She was certain that line was meant for her. She was not going to make old age, and it wasn't going to be any illness that takes her—it was going to be him. He was going to be the death of her one way or another. So what do you do when you know the man you are married to is going to be the death of you? *Do I leave?* she thought. *Don't be dumb. He would never let that happen, so I have to stay. Stay and let him abuse me.* It wasn't always physical; it was the mental abuse, the arguing and the way he controlled her. *But why? How did it get to this?* At 32, Hannah had imagined her life far different from this. She imagined living in a house in the suburbs with kids, two or maybe three. Having coffee with the neighbours while all the kids played in the yard. She imagined laughter and fun and a real life. Not this life. Stuck in this dark apartment day in and day out with only one purpose—to be at the beck and call of her husband. Not allowed to work, no social life. She was lonely and depressed.

She snatched up her keys from the bowl and let the door slam behind her. She didn't care if the noise of the door woke anyone up; if it did, hopefully, they would be gone by the time she got home from the market. She made her way down the stairs and out into the daylight. The sun was warm on her face. She breathed in the morning air, fresh and scented by the flowers growing in the front yard. For a moment, she was in a world of her own until a voice brought her back to reality.

'Oh dear, what happened to you?' It was Mrs Buckley form two doors down. The kind old lady came over to Hannah, and with a concerned look, she put her hand on Hannah's arm. 'I heard the arguing last night, but I didn't think it was that bad.'

'Hey, Mrs Buckley,' Hannah said timidly. 'It's nothing. It was an accident. I slipped on the wet floor and hit my head on the cupboard. No need to be concerned.' As convincing as her words were, she knew her neighbour wasn't buying it. They have been neighbours for a decade now; and when Hannah and her husband argued, it was usually loud, and she knew the other residents could hear what was going on. With a big smile, Hannah turned with a wave and walked into the warm summer morning.

'You know where I am if you ever need to talk or anything!' her neighbour called out after her. 'Anytime, day or night, you just knock on my door!'

Hannah turned back over her should and nodded at the old lady, whispered thanks, and continued on her way.

Chapter 2

The market was abuzz with the early morning gathering of people coming to get their fresh fruits, vegetables, meats, and fish. The market stall owners were standing on their crates, trying to catch the attention of passers-by by yelling and bantering with one another in the most comedic manner. Hannah loved everything about this place; it was fun and light-hearted, and the smell of the food was sensational. She stopped at her favourite bakery stand and selected a variety of breads and buns. She leaned closer to the counter, breathing in the warm and inviting scent. With a grin from ear to ear, she handed over her money, thanked the girl behind the counter, and took her treats. Hannah turned away from the counter, feeling on top of the world when it happened. She looked up from her shopping bag into the crowd when she saw him. He saw her. Their eyes locked, and she suddenly felt warm all over with a tightness in her stomach. She held his gaze for what seemed like an eternity, and with a sudden jolt, she broke eye contact. Hannah turned away from the crowd and frantically looked for the nearest exit. Hannah hurriedly moved through the people, desperately trying to get to the door. Outside, Hannah was struggling to breathe; she was hot all over and felt a tingling in her skin she wasn't familiar with. She leaned back on the wall, took several deep breaths, and composed herself. *What the hell was that?* she thought to herself.

Looking at the one bag of shopping she had got, Hannah knew she had to go back into the market and finish what she had started. Nervously, Hannah stepped back through the door and into the sea of people. She knew this place like the back of her hand, so she finished her shopping quickly and went home.

He was here under sufferance. His younger sister had dragged him here on a Sunday morning, again. It was busy and loud, and he hated the smell of the fish. He couldn't think of a worse place to be on a Sunday morning; he would rather still be at home in bed or lounging on the couch, watching a bad movie. He stood there sulking like a child when his sister shoved some weird-smelling vegetable under his nose. He scrunched up his face, swiped at whatever it was, and turned away. This was when he saw her. She was the most amazing thing he had ever seen. Standing there at the bakery, she had a smile that was as bright as the sun. He could see how she was in her element. The noise of the market started fading, and he could only see her. His feet felt like they were stuck to the floor; he just couldn't move. He was mesmerised by her. Then she turned and looked straight at him—not just in his direction, but right into his eyes. His heart started beating faster, and his palms were sweaty; their eyes locked on each other. Now the whole world disappeared, and only she existed. His sister tapped his shoulder to regain his attention, and when he looked back, she was gone. He turned and scanned the market but couldn't see her anywhere. He became agitated when his sister tugged his shirt and ushered him away. For a brief moment, he now knew she existed—she was the one.

Chapter 3

The walk back to the apartment block let her clear her head. *Who was he?* she thought to herself over and over. She caught herself smiling in the reflection of a corner store window. It made her heart skip a beat, and she quickly pulled her thoughts back to what was waiting for her at home. Her heart sank, and she felt heavy; her body started to ache. She rounded the corner and saw him standing on the balcony in grey trackpants and a black tank top, smoking a cigarette. He spotted her and just stared as she approached the apartment block. His stare was angry and enough to instil fear into anyone who didn't know him. Hannah was scared of who her husband could become when he was angry and didn't want to do anything to start a fight with him. She scurried up the stairs, took a deep breath, and entered the apartment. Without lifting her eyes from the floor, she made a quick dash for the kitchen, unpacked her bags, and started to prepare lunch with the food she just purchased at the market. As Hannah unwrapped the bread, the amazing smell was overwhelming; and for a moment, while she savoured the aroma, she forgot where she was. Lost in her own little world, Hannah didn't notice Sean come into the kitchen. He came up behind her, leaned up against her back, and started kissing her neck. Her body stiffened, and her skin went cold. She shrugged him off and continued making lunch.

'Don't be like that,' he said, his voice stern and controlling. 'If you just did what I asked, then I wouldn't have to lose my temper with you. But you have a smart mouth and just have to be difficult, and it drives me insane. I love you, but Jesus, you're a pain in the ass to be around.' He kissed her again and left the kitchen.

Hannah finished making lunch and placed it on the table. 'Lunch is ready!' she called in the most stable voice she could muster and then proceeded to clean up the mess. Within a minute or so, bodies began migrating from the lounge and stumbled into the kitchen. Like a horde of hungry swine, they proceeded to engulf the food that had been prepared for them. The din of their voices gave her a headache, and she moved herself into the lounge and cleaned up after them.

Later in the evening, with the apartment tidy again and guests all gone, Hannah took a moment to herself and went to hide in the balcony. Alone in the balcony she sat, staring out at the setting sun and enjoying a moment to her thoughts. As she sat there mesmerised by the afternoon glow, her thoughts took her back to the morning at the market. She closed her eyes, and his face was there. Across a sea of people, there he was, looking at her like she was the only person who existed. Her body relaxed into the chair, and the warmth of the sun melted away her darkness and gave her a sense of being. It was a feeling that she hadn't experienced in what seemed like forever. She liked the way she felt right now. In the back of her mind, she knew it wasn't real, but the fantasy that was growing in her head made her feel special. She kept her eyes closed and took that moment from the market and started creating a story. There he was, this handsome man, staring at her through the crowd. She stared back. She felt young and beautiful. The crowd parted, and he started walking over to her; she stood still and waited for him. He stopped right in front of her, and without a word, he put his hand on her cheek and motioned her face towards his. He leaned in and kissed her lips. She had butterflies racing through her stomach, and she kissed him back. Romantic music filled the air, and the fairy tale had its ending.

Hannah breathed in deep and opened her eyes again. What she wouldn't give to have a real moment again with someone who thought she was the most beautiful person in the world and with a kiss could make the earth stop turning! The sun finally gave way to the night, and she re-entered the apartment and went to bed. Tonight he left her alone, and she was grateful for a moment of peace.

Chapter 4

The weeks all seemed the same: He got up. Hannah prepared his breakfast. He went to work, and she was left alone. Hannah filled her days with cleaning, cooking, and reading. Her only outing was once a week, a trip to the library before she went to the grocery store. Reading was Hannah's way of escaping her life and becoming someone else. She particularly like stories set back in medieval times. Kings and queens, knights rescuing their princesses from evil. Hannah was a romantic at heart and dreamed of her white knight one day riding into her life and taking her away from here.

Hannah married Sean right out of high school. They were childhood sweethearts, and she thought he was perfect. He was strong and smart; everyone liked him, and he liked her. They were great together, so it was no surprise when they married and moved into their own apartment. It wasn't too long into the marriage when life became boring. Sean still worked for the same construction company, and Hannah was still his housewife. She couldn't remember when exactly the arguing started. He was probably drunk on a Friday night after drinks with the boys at the local pub; she was bored and started nagging at him the moment he walked in the door, and now it was just part of their routine.

On the way to the library, Hannah passed a quaint little café. It was small on the inside and always smelled great; they had a nice garden down the side, where there were tables and chairs for diners to enjoy their meals outside. It was nothing fancy, but was always filled to the brim at lunchtime. As she walked by, something caught her eye—a sign in the window stating 'Help Wanted – Enquire Inside'. This got Hannah's attention, and for the first time, she wandered inside. Hannah waited patiently in line, all the time looking around and taking it all in. The floors were wooden, the walls exposed brick with various pieces of art hanging in no particular order, big windows in the front, and a side door leading out to the tables outside. There was music playing in the background; it seemed to be current music. *The radio perhaps*, she thought. The tables were wooden with matching chairs and in the centre had a small vase with a coloured flower. Although the place seemed full of people, it wasn't overly noisy. Hannah had a great feeling about this place, and when she got to the front of the line, she was just about bursting with excitement at the thought of working here.

'Hi, what can I get for you?' said a cheery young girl.

'I'm here about the "Help Wanted" sign in the window,' Hannah replied, trying to keep her enthusiasm in check.

'Hey, cool. Let me just go grab the manager for you. I'll just be a sec.' Then the young girl disappeared into the kitchen. A short moment later, an older lady—maybe in her mid-fifties—appeared with a welcoming smile.

'Hello, I'm Lucy. Thank you for coming in. Please come and take a seat over here, and let's have a chat.' Lucy gestured to a small table in the corner, and Hannah immediately felt relaxed. 'So . . .,' Lucy started and looked at Hannah with a questioning glance.

'Hannah.'

'So, Hannah, please tell me a bit about yourself and why you would like to work here.'

Hannah sat up straight, folded her hands together on the table, and smiled at Lucy. 'Well, I'm 32 and been a housewife all my life, and I really think now is the time I did something for myself. I don't have any qualifications or experience, but I can promise I will work really hard, and I won't let you down if you give me a chance.' Hannah blurted it all out in one breath. She didn't think about what she was going to say; it just sort of came out. Lucy sat back in the chair and smiled at Hannah.

'I like you. You have enthusiasm and a friendly face. The job is Monday to Friday for the lunch shift, three hours a day, maybe a little more, depending on the crowd. You would start by learning the till and getting orders to the kitchen, and when you have got the menu under control, you would rotate with the others waiting and clearing tables. How does that sound?'

'Just perfect! I can't wait! When do you want me to start?'

Lucy laughed. 'Come in a bit before opening on Monday, and we will show you what you need to do and get your training started.' Lucy stood up and extended her hand to Hannah. 'Welcome to the team, Hannah.' Lucy took Hannah's hand in both of hers and held it just for a second. 'You will need a plain white T-shirt, black pants or skirt, and comfy shoes. Think you can manage that?'

'Easy done, and I will see you Monday!'

Hannah left the café on top of the world. This was to be her secret; there was no need to cause trouble by telling Sean as she already knew what he would say. He would forbid it. In his mind, he was the man, and the man was the income earner. She, being the woman, should be home looking after him. Hannah didn't understand why his mindset was stuck in the Fifties, but it just was. She was convinced he needed to control her, and keeping her at home was his way of staying in control. With a skip in her step, she continued on her way.

Chapter 5

H annah woke early that Monday morning, eager to get to her new job. After tossing and turning impatiently for about half an hour, she decided she would get up. She looked at the clock, and it was a bit before seven; she was never up this early during the week. Her normal routine was to wait for her husband to get up after the first snooze of the alarm at ten past seven, and then he would take up residence in the bathroom for around half an hour. This was when Hannah would get up, stay in her PJs, and go to the kitchen. She always made Sean breakfast; she figured it was the least she could do seeing he worked and she didn't. But not today. Hannah got up before Sean, took a quick shower, and dressed. She didn't wear the clothes she had picked out for her first day of work, rather just a comfy pair of trackpants and a baggy T-shirt. She was in the kitchen humming to herself and making Sean his breakfast when he came in.

'You're in a good mood this morning,' he said in a gruff voice. 'I don't normally get bacon and toast on a Monday, so what's going on to make you this happy?' Hannah turned and placed a plate in front of her husband and smiled.

'Nothing in particular. It's just a beautiful morning, and I felt like making sure you had a good breakfast today.' She turned back to the sink and started cleaning up, almost giggling to herself as the excitement of the day started building up in her.

Sean finished his breakfast, got up from his seat, and stood behind his wife at the sink. He put his arms around her waist and whispered softly in her ear, 'Thank you.' He released her from his hug and paused for a second. Something seemed different about her today; he frowned as he couldn't figure out what the unusual good mood was about. Sean kissed Hannah on the back of the head as he started to walk away.

'See you tonight, love.' Hannah stopped what she was doing and turned towards the door to watch Sean leave.

'Have a nice day, Sean! See you tonight!' she called after him.

When the door closed, Hannah sat at the kitchen table with a cup of coffee and stared at the clock. She was becoming impatient; she just wanted to get to work. She looked at the clock again, 8 a.m. She needed something to keep her mind busy while she was waiting. Hannah picked up her coffee and went to the lounge, where she flopped on the couch. After searching down the sides of the cushions for the TV remote, she grumbled to herself, 'Why can I never find the damn thing? Is it so hard to leave it on the table?' She arched her back over the arm of the couch and noticed the remote was there the whole time. 'Well, that's a first,' she said to herself with a sigh. Turning the remote around the right way and pointing at the TV, she pressed the on button. Nothing. She pressed the button again vigorously about ten more times, and still nothing. 'Seriously!' she yelled and angrily started pulling the back off the remote to fiddle with the batteries. She pressed the button again, and the TV finally made some noise; and within a few seconds, there was a picture. Now the big question was, what to watch? She ignored the free to air channels as there was never anything good to watch at this time of the morning, and she went to the menu of the paid TV provider. Hannah wasn't a big fan of reality TV, but she came across a show that had a camera crew following a woman who was about to confront her partner while being caught in the act of cheating.

As sad as the situation was, with the angry woman ripping into her husband while the mistress was screeching in the background, Hannah found it a little on the funny side. *Who would seriously air their dirty laundry like that for the whole world to see? Doesn't anyone keep their personal lives to themselves anymore?* Hannah didn't really get the whole reality TV phenomenon, which had seemed to have taken over in the past few years. She started to wonder how she would handle finding out her husband was cheating; she wasn't even sure she would know how to tell if anything was going on. She knew she was fairly naïve, but she also trusted Sean, and he rarely was away from her except during the day when he was at work. The occasional fishing trip with the boys or footy match during the winter. If anyone had the opportunity to cheat, it was definitely her; she was home all day and bored most of the time. Plenty of time and reason to find a friend with benefits. Hannah chuckled to herself, knowing she would never do that to Sean; she might be unhappy at times, but she was loyal to him all the same. Unconsciously, her mind quickly turned to the image of the man from the market and how she felt every time she let herself think of that moment. What would happen if she ever met him again? Was she capable of an affair? Hannah shook her head, dismissing the idea.

Oddly, the show made her feel better, and she decided to go and get ready for work. Hannah changed into a white T-shirt and black pants as instructed and stared at herself in the mirror for a few minutes. She had worn this combination of clothing many times before, but today it was different. Today this was her uniform, and for the first time in her life, she was about to earn her own money. She knew it wasn't going to be a lot of money, but she would have earned it all by herself. The thought of this made Hannah stand up straight and feel proud of what she was about to do. Next, she tidied her hair into a ponytail and brushed her teeth. She put on comfy shoes next, and she was ready to go. It was still a little early, but Hannah left the apartment anyway. She would take her time walking to the café, trying to be as relaxed as she could. The closer she got, the more nervous she got. One block to go, and she was there. When she saw the building, she took a deep breath and headed for the front door.

Chapter 6

A
t exactly 7 a.m., he was startled awake by his alarm clock. Ryan
hated Monday mornings. *Why do the weekends always go so fast?*
he thought to himself as he headed for the shower. Ryan was
34, tall, slim, and very single. He didn't mind being single too much as
it meant he didn't have to worry about anyone but himself, which right
now suited him just fine.

Ryan sat at the kitchen counter and poured himself some cereal
for breakfast. He was conscious of his diet, so he tried to pick healthy
cereals and not the ones he really wanted, which were usually 50 per
cent sugar. He figured he wasn't getting any younger, so he'd better
start watching what he ate. He had already retrieved the paper from
the porch and immediately went to the sport section. He wasn't a huge
sports enthusiast but liked to keep on top of the weekend's results as
it was a guaranteed conversation in the break room at lunchtime on
a Monday, and he liked to be able to add to the conversation even if
he didn't really care. As he was flicking through the rest of the paper,
Ryan's cat, Bruce, jumped up onto the counter to get his attention. Oh,
he got attention all right; as he landed on the counter, he landed on the
side of the half-empty bowl and sent it spinning right into Ryan's lap.

'Oh, for crying out loud, Bruce!' he snapped as he shoved the cat
off the counter. 'Now look at me. Just great! Now I'm going to have
to go change.' With that, he snatched up the dish, dumped it in the
sink, and stomped back to the bedroom. Agitated, Ryan unbuckled
his belt, dropped his pants, and flicked them off with his foot into the
direction of the hamper. Bruce wandered into the room and rubbed up
against his bare legs, purring loudly like he had done nothing wrong.

Still grumbling to himself, Ryan leaned over and gave Bruce a scratch behind his ear. Then Ryan went to the closet, took out another pair of pants, and dressed for the second time that day.

Back in the kitchen, Ryan grabbed a cloth and cleaned up the remnants of his breakfast off the floor. Bruce came over again, still purring and looking for attention. 'Times like this I wish you were a dog. Then you could clean up your own mess.' Over at the counter. Ryan filled up Bruce's food bowl and topped up his water. 'Now try to stay out of trouble while I'm gone.' Bruce gave a small meow as if he understood Ryan and pranced over to his food bowl.

It was a beautiful morning outside. Ryan contemplated whether to drive or bike it to work today; he looked at his watch, and after having to change and clean up the mess Bruce made, he thought he might be pushing it to be at work on time. He opened his car and sat heavily into the driver's seat. 'OK, baby, don't be giving me any grief this morning.' He put the key into the ignition and turned. With a purr smoother than Bruce's, the little Toyota started. 'That's my girl,' Ryan said with a smile.

It wasn't a long journey to work, but it was very stop-start in the traffic. This frustrated Ryan and many of the other commuters on the road, but he decided not to let it get to him today. He leaned over and turned up the radio, and without a single note in key, he belted out the song. Ryan looked out his window, and realising that his out-of-tune melody was being heard by the older lady in the car next to him, he gave a little nod and smile and sang even louder. His act was appreciated by his neighbouring commuter, who had a good laugh and drove off with a wave. Chuffed at himself for making someone's Monday drive a little more interesting, Ryan smiled the rest of the short journey to work.

Ryan parked his car not too far from the building and walked at a leisurely pace to his workstation. He worked at a company that engineered and manufactured automotive parts. Ryan wasn't one of the engineers; he wasn't anywhere that smart or dedicated. He worked in the shipping department. All Ryan had to do was speak with his allocated customer base, place their orders, and make sure they got delivered on time. Not rocket science by any stretch, but his boss always told him and his co-workers that it was one of the most important jobs in the company. If the company didn't get orders in, the factory and engineers would have nothing to do. It sounded good, and his boss had a way of embellishing the statement so well it made a mundane job tolerable.

Coffee first, he thought to himself once he pushed the on button to his computer. He grabbed his mug and wandered down to the break room. True to form, the conversation about the weekend's sporting results was in full swing.

'Oi, Ryan!' Alex yelled at him as he made his way to the coffee machine. 'Please tell me you watched the game on Saturday night. Was it or was it not the best game of football you have EVER watched in your entire life?'

Ryan looked over with a smile, and before any words could leave his mouth, Alex had already turned his focus onto the next person innocently making their way for their morning caffeine hit. It made Ryan chuckle as he walked back to his workstation and thought to himself he could retire if I had a dollar for every predictable conversation that happened here.

The morning went quickly that day—no grumpy clients with missing orders, the boss was extra cheerful, the factory was running smoothly, and all his new orders were in stock. Ryan looked up at the clock and was surprised when it was almost midday; he was getting hungry since he didn't get all of his breakfast. Alex wandered past his desk and stopped when he too noticed the time.

'Hey, what you doing for lunch today?' Alex asked with intention in his voice.

'Dunno, hadn't really given it any thought yet. Why? What did you have in mind?'

'How about we head over to that little café a few blocks down? The food is always good, and since I'm still in recovery mode, a good feed is in order.'

'Self-inflicted, I take it?' Ryan said with no sympathy.

'Oh yeah, freakin' awesome party Saturday night at the place of this chick I met the other weekend. Oh man, she has legs that go all the way up, and I will give you all the details if you come with me.' Alex was standing there with a dirty grin. How could Ryan refuse? He needed a few dirty details to make up for the complete lack of action in his own life. And with the promise of a good story, they headed out for lunch.

It was only a five-minute walk to the café, but it seemed only a minute with Alex freely giving up all the details of his weekend rendezvous with his latest conquest. Ryan didn't know where he found these girls or how he convinced them to spend the night with him, but he seemed to have a different girl every weekend, Ryan thought to himself. Not that he was judging him—each to their own, and maybe he was just a bit jealous as he just couldn't ever seem to get a date. With an evil chuckle from Alex, they walked into the café. Ryan scanned the shop to find a quiet table to sit at where Alex could finish his story without offending too many people. Alex shoved his elbow into Ryan's arm and gestured to a table by the door leading out into the al fresco seating area. They took a seat, and a chirpy young girl handed them menus and told them to order at the counter when they were ready. Didn't take them long; there was only one thing either of them ever ordered here—schnitzel and chips covered in gravy. Alex chucked some money Ryan's way. 'Hey, can you order for me and get me a large Coke to go with? Thanks, man.'

'Yeah, all right.' Ryan got up from the table and made his way to the counter. He wasn't really paying attention when a girl's soft voice brought his eyes to her direction.

'What can I get for you?' she repeated with a stammer in her voice. He was mesmerised and for a moment said nothing. It was her. It was the girl he saw from a distance at the markets a few Sundays ago.

'Um . . . yeah . . . ah . . . two schnitzel, chips, and gravy and two large Cokes please,' Ryan muttered. The girl looked down at the register and hesitantly placed his order.

Lucy walked up behind her and smiled at Ryan. 'Sorry, Ryan. It's Hannah's first day, so she's just getting used to the till. Can I get you boys some drinks?' Hannah, her name was as beautiful as she was. 'Ryan?' Lucy prompted again, raising an eyebrow.

'Ah, yeah . . . Two large Cokes please, Lucy.' Lucy smiled at him and prompted Hannah on how to enter the drinks.

'Twenty-one thirty for the two meals and drinks.' Hannah's voice was barely audible, and she still didn't look up from the register. Ryan handed over the money and put the change in the tip jar sitting on the counter.

Ryan went back to the table and sat down, staring off into the distance. 'Ryan . . . Dude, you OK?' Alex said, looking at his friend with concern. 'Ryan!' Alex said sharply. Ryan brought his attention back to Alex.

'It's her.'

Chapter 7

After her unusual Monday morning, Hannah made her way to the café, ready to start her very first job. She arrived ten minutes early—excited, eager, and nervous all at the same time. Lucy greeted her at the counter with a smile that could light up the night. 'Welcome, Hannah! Let's get you ready.' After half an hour of meeting the other staff and a quick orientation of the register, Lucy opened the front door. Within a few minutes, hungry patrons started filling the tables. Armed with her 'In training' badge, Hannah started taking orders; they weren't too complicated, and so far, all the customers were friendly and patient. Most of the people that frequented Lucy's place were regulars and were happy to let Hannah take her time in getting the hang of the register.

Everything was going better than Hannah had ever dreamed of when someone caught her eye. Hannah was watching the customers come in through the front door when she recognised him. His soft brown hair was short but messy. He was tall, slim, and good-looking. Not movie star 'I know I'm hot' good-looking, but easy on the eyes and someone you'd definitely take a second look at. He was with some joker who was clearly suffering from the weekend's activities, but he seemed to be humouring him. They sat by the door that led to the side garden as the joker continued his very animated story. She became distracted with her thoughts, curious as to what was so amusing.

Hannah was quickly brought back to reality when he stood up and made his way to the counter. She became agitated whilst serving the customer in front of him as her nerves became evident. Lucy was hovering behind the counter, watching her when she saw Hannah look up at the man and then down with shaking hands. Lucy had been around long enough to pick up on these things, so she stayed close and kept a watchful eye on her new recruit.

Then the moment came; he was next. Her stomach was in the back of her throat, and she felt her body temperature rise. Her voice could barely be heard. 'Hi, what can I get for you?' Silence. He wasn't paying attention. Hannah repeated herself, this time a little louder and slightly more assertive. 'What can I get for you?' He lifted his head and made eye contact. She was breathless. The world around her seemed to disappear, and her body started to numb.

'Um . . . yeah . . . ah . . . two schnitzel, chips, and gravy and two large Cokes please.' Hannah struggled with placing the order in the register, but Lucy was right behind her and jumped in.

'Sorry, Ryan. It's Hannah's first day, so she's just getting used to the till. Can I get you boys some drinks?'

She saw Lucy move to the drinks fridge and organise the Cokes, and she hesitantly took the money and completed the transaction. Ryan went back to his table, and Hannah breathed again; her light- headiness started to ease. *What just happened?* She didn't understand these feelings about someone she had never actually met before. She now knew his name and knew he worked close by. She felt her body cool down, and she regained control of her thoughts. The more customers came in for lunch, the more she focused on her job and less on the man who had without warning stole her concentration.

Before she realised it, Hannah's first shift had finished, and she was exhausted. She sat at the table closest to the counter to take a breather, and almost immediately, Lucy joined her. 'You did good today, chick. How do you feel?'

'Amazing and totally knackered all at the same time.' Hannah giggled and rubbed her eyes.

Lucy put her hand on her arm as she rose from the chair. 'So will we see you again tomorrow?'

'Oh yeah, for sure. I can't wait.'

It was around a quarter past two when Hannah left the café after her very first shift; she was a flurry of emotions—happy, as she was finally doing something for her that was outside of the apartment, and exhausted, as she had never worked a day in her life. She was distracted by the man who was now a regular in her dreams, and she was disappointed about having to go back to her prison. She stood up straight, took a deep breath, and started walking.

As she walked, she started thinking about keeping this secret from her husband; if she could, then she might just be able to have something to look forward to, and things wouldn't be so bad. Getting out of the house every day for just a few hours, meeting new people, and earning a few dollars might just be the answer to getting herself out of this rut she was in. If she became a more positive person, happy and energised, then maybe she could learn to tolerate her husband better. If she was better to him, it might have a twofold effect, and maybe he might be nicer to her. Couldn't hurt, right? And it had to be better than the current situation.

By the time she got home, she had made up her mind: today was the first day of a better life for her and her husband. She was determined to make this work.

With a skip in her step, she bounded up the stairs and let herself into her apartment. She put the radio on and started signing to the song that was on. She opened up the curtains and windows and let the magnificent day in. Hannah looked around the apartment, and with a renewed energy, she started her chores.

In what seemed like five minutes, the front door opened, and Sean walked in. Dirty and tired, he saw his wife singing to herself and dancing around while cleaning up. He stopped and just watched for a while. Wow, he hadn't seen her like this since early in their marriage. As she turned around, the sun hit her face, and he saw her smile; it took his breath away. She was still as beautiful as she was when he had to have her in high school. Why hadn't he seen this in so long? Then he started thinking about how they didn't seem happy at the moment and how it had got to this. He hated his job, and he hated the tiny apartment that they had lived in since they got married. But he couldn't tell her that. He couldn't tell her he felt like a failure. No! That just wouldn't happen, and with that, his anger came flooding back.

'What's got you in such a good mood today? What have you been doing?' he said in a harsh tone.

Hannah was startled by his presence as she hadn't heard him come in. She slowly and coyly wandered over to him, kissed him firmly on the lips, and whispered, 'I love you.' She stepped back and, with a smile, said, 'Hungry? How about I get dinner started?' Then she turned her back to him and set off for the kitchen.

Sean felt his anger subside, and for a brief moment, he was glad he married her; even in their disappointing life, she still loved him. He followed her into the kitchen, sat at the table, and watched her cook. When the food was ready, she placed a plate in front of him. He looked up with a sadness in his eyes and a slight hint of a smile and thanked her. The mood was soft that night—barely a word said, but no tension or anger. They watched TV together, and when the movie finished, he offered her his hand and led her to bed. He didn't touch her in his usual way that night, but he was attentive and gentle. She kissed him back for the first time in a long time. The more she kissed him back, the more she felt passionate. The more she felt passionate, the more he responded; and when it was over, she cuddled in under his arm and fell asleep.

Chapter 8

The sun was warm, and Hannah was standing under a beautiful oak tree; before her stood Ryan. He was tall and handsome. Dressed in cargo shorts and a white linen shirt that was unbuttoned far enough she could see his chest, he was picture-perfect. She looked up into his eyes, and as the sun danced on his face, she felt herself fall deeply in love with him. The breeze tossed her hair around, and Ryan cupped her face with his hands. His hands were big and soft, and as his fingertips touched her cheek, she got goosebumps all the way down her body. He smiled down at her, and without a word, he kissed her. Her body felt hot, her heart raced, and she had an overwhelming sensation flood her body. She had to have him right there and right then. The kiss lasted a few minutes, and the longer he kissed her, the stronger the desire grew. When the kiss ended, Hannah ran her hands up his chest and started undoing another button. Ryan looked down at Hannah, tilted his head to the side, and smiled with acknowledgement to her advances. He put one of his hands behind her back, and the other took her hand; then he slowly lowered to the ground, beckoning her with him. She lay back on the soft grass and looked around her; she saw they were in the middle of a field with a picnic set up just near where she lay. Not another person to be seen, and the only sound she could hear besides her heartbeat was the chirping of the birds somewhere off in the distance. As she lay there with now him over the top of her, she felt his hand run up her inner thigh. Her burning desire for Ryan was at its peak, her body was so hot, and her breathing so fast she thought she was going to pass out.

'Hannah . . . Hannah . . . Hannah . . .' She could hear him saying her name.

With a sudden gasp of air, Hannah sat upright in bed; and as she became aware of where she was, she saw Sean in the dim light sitting up next to her.

'You OK? You were tossing and turning and really hot and sweaty. Was it a bad dream?'

'Yeah,' Hannah said, taking a deep breath and feeling her pulse return to normal. 'I was lost and couldn't find you,' she lied. Hannah lay down again, now wide awake.

'It's OK. I'm not going anywhere,' Sean replied sleepily, put his arm over her, and drifted back to sleep. Hannah lay awake for what felt like an eternity. The one thought kept going through her mind: was she really capable of being with someone else? Could she have an affair and get away with it? Sean finally rolled over, and Hannah wriggled around to get comfortable. She started to feel guilty at her thoughts, but at the same time, she started feeling alive again. She liked feeling sexy and thinking someone else out there might find her beautiful, but acting on her feelings was a very different matter. Hannah honestly believed that she could never do it. As she closed her eyes again, she convinced herself that just dreaming about it wouldn't do any harm.

Chapter 9

It had been a couple of weeks since her first day of work. Hannah had opened her own bank account at a branch in a neighbouring suburb where no one knew her, and the balance was growing. It was becoming a nice little nest egg all of her own. Ryan came in two or three times a week, sat at the same table, and ordered the same meal every time. The more he came in, the longer the conversations went. The first few times were pleasantries; and then they started becoming more meaningful, like what they did on the weekend or what movies they watched, and a friendship started to develop.

It was an ordinary Tuesday night, and things were so much better at home. Because Hannah was only at work for the lunch shifts, she was always home before Sean and made sure dinner was always started by the time he got home. Hannah was happy; she smiled so much more, and Sean responded with less angry tones.

As she sat back on this night, she knew she was in the wrong by hiding her job but figured why rock the applecart when things were so nice now? If she could keep it up, then who knows? Maybe their marriage had a fighting chance of surviving. They were having a pleasant conversation over dinner when Sean's phone rang. He looked at the number, rolled his eyes, sighed, then excused himself. Hannah couldn't quite hear what was being said in the other room, but from the tone and the sudden outburst of laughter, it was a friendly conversation and let out a sigh of relief. She slouched in her chair a little and continued eating her meal. Sean returned to the table with a smirk on his face.

'Sooooo', Hannah said with an increasing curiosity, 'who was that?' She smiled slyly at Sean so as not to seem imposing.

'That, my dear, was Dave. He's getting the boys together this weekend for a fishing trip to the coast, leaving Friday night and getting back Sunday arvo. Sounds just like what I need—a break with the fellas, knocking back a few beers and throwing the line in. I figure I work hard, not that you probably understand that, and hanging out with the boys sounds just what the doc ordered. You will be OK here on your own, right?'

'Yeah, I guess I will be OK. I can always go see Mum and Dad if I can't cope without you at night.' Hannah knew she would be OK, and her stomach started fluttering with the excitement of a few days alone. She sat back in the chair and tried to remember the last time she had a night to herself. She could get a bottle of wine, run a hot bath, get a chick flick, and totally relax. She looked back at her husband and asked, 'Do you want me to cook some stuff for you to take—you know, just in case the fish aren't biting?'

'Yeah, babe, that sounds great. And I will give you something to do for the next couple of days. I'll leave some cash out for you tomorrow to go to the store. And while you're there, why don't you grab yourself something special, like that fancy ice cream you're always trying to get me to eat?'

With a grin from ear to ear, Hannah nodded, stood up from the table, and cleared the plates. 'Want help with the dishes?' It wasn't really a question from Sean as even when Hannah would say yes, he would promise to come back in a few minutes but never would.

'No, it's all good. You go put your feet up and find us something to watch.' Hannah wanted a few minutes to herself to daydream about having a weekend alone. Once Sean left the room and she could hear the TV, her thoughts immediately went to Ryan. *I wonder what he is doing this weekend* was her first thought. Hannah looked over her shoulder to make sure Sean was in the lounge; then she turned back to the sink to continue with her fantasy. Maybe if he came in this week for lunch, she could probe a little; and if he was going somewhere close by, she could just happen to be there. She mentally started going through her closet to work out what she would wear and where she might just happen to bump into him. She giggled a little to herself and finished putting the last of the dishes away.

'Hey, are you coming in here yet? The show's about to start.' Hannah jumped a little as Sean's voice called from the lounge room, and for a moment, she felt guilty about her thoughts. *It's not cheating if I just think about it*, she thought. *It's not like I would ever do anything.* Hannah took a deep breath and convinced herself she hadn't done anything wrong and never would and went to join her husband in the lounge room.

Chapter 10

Ryan was up extra early that Wednesday morning; he had a spring in his step as he headed for the bathroom. Bruce trotted behind him down the passage, purring loudly. Ryan stopped at the bathroom door, bent over, and patted Bruce on the head. 'You're in a good mood this morning, buddy. You got some last night on your midnight wander?' He chuckled and thought to himself, *At least one of us has a social life.*

While in the shower, Ryan caught himself daydreaming about Hannah again. She was so mesmerising; her bright, beautiful smile got him every time. He really looked forward to work these days just so he could take his lunch break and go and see her. He knew she was married; the ring gave it away, but even so, he knew he had a big-time crush on her. *I wonder*, he caught himself thinking, *is she happily married?* He shook his head and was slightly disgusted with himself for thinking that. Married women are not on the menu—no way. He knew the trouble that came with that. Anyway, he kept dreaming. *It is just a bit of harmless flirting—more like being friendly, really. And she wouldn't think anything of it. She is so nice to all of her customers that she probably doesn't really notice me. But what if? Stop it,* he told himself. *She's just being nice to you 'cause you're a regular customer, that's all.*

Ryan turned off the shower and went back to his bedroom to get dressed with Bruce right at his feet again. Sitting on the end of the bed, Bruce pawed at Ryan, looking for attention. Ryan stopped what he was doing and scratched him under the chin.

'One day, buddy, I will surprise you and bring a beautiful girl home. You'll see.' Bruce jumped down from the bed and walked out. 'Pfft! Don't believe me, huh?'

Ryan followed Bruce back into the kitchen; he filled the kettle and switched it on. He got his favourite mug from the cupboard and leaned back on the counter, waiting for the kettle to finish boiling. Over the noise of the kettle, he heard his phone buzzing on the table. He looked over to see who it was but couldn't quite make it out. Ryan finished making his coffee and went to his phone. It was his sister. He knew if he didn't ring her back, she would pester him all day. He also knew what she wanted. His sister thought of herself as his personal matchmaker. She hated him being alone, and no matter how many times he assured her that he was fine being single, she kept trying to set him up with someone. With a deep breath and a sigh, he called her back.

'Hey, little sis, what's up?'

'Oh, you know, the usual . . . same crap, different day. So I was thinking, right?'

'Yeah, I figured that.'

'No need to be a smart-ass. There's a new girl at work, and she's just moved here and doesn't know anyone. And I thought you, me, and a couple of others should take her out Saturday night and let her get to know a few people. You know, help her settle in and all.' Ryan could hear the devious thoughts going through his sister's head. By helping her meet people, she really meant set him up with her. His sister just couldn't help herself.

'Well, actually, sis, I have plans this Saturday night. So sorry, but you're just going to have to entertain her yourself.'

'Plans? With who, and why am I just hearing about this now?' His sister seemed to be a little annoyed that she didn't know about her brother's every movement.

'Because there's nothing to tell you yet. There's someone I am getting to know, and until there's something more, you don't need to know about it.' Ryan wasn't exactly lying to his sister, just embellishing the actual truth just a little. He was hoping this would be enough to get her off his back and leave him alone for a while.

'Oh come on, you have to give me more than that. What's her name? Where did you meet her? What does she look like? How old—'

'Stop! All right, I will give you a few details, but don't get all excited as I don't even know if it will go anywhere. Her name is Hannah.' He figured telling his sister her name wouldn't do any harm; there were probably hundreds of Hannahs around. 'I met her through work.' Well, that was kind of the truth. 'A bit shorter than me, dark hair, and has the most amazing smile.' Ryan started to drift off as he was describing her; he could see her perfectly in his head at the café standing behind the counter and her smile lighting up the room.

'Oh my god!' his sister squealed. 'I've never heard you talk like that about anyone before! The way you just said that, you have a major thing for her, don't you?' His sister was laughing excitedly at him.

'Just settle down. We're just friends, all right? I gotta go, or I'm going to be late for work.' Ryan cut his sister off from any more comments and hung up.

He sat in the chair staring at the empty mug for a few minutes. He was feeling deflated; he knew there would never be anything more than just being friends with Hannah.

Bruce jumped up on the table and rubbed up against Ryan's face. He smiled at the cat and gave him a good scratch.

'Time for me to go now, buddy. You behave, all right?' Ryan got up, collected his things, and left for work.

Chapter 11

Right on cue, Ryan walked into the café, wandered over to what was now known as Ryan's table, and took his seat. He always sat facing the counter and always looked around until he saw Hannah. He couldn't see her at first but then heard laughter come from the kitchen, and then he heard her voice as clear as day. He couldn't make out what she said, but he heard her; her voice was bright and happy, and that made him feel good. In just a few seconds, she appeared from the kitchen, and he caught his breath. He didn't know why, but she looked amazing today; she was wearing the same white T-shirt as everyone else and had an apron tied around her waist, but she just seemed to be glowing. She looked in his direction and made eye contact. As she started around the counter to come and say hi, Ryan started to get all fidgety and a little nervous.

'Hey, Ryan, how are you today?'

'Yeah, not bad, thanks.' He leaned back on the chair, trying to look casual and to hide his building affection for her.

'Any point in me asking what you want? I know, I know . . . One day, you will surprise us all and order something different. So the big question is, is today that day?' Hannah said, smiling and lifting one eyebrow at Ryan.

'Now that would just make you all think something was wrong, and I couldn't do that to you now, could I?' Ryan chuckled. He saw Lucy at the counter and raised a hand to acknowledge her. He shuffled in his chair, trying to get his wallet out so he could pay Hannah for lunch; she now took his order at the table since he was here several times a week and had the same thing every time.

'So, young lady, what was all the laughter coming from the kitchen about? I could hear you from the street.' He couldn't but was desperate to make conversation.

'Well, if you must know', she started, 'I was telling the others that I am home alone this weekend, and we were having a giggle about all the bad things I could do to get myself in trouble.' Hannah finished with a cheeky grin.

As she finished the sentence, Ryan fumbled and dropped his wallet on the floor; he leaned over to pick it up and hit his head on the table. 'Oh, for the love of . . .,' he said a little loud and with a hint of pain. Hannah tried hard not to laugh and offered to get him some ice, but he waved his hand at her. 'Not necessary, thanks.' His voice was a little harsh, but she could see he was a little hurt and probably a little embarrassed. She put her hand on his shoulder in comfort and then left to place his order with the kitchen.

Holding his head for a minute, he didn't look up from the table; his ego was bruised from headbutting the table, and his mind started to wander. *So she is home all alone this weekend . . . interesting.* Not that he would ever do anything about it, but it gave him enough to let his imagination take over. *What will she do on her own? I wonder if she will go out . . . to the movies maybe. Where is the closest movie theatre to her? Does she even live close by? Well, I have seen her here and at the markets near here, so more than likely, she doesn't live too far.*

Lost in his thoughts, he hadn't noticed Hannah come back over with his lunch.

'Is it a good place?'

Startled, he looked at her blankly. 'Is where good?' He was confused at the question.

'That place you've been in your head for the past ten minutes. You've been somewhere else and grinning, so I was curious as to if it was a good place.'

Ryan looked down at the table, too nervous to make eye contact. 'Yeah, it's the perfect place.'

'How's the head?' This made Ryan look up at Hannah.

'It's fine, thank you for asking.'

Hannah looked down at Ryan with a softness he hadn't seen before; she looked really concerned. 'You're welcome. Let me know if you need anything else, OK?' Hannah turned and went back to serving the other customers.

'OK,' he said softly, and as he ate his meal, he made a mental list of all the things he wanted her for, but could never ask. His head started to thump, so he finished quickly and made a quiet exit.

Chapter 12

F riday at last, Hannah was helping Sean get ready for his weekend away. All the boys took the day off to get an early start on the road trip. She was packing the last of the food she had prepared into the cooler when Sean came up behind her and grabbed her tight around the waist.

'You'd better be a good girl while I'm gone. Don't want to hear any stories about you when I get back. You hear me?' He then turned Hannah around and kissed her hard. She pulled back from him and laughed.

'Oh, there will be stories. You won't believe the things I have planned,' she said slyly. 'Have a great time and bring me back a bucketful of fish.' Her tone was happy but controlled; she didn't want to come across as too excited that he was going to be gone for three whole days.

She walked with him to the front door and saw him off; she could hear the others down in the street waiting for Sean to come down. She closed the front door and went to the balcony just to make sure he left. As she looked down at the car, the boys yelled up to her that they would take good care of him and not to worry. She smiled brightly back at them and waved as the car pulled away from the kerb.

With a big sigh of relief, she came back into the lounge room, and with her hands on her hips, she looked around the empty apartment. *What to do first?* she thought to herself. *I could walk around naked eating ice cream or put on my radio station really loud and belt out a few tunes or just sit on the couch with my feet up and watch whatever I please.* As she plopped onto the couch, she knew her choices were endless. She leaned backwards, and with her fingertips, she willed the remote for the television to come to her. After a few moments, she grabbed the remote and turned on the TV. What to watch was now the biggest decision she had to make. She flicked through a few channels, and then a movie trailer caught her attention. *Looks OK*, she thought to herself, wondering what time it was playing tonight. And with that, she leapt up from the couch and went to find her phone. After flicking through the cinema app, she finally found the movie. Six o'clock. Yes, that would be perfect; she would finish work a bit after two, come home to do her chores, shower; and she could be at the movies in plenty of time. Done! Hannah had made up her mind, and her night was planned.

Now that she had her evening sorted, she was at a loose end to what she was going to do for the next couple of hours before work. The library? Hannah hadn't been to the library in a long time since she started work, and she missed that part of her day. She grabbed her purse and a jacket and left the apartment for the library. It was a nice day outside—a little on the cool side, but at least the sun was out.

She walked past the café on the way to the library and noticed Lucy already there unstacking the chairs. Hannah opened the front door and poked her head inside.

'Hey, Lucy, how are you today?'

'Well, hello there, Hannah! I'm just great, thank you for asking, and how are you on this lovely morning?'

'Amazing, thanks. I have a few days without my husband, so I plan on doing all of the things I would never normally get a chance to do.' In the background, Hannah heard the phone ring.

'Two secs, love.' Lucy gestured at Hannah to come in and disappeared into the kitchen. The conversation was short, and within a minute, Lucy was back out in the dining area. 'Ah, that's a shame. Nicky is sick, so she won't be in today. Didn't think she was looking too well yesterday, so best she stays away. No need to put the customers off their lunch.'

'Oh no, that's not good,' Hannah said with concern. 'I'm not doing anything just now. I can stay and help set up if you like?'

With a big smile, Lucy nodded. 'That would be a big help for me, thank you.'

'Of course.' Hannah smiled back at her boss. She really liked Lucy, and during the past few weeks, she had been so good to Hannah that she was more than happy to help out.

The two women busied themselves setting up the tables for lunch while gossiping and laughing, and after a little while, the other staff started arriving and joined in on the fun; in no time at all, customers were coming through the front door, hungry for the delicious food that was being prepared for them.

The atmosphere was electric today; the staff were all full energy, and the customers were feeding off that energy and joining in on the banter. It was a little after twelve thirty when Ryan arrived for his usual Friday lunch. He was joined by Alex, who was really getting animated in his story, but that was just the way he was. Ryan laughed, and the two men sat at the same table by the door as they always did.

Hannah walked past the boys while taking food to another table when Ryan piped up, saying, 'So big plans for the weekend then?'

Hannah smiled back over her shoulder. 'Yep, taking myself to a movie tonight. Going to go and see that new action flick that's just come out. Saw the trailer this morning, and it looks good. Just hoping the best bits weren't in the trailer. You boys got trouble to get yourselves into?' Hannah stopped at their table to wait for the response when the bell from the kitchen rang. 'That's me.' She smiled. 'Have a good one, and I want to hear all about it next week, OK?'

Ryan sat there and thought that thought he knew he shouldn't. *Movie, huh? Looks like I know what I am doing tonight.* With a self-satisfied smirk, he leaned back in his chair and brought his focus back to Alex.

'So, Ryan, want to come out with me tonight? I know this chick who is having a party, and she has friends who will do things to you that you only dreamed of.' Alex knew Ryan wouldn't come with him but always asked. One day, his friend might actually relax and learn how to have fun.

'Sorry, man, got plans already for tonight. But thanks anyway.'

Alex laughed out loud at Ryan. 'You? You have plans? Oh, this I got to hear! So, big man, what are these plans of yours?'

Ryan suddenly felt himself get hot as he was put on the spot by Alex. When he said he had plans, he didn't think that Alex would actually ask what they were. Ryan fidgeted in his chair as his mind raced, trying to think of something quick. It had to be interesting to get his friend's approval, but not too interesting that he would want details next week.

'My sister and a group of her friends are going out, and she just wouldn't stop until I agreed to go. Her friends are a pain in the ass, but at least if I go, this will get her of my back for a while.'

Ryan felt uncomfortable with the awkward silence that followed while Alex considered his plans. 'If you get bored and want to actually have some fun, text me, and I will let you know where the party is. Show you what you've been missing out on.' Alex scanned the room and locked on to Hannah. 'Hey, what do you think of her? She looks like your type. Maybe you should ask her out.'

'Bro, she has a wedding ring on, or did you miss that?' Ryan dismissed the question with a shake of his head.

'As if that counts for anything these days. You want to know how many married chicks I've had? They are all the same. They don't get the right attention at home, so they want a quick fix. Just got to tell them they are the most beautiful girl you've ever met, and bam, you're in! Just be careful, though, and don't let them get emotionally attached. That's a shit fight you don't want. And DON'T ever give them your number. Want me to suss her out for you? Or even better, maybe I will work my magic on her. What do you think?' Alex let out a creepy little laugh with that last part, and Ryan shot him a dirty look.

'How about you just leave her alone? Not every girl is like that.'

'Geez, man, lighten up. I was just having some fun.'

'Yeah, I know. Come on, we'd better head back.'

As the two men weaved through the tables heading for the door, Alex tried to lighten the mood again. 'So how is your sister? Maybe I should get her number from you.' Ryan laughed at his friend.

'She annoys the crap out of me at times, but I don't hate her that much that I would let you near her.'

Alex punched his friend in the arm and retorted, 'That's harsh!'

Chapter 13

With a mighty explosion, the screen was filled with bright red and orange flames. The hero emerged from the fire carrying in his arms the female love interest, who was gazing up at him with love-struck eyes, and then the credits started rolling up the screen. The theatre lights slowly started coming back on, and Hannah checked her surroundings to make sure she hadn't left anything behind. She hadn't noticed, but two rows behind her, she was being watched by Ryan. She shuffled her way out of the row and headed for the door. Just outside, she stopped at the bin to dump her popcorn box and drink cup when someone bumped into her.

'Oh, so sorry,' came the male voice, which she recognised. She smiled to herself and turned around.

'Well, hello there,' Hannah responded happily. 'What did you think of the movie?'

'Was OK, but why do they have to ruin a perfectly good action movie with romance? Without that part would have been great.'

'Hahaha! Yeah, I know what you mean.' Hannah moved away from the bin and started for the exit. 'Was pretty cheesy, but still had enough good bits to make it OK.' Hannah felt a little nervous being next to Ryan outside of the café. where she was in control of her feelings.

Ryan walked next to Hannah, and they left the cinema. 'Where are you parked, Hannah?'

'Oh, I don't drive, so I'm going to go and wait for the bus. But you enjoy the rest of your night, OK?' Hannah started walking away towards the street corner to where the bus stop was.

'Hey, wait up! Let me give you a lift home. I can't let you get on the bus alone at this time of night. What if something happened to you? I would never forgive myself.' Ryan stood there with his hand beckoning her back to him.

Hannah paused for a moment, not sure what to do. 'OK then, that would be great as long as you are sure it's not out of your way.'

'Wouldn't matter if it was. The important thing is you get home safe.' Ryan smiled at Hannah. He spoke softly, and his eyes showed her he was concerned for her safety, and for a second, she held his gaze. She walked back to him, and in silence, they made their way to Ryan's car.

Reluctantly, Hannah got into Ryan's car; it was not that she didn't trust him, but she really didn't know him. So she was now alone with a man she had thought about since that moment in the market and had now got to know him while working at the café. He was exactly who she thought she would be with—a gentle soul who was kind, caring, and someone who she knew would go out of their way for her. But it wasn't like she didn't love Sean, but he could be mean and treated her more like a possession—someone who was there only to do what he wanted. She didn't feel like an equal around him most of the time. It had been better lately; but in reality, it was only because she had made changes in her own life, and those changes would always be her secret.

They pulled up in front of the apartment complex. Hannah turned to Ryan. 'Thank you for the lift. I really appreciate it. I know I don't really know you, but I am really grateful. I was a bit worried about getting the bus on my own at this time of night.'

Ryan tilted his head slightly and smiled. 'You're very welcome. I couldn't leave there knowing you were getting the bus.' He paused for a moment. 'Hey, this is kind of out of the blue—and feel free to say no—but I was wondering if you were doing anything tomorrow. There's a "come and try" cooking thing at the market in the morning, and I was hoping you would come with me. It's not something I would go to by myself, and I really need to learn how to cook.' He sat back in the seat and stared out of the front window, waiting for the rejection. What was he thinking? She would never agree to go with him. He felt a sudden rush of heat in his face, and his body slumped in the seat.

'You know what? That actually sounds like fun! I love to cook, but I'm not very good at it. What time does it start, and where should I meet you?'

Ryan sat up straight. He was surprised at the response. 'Ah . . . yeah, starts at eight thirty, and we need to meet the lady at the main entrance. Want me to pick you up on the way?'

'Nah, it's all good. I will meet you there at a quarter past then,' Hannah said with a smile that could light up the darkest of nights. She opened the car door and stepped out. Before closing the door, she leaned back in and said, 'Again, thank you so much for the lift home.'

She gently closed the door and walked away without a second look. Ryan watched her until she reached the stairs; his heart was racing, and his mind was all over the place. He couldn't believe he was going to get to spend the day with her tomorrow. He drove home a little faster than normal and burst through the front door. Bruce was curled up on the sofa; his lifted his head and gave Ryan an annoyed look for being woken. Ryan scooped up Bruce from his sofa and held him in the air. 'Oh, buddy, you're not going to believe how my night went!' Ryan sat heavily into the sofa, put his feet on the coffee table, and turned on the TV. Bruce curled up in his lap and went back to sleep. Ryan knew tomorrow was going to be a great day.

Chapter 14

Hannah loved the market—how she loved the smell and the noise and the hustle and bustle of the shop owners interacting with the customers. It was organised chaos, and she loved it. It was right on eight fifteen, and she was in the main entrance. She spotted a sign saying 'Can't cook? Then you're in the right place. Cooking class starts at eight thirty sharp!' She smiled to herself, made her way over to the sign, and overheard a couple bickering about what they thought the day would entail. She had been there barely a moment when the very familiar sound of Ryan's hello was behind her. He leaned in for a hug and told her how glad he was she could make it and how much he was looking forward to finally being able to make something more than toast or cereal.

They made small talk for around five minutes when a loud Italian woman came over and immediately took control of the group. They paid the fee and quickly tried to keep up with their teacher for the morning. Although she was a larger woman, she sure was quick on her feet and within a minute had all of the groups set up at a makeshift kitchen in a back corner of the market. Hannah looked around at her surroundings as she had never been to this part of the market before. She smiled at Ryan and couldn't wait for the class to begin. She felt a little weird being here with Ryan as she thought this was something that she and her husband should be doing together, not with some guy she met a few weeks ago. Her worry eased when she reminded herself that Sean would never agree to do something like this with her. He would have laughed straight in her face and told her not to be stupid. Hannah glanced up at Ryan, who was completely focused on the teacher. He was beautiful, she thought to herself; and at that moment, Ryan looked over at Hannah. She quickly turned away, feeling herself turn red. After that, she focused completely on the class.

The class was a blast; it was loud and fun, and they giggled every time they got told off by Mamma for not taking it seriously. Neither of them was particularly proficient in cooking, but they gave it everything they had. And after the hour-long class, they had in front of them the worst-looking pasta dish either of them had ever seen. When Mamma came over to inspect the dish, she gave them a look of disgust and rolled her eyes. Mamma picked up the plate and showed it to the rest of the class, telling them that this was not how pasta should look. She placed it back in front of the two of them and laughed. Although it looked terrible, it tasted pretty good; and for the next fifteen minutes, they got to enjoy the fruits of their labour.

The conversation was easy and free-flowing. She learned about his job and his sister, who was constantly interfering with his life. Hannah was kind of glad she didn't have any siblings after hearing the stories about Ryan's sister. When the class was over, Ryan gestured towards a coffee stand. *Perfect*, she thought. That was exactly what she needed. There was something about a hot cup of freshly made coffee that made you feel instantly better. And then for next couple of hours, they continued their conversation amidst the chaos of the market.

It was just before midday when Hannah became aware of how late it had become.

'I'm so sorry,' she said with a panic in her voice. 'I had no idea of the time. I'm sure you have much better things to do than spend your day listening to me talk.'

'Actually, I am really enjoying the conversation,' Ryan said cheerily. 'It is really nice to talk with someone that couldn't care less about sport.'

'Ha ha ha ha. Well, then I'm your girl.' Hannah relaxed again; she felt comfortable in Ryan's presence. He never made her feel like he was better than she was, and it was nice to have someone actually listen to what she had to say. She knew she wasn't worldly or a genius in any way, but she was having a great time talking about not much at all; and she really didn't want to leave, and she didn't want for the day to be over either.

'When was the last time you went to the museum?' Ryan asked with a cheeky grin.

'Oh . . . geez . . . um . . . wow, probably not since school. So a few years. Why?' *Well, that was an odd question*, she thought.

'Want to go? I know it sounds boring, but it's actually really cool.'

'Sure, why not!' Hannah smiled her big smile and a chuckle and grabbed her bag. 'Let's go!'

It was only a short walk from the markets to the museum, and it was a beautiful day. The sun shone bright high in the sky; there was not a breath of wind, and birds were flying overhead. Watching a flock of birds always fascinated Hannah, the way one bird would suddenly change direction and the others all followed. The conversation continued with ease, and the two new friends were getting to know each other better.

Outside of the museum, Ryan spotted a food truck. 'Hungry?'

'Yeah, actually, I am a bit. Do you know what they have?'

'Not sure, want to go and check it out? Otherwise, there's a kiosk inside'. Hannah followed Ryan over to the food truck. It was a fairly basic menu of hot dogs, sandwiches, and cans of drinks. Hannah ordered a hot dog, and Ryan the same. They found a bench set and quickly devoured the food.

'Oh my god, that was so good!' Hannah said, using a thin napkin to wipe the mustard from her lips.

'I know, right? Sometimes the most basic food is the best.'

Hannah broke into laughter when she saw sauce on Ryan's chin.

'What's so funny?' Ryan grinned. 'Do I have food on my face?' Unable to speak because she was laughing at him, Hannah handed him her napkin and watched him clean up.

'Better?' he asked.

'Perfect,' she replied.

Two hours and twenty minutes later, they had seen all there was to see; they discussed the dinosaurs and early humans and had a long conversation about the various war memorabilia displayed and the atrocities of war.

Without thinking, the two left the museum and took up residence in a quaint little bar not too far away, where they ordered some wine and dinner; the conversation continued well into the evening. Hannah wasn't much of a drinker, and it didn't take long for her to feel tipsy. Ryan went to order another bottle of wine, but Hannah felt like it was time for her to go home. She was having a wonderful time and didn't want to make a fool of herself by getting drunk. As they exited the bar, Hannah tripped on the step, and Ryan caught her.

'I think I'd better escort you home, young lady.'

'Noooooooo, don't be silly. I'm a grown woman!' There was a distinct slur in her words. 'I'm very capable of getting myself home.' She stood up straight and tried to put on a serious face. As she turned to start walking off, she missed the kerb and landed with a thud in the gutter. Ryan helped her up and flagged down a cab. It was a very quiet ride as both her knee and ego were bruised. It wasn't too long when the cab pulled up at the front of her apartment. Ryan exited first and helped Hannah out of the cab. He tossed a twenty on the front seat and thanked the driver for the lift. With one arm around her back, Ryan carefully helped Hannah up the stairs to her front door. Hannah put her hand in her bag and fossicked around for the keys, her agitation ever increasing as the pain in her knee got worse and her keys just seemed to be avoiding her grasp. She let out a small wince. Ryan put his hand on her shoulder.

'It's OK. Take a breath and relax. Once we're inside, I will show you my expert first aid skills and take care of that knee.'

With a deep breath in, Hannah calmed down and fought back the tears; she found her keys, opened the front door, and gestured Ryan in to the lounge room while she continued into the kitchen to look for anything that resembled medical supplies. With a bottle of antiseptic and some cotton wool, she limped into the lounge room. Ryan got up from the couch, perched himself on the coffee table, and let Hannah sit down in front of him.

With gentle hands, he lifted her leg onto his knee and surveyed the damage. Without warning, he broke out into laughter.

'Sorry, but it was pretty funny. I know that it hurts, but you spun like a top and landed square on your arse in the street.' And with that comment, Hannah laughed and laughed. She hadn't laughed that hard in a long time. Once the laughter stopped, Ryan had another look at Hannah's knee.

'It's not too bad, princess. Sit still, and I will have this cleaned up in no time.'

His hands were gentle, although the antiseptic stung like hell. Once he had her knee cleaned up, he stood up from the table and looked down at her.

'Looks like my job is done here, so I will leave you in peace.'

Hannah did her best to get up from the couch gracefully and hobbled behind him to the front door. She had a sudden rush of sadness surge through her body. She didn't want him to leave, but she knew he had to. If he stayed any longer, she knew she was going to let him do something that she would regret, and she was never going to be that person. No matter what issues she and Sean had, she was not a cheater and never would be. The thought of Ryan kissing her right now gave her feelings she hadn't had for such a long time. Ryan stopped in the doorway as he left her, leaned close to her, and gently kissed her on the cheek. Not in a way that was forceful or inappropriate, but in the way good friends say goodbye. He could smell her perfume and wanted to kiss her lips but pulled back.

'I hope you knee feels better in the morning. Enjoy the rest of your weekend, Hannah.' And with a slight glance back, Ryan left.

Hannah closed the front door, breathed in, and held her breath. For what seemed like forever, she just stood there leaning on the door and argued with her thoughts. In one thought, she told herself she hadn't done anything wrong; and in the next, she knew there was potential for something to happen.

'Just friends,' she stated aloud to herself and walked to the bedroom. 'And never anything more.' Maybe if she said it out loud, she would convince herself that she felt nothing more than just being friends with Ryan. But she knew deep down, she was lying to herself.

Chapter 15

After a peaceful sleep, Hannah woke to the sun beaming into the bedroom, filling her with enthusiasm to get out of bed. She threw back the covers and sat up. She turned and put her feet on the ground; it was at that point her knee reminded her of the night before. She gingerly walked to the bathroom and turned the shower taps on. While she was waiting for the hot water, she peeled the plaster from her knee and looked at the damage. It wasn't too bad; she had had worse injuries.

Hannah stepped into the shower and let the warm water run over her body. She squeezed body wash onto the flannel, and as the soap lathered on her skin, she took a deep breath of the fragrance in; it smelled of wild orchid, and the lather was thick and creamy on her skin. It was the one small indulgence she could have every day.

After she had finished in the shower, Hannah wrapped a towel around her wet body and walked back to the bedroom. She looked at the time, 8.30. OK, so she had hoped to sleep in today, but never mind; she was sure she would find something to amuse herself with. She opened her closet and looked at her clothes. Old and faded, she was sick of everything she owned. She wanted something new—a fresh, new style. While she flicked through her clothes, getting more disappointed as she couldn't find anything she wanted to wear, she had a thought. What if she took some of the money she had earned over the past couple of weeks and took herself shopping? She instantly felt her mood improve, and she giggled a little. *Oh wow,* she thought to herself, *when was the last time I went shopping for me and only me? Must be forever ago.* She had made up her mind; she was going shopping. Just one new outfit was all she needed, and she didn't want to spend all of her money she had earned—just a small treat. She yanked a T-shirt off its hanger and quickly paired it with some jeans. She found her comfy flats by the door, grabbed her bag, and was off. A little adventure just for her.

The apartment wasn't too far from anywhere, which meant Hannah could pretty much walk most places or just take a short bus ride. There was a small shopping mall about fifteen minutes away. It was a magnificent morning for a walk; she took in all of the sights and sounds of the neighbourhood. She knew her weekend alone would be over soon, so she should make the most of her temporary freedom. For the first time this weekend, she really felt that she didn't want her husband to come home. She could do whatever she wanted and whenever she wanted, with no one telling her what she should be doing and no one watching over her every move. She prayed that he had a great time away with the boys and would return in a good mood. If he came home hungover, he was going to be awful to be around, and he would start at her the moment he walked in the door. She shook her head and told herself not to think about that and to enjoy the day.

She walked through the car park and towards the mall entrance. She located an ATM on the outside wall and took out a small amount of cash from her secret bank account. Just enough, she thought, to herself to buy something small as a reward for her hard work. It may not seem like a hard job to the rest of the world, but for someone who had never worked before, it was hard—and keeping the secret from her husband was even harder.

The smell of fresh hot coffee filled the air, and she decided that she would indulge in a cup before she headed into the mall. She placed her order and sat at a small table outside in the sun. In only a few short moments, the waitress delivered her drink, and she savoured that first sip. She sat back in the chair, and for a while, she watched the people go in and out of the mall. She loved watching people interact, especially the parents with small children—the way the children clung to their hands and were completely dependent on that person. In a small way, she was glad she didn't have any children. The apartment, for a start, was far too small; and she didn't want to have a child exposed to Sean's temper. It just wouldn't be fair. But she did yearn for that interaction that a mother and child share, someone to love who would love her back unconditionally.

Coffee finished, Hannah vacated the seating area of the coffee shop. She walked through the glass doors of the mall entrance and stood almost dazed at where to start. She reminded herself that she only had a small amount to spend and not to love everything she tried on. She wandered in and out of the small boutiques and had not bought a single thing. She felt disheartened as everything was designed for a much younger person, and now she just felt old. There were a couple more stores down one last alley. *Might as well look at all of the stores,* she thought. *Could be a while before you can do this again.* She slowly walked around the corner, which was occupied by a jeweller. She stopped to gaze at all the beautiful shiny treasures when she saw something in the reflection of the shop window. She turned around and felt the ground disappear from under her feet. She was breathless like she never had experienced, and her knees almost buckled beneath her. It must have been only a second or two, but it felt like an eternity. She caught her breath and stumbled into the jeweller's. She must have looked sick because a concerned assistant came straight over to Hannah.

'Oh dear, are you OK? Here, come over here and sit down.' Hannah sat on the chair offered to her and put her head in her hands. Before she knew it, the assistant was back with a glass of water. 'Here, drink this, dear.'

Hannah took a mouthful of water and looked up to the lady who had helped her. 'Thank you,' she muttered barely loud enough to be heard. She sat for just a minute, then stood up; she smiled at the kind stranger and insisted she was OK to leave. She looked outside the store and no longer could see what almost crippled her. She left the mall from a side door and started the walk home. She felt nauseous, and every step was a struggle, but she finally made it home. She dragged herself up the stairs and into the apartment and collapsed onto the lounge. This was a feeling she had never experienced before, and she just didn't know what to do next.

A darkness started to engulf Hannah. She started pacing around the apartment, going from room to room, picking up nothing and not doing anything, just aimlessly wandering. The minutes ticked slowly on the kitchen clock. She heard every second pass. Her skin became hot. Her heart beat faster. Her breath short and sharp.

She was angry. Through her entire life, she had never experienced true anger—an anger so deep her body was staring to go numb.

How could this happen? What had she done so wrong that she was to be punished in this way? And not in the normal 'unhappy, mildly abusive marriage' way she had become accustomed to, but in a way she was now being made a fool of. A sneaky, underhanded, behind-her-back type of punishment.

As she wandered out onto the balcony for the fourth or fifth time, she stopped her thoughts for a moment. *If I hadn't randomly gone shopping, would I have ever found out?* It was a legitimate question, and now that she knew, would the truth come out without her having to push for it? The biggest question racing through her mind was, *How long has this been going on?*

Hannah leaned against the railing and dropped her head. The anger morphed into sadness. At first, she could hold the sobbing in. Her body started to shake, and she no longer had the strength to stand. She slowly collapsed to her knees, and then she turned her back to the balcony rail and hugged her knees. It really hurt; she was crying out loud now, and the tears ran down her cheeks. In her head, the same word just kept repeating. *Why?*

She must have sat there on the balcony for an hour or so sobbing, hurting, questioning herself about the why. She had no answers, just an emptiness in her heart. Hannah grabbed the railing with one arm and pulled herself to her feet. In a trance-like state, she walked to the bathroom and turned on the shower. She undressed and stepped under the water. The warm water ran over her body and almost breathed life back in to her. She looked up at the showerhead and let the water run directly over her face. She let the water wash the tears away; she let the water remove the evidence of her pain. With a deep breath, Hannah stepped out of the water and turned off the taps. She moved out of the shower recess and on to the mat in front of the mirror. She looked at the steam-covered mirror and used her hand to wipe it clear. She stood there naked and wet, just staring at the image in the mirror. She almost didn't recognise her own reflection. Staring back at her was a woman who was tired, sad, and angry. Her lips frowned, her brow dipped, her eyes dark. She stared at herself for another minute, and then speaking as if it was to another person, she said aloud, 'Get a grip. You're better than this.'

Hannah dried herself and redressed. It was still the early afternoon, but the day seemed to be dragging. It wouldn't be long until Sean was home from his boys' weekend away. Her head felt light and dizzy, but she was doing her best to try to collect her thoughts and get back in control of her emotions. This was so unlike her; she just couldn't shake it.

Hannah went to the kitchen to see what she could cook for tea; she was unenthused and still felt heavy. Maybe Sean might bring home some fish? But it wasn't worth the risk of not having a meal ready. Hannah put on her shoes, grabbed her purse, and once again headed out. She didn't have to go far to find the local supermarket. She entered the store and headed for the meat counter. With very little interest, she took a number and perused the display.

'Well, hello there.'

Startled, Hannah turned around to see Ryan standing right behind her. Uncontrollably, her emotions came to the surface, but she was able to steady her voice enough to get a hello out.

'Everything OK?' Ryan tilted his head and had a look of concern on his face.

Hannah couldn't get into it here at the supermarket meat counter, so she held her breath and assured Ryan everything was just fine. She turned back towards the counter just as her ticket was called. Hannah placed her order and quickly left the counter between two older ladies who had suddenly had put themselves between her and Ryan. A quick sidestep down the nearest aisle and Hannah could compose herself. Her breathing became heavy and fast, and she could feel the anger rising again. She didn't know whom she should be angry at; she just knew it wasn't her fault, was it? Goddamn it, doubt came creeping in again. Was all this because of something she had done? Was she just too naïve? Far out! She just needed to get the things she needed for tea and get out of there.

Hannah left the check out and scanned the front area of the supermarket for Ryan; he was nowhere in sight, so she made a dash for the door.

'Hey, what's going on?' Ryan was waiting just outside of the door where he couldn't be seen from the checkouts.

'Don't know what you mean,' was Hannah's reply as she tried to pass him without making eye contact.

Ryan grabbed her arm aggressively and stopped her from walking away. 'So we go from having a great night last night to now you not even making eye contact or having a conversation with me? What's with that?'

Taking a deep breath in, Hannah looked up and stared right into his eyes. 'We can't be friends, Ryan, so please leave me alone.' She yanked her arm from his grip and hastily walked away, fighting back the tears.

Hannah gritted her teeth, trying to control her anger; she wanted the whole world to just leave her alone. Was that too much to ask? 'Just leave me alone,' she said to herself over and over on the short walk home.

Home again, she was now grateful for that small space where she could be where no one else would bother her. Back to the kitchen to do what she needed to do—she needed to cook so Sean would have a hot meal when he returned home.

Before she knew it, she heard the key in the front door. Finally, Sean was home. Hannah rushed from the kitchen and threw her arms around him.

'Hey there, I wasn't expecting such a welcoming!' After a short embrace, Sean pushed Hannah away; looking at her face, he could see she wasn't OK. 'What's happened?'

'I just missed you so much. I didn't like being here alone,' was her reply. Sean tilted his head to the side. He could tell there was more to the story but wasn't ready to push the issue as he had just got home. He kissed her on the forehead and walked to the bedroom, calling behind him, 'Tea smells great, and I'm starving!'

They sat at the kitchen table in silence. Hannah couldn't speak without the tears welling up in her eyes, and Sean just looked tired. So there they sat, husband and wife, not saying a word, knowing there was something that needed to be said; but neither of them had the inclination to say it.

When the meal was finished and the dishes cleared, Sean went and turned on the TV, and Hannah went and sat on the balcony. The tension was obvious, and neither wanted an argument. So they kept to themselves until the day was over, and they both went to bed without a single word being said.

Chapter 16

It was just another Monday morning. Sean got up and got ready for work. Hannah got up and made him breakfast. There were pleasantries and a small kiss as he left, but neither mentioned the night before.

Hannah shut the front door and went back to the kitchen to make a cuppa before getting ready for her own job when she noticed Sean had left his phone on the table. She stood for a moment, contemplating if she should try to catch him at the bottom of the stairs or just leave it. Hannah went to the balcony and saw that his car was already a few houses away, so it was too late to catch him.

Hannah walked back into the kitchen and stared at the phone again. *So do I have a look, or do I just leave it?* she thought to herself. She pushed the phone around a bit with her fingers, almost picking it up several times. *Would he look at my phone if I left it here? Yes, he would, but I'm not him.* She finally justified what she was about to do to herself and picked up the phone and unlocked the screen. She had never looked at his phone before; she never had a reason to look, but she now found herself in a position where she didn't care about his privacy.

Hannah's first instinct was to open his text messages. What she saw next hit her like a sledgehammer. At the top of the list was a message to his best mate and was sent after he had got home yesterday.

'Yo man, freakin hot. Holly crap where did you meet her?? And thanks, she was exactly what I needed.'

Hannah suddenly had that sinking feeling again, her legs went weak, and she pulled a chair out from the table and slumped into it. She felt the tears coming. Biting her lip and taking in a deep breath, she went to the next message down. Hannah assumed it was from the mystery woman she had seen Sean with at the mall. She scrolled down to the beginning of the conversation, which started Saturday lunchtime.

'Hi Amy, I'm Sean, my buddy Matt gave me your number. Any chance of hooking up later?'

'Hi Sean, yeah sure, Matt can give you the address and come over around 6, having some girlfriends over and going out for drinks so bring Matt and a couple others. We will make sure you have the night of your life.'

'Awesome see you then.'

The conversation then changed to Sunday morning from Sean to Amy.

'Hey there beautiful, wow, you are so amazing. What a night. Again wow.'

'Well hello there. It was a great night, the girls had fun and so did I. Any chance I can see you again?'

'Sure, want to do a late breakfast this morning? There's a mall not far from you, I can meet you there.'

'Perfect, see you there at 9.'

'Awesome.'

It was her. Hannah's heart sank deeper. Why would he do this to her? Things had got better, they weren't fighting much anymore, there was intimacy like when they were first married, and she was happy again. The conversation continued mid-afternoon, this time Amy to Sean.

'Hey babe, thanks for breakfast and coming back to mine to keep me company for the afternoon. Can't wait to see you again. When do you think you will be able to get away for a couple of hours?'

'God you are so sexy, how bout I come to you Wednesday night? I don't know what you have done to me but you're all I can think about.'

'Yeah I know what you mean, I just keep thinking about last night and again today, you were sooooooooo amazing and did things to me no man ever has.'

'Tell me about it, my ex-wife never got me off like you.'

Ex-wife! What the hell? He has told her we are divorced. Hannah's mood went from heartbroken to furious in an instant. *How dare he cheat on me and tell her he is divorced!*

'Hey sexy', he continued, 'what's the chances of a pic to get me through till Wednesday.'

That's where the conversation ended. Hannah felt hot all over, her teeth were clenched, and her knuckles white from holding the phone so tight. She stood up with such force she hit her hip on the edge of the table. The pain surged through her, which only intensified her anger. She went to her bag and yanked out her phone. Back at the table, she sat and contemplated copying Amy's number into her phone. As Hannah was saving the number, Sean's phone buzzed. It was Amy, and she had sent the requested picture. Hannah stared at the image on the screen of a scantily clad brunette standing in front of a full-length mirror with a pouty look on her face. It made her sick inside. With the image burned in to her brain, she clicked out of the messages and locked the phone. She felt herself slipping into a dark place. She closed her eyes and saw the messages flashing in front of her: 'Come to you Wednesday night', 'ex-wife', 'you're all I can think about'. Hannah opened her eyes and started to think about what she would do from here. She went to the bedroom and changed into her work clothes. Hannah decided to leave a little earlier for work and take her time walking; she hoped this would clear her mind and let her think more rationally. She left the apartment and started the walk to the café.

Lucy was as bubbly as normal, and Hannah started to lose some of the anger that had built up inside. While preparing for opening, a thought sent a jolt through her body. *Oh crap, what if Ryan comes in today? Oh no, oh no, oh no . . . I was so mean to him yesterday at the supermarket*, she thought to herself. In a daydream, she stood staring into space and tried to think why she had reacted that way when he was just being his usual friendly self. She wasn't sure if it was guilt, anger, or both. Hannah knew she had feelings for him. Although they were not strong, she knew if she spent any more time with him, they would become more, and that would be wrong. Her guilt started to bring her mood down again, and she started getting pains in her stomach. Far out! Could her life get any more complicated right now? She felt her eyes sting, and that brought her back to the now in which she suddenly noticed Lucy standing in front of her.

'Where on earth were you just now?' She tilted her head slightly. 'Do I want to know?'

Hannah did her best not to fall in a heap right then and there. 'No, Lucy, you really don't want to know.' She dropped her head slightly, picked up a tray of condiments, and started setting the tables.

Before long, the café was open, and customers started dribbling in. Hannah took her place behind the counter and did her best to smile and greet them with a friendly hello. As much as she was trying to focus on the customer in front of her, she always had one eye on the clock. She could see the minute hand creeping closer and closer to twelve. That was his time; he always came in a few minutes after twelve.

Chapter 17

Ryan had the worst night's sleep in a long time. His mind was fixated on the encounter with Hannah at the supermarket the day before. He couldn't find a reason why she had snapped at him like that. He tried to recall the events of Saturday night and replayed everything he said and did. He thought he had been a gentleman; he kept himself at a good distance so as not to come across as hitting on her, but still being a little flirty, although he really wanted to. He knew she was married, and that was a line he was not prepared to cross. When he noticed she was getting drunk, he just stayed near her to make sure she didn't get into any trouble; and when she fell and hurt herself, he made sure she got home and helped her with her injuries. Was she angry because he didn't make any moves on her? He was totally confused. Frustrated, he got up and got ready for work but lacked any sort of enthusiasm. Bruce was being more annoying than normal, so he left his apartment early and decided to walk to work.

Arriving at work early gave Ryan the time to go to the break room and get his morning coffee without having to make small talk to anyone, especially Alex. He just wasn't in the right frame of mind to start the day with him. A thought suddenly came to him; he knew it was a bad idea, but he had Hannah's number. Maybe he should send her a text to see if she was OK. Maybe she just had a bad day and snapped at him without realising she had done it. He smiled to himself and went back to his workstation. He started typing the text when he changed his mind. Maybe she snapped at him because she really just didn't like him. He sighed to himself, turned on his computer, and pushed his phone to one side.

As predictable as ever, Alex wandered over to Ryan, story in full swing before Ryan could say anything. In an attempt to humour Alex, Ryan sat quietly, listened to each word, and just waited the conversation out. In less than ten minutes, Alex walked away, grinning proudly at the weekend's events, looking for the next person to tell all about it. Sitting at his desk, Ryan thought back to Hannah. It was frustrating him to no end not being able to work out why she snapped at him yesterday.

A short time had passed, and Ryan had busied himself when his phone started vibrating and buzzing around his desk. He picked it up and was curious at the partial text message that was on the screen. He opened the message to see a photo of himself and Hannah at the bar with the message 'Is this her?' Ryan felt his face burn; he sat upright in his chair and scanned the office to see if anyone was around. He never once thought that someone might actually see them out together. He sank back down and looked at the photo again. It was taken from the back of the bar through the crowd. It was later in the night when Hannah was relaxed and laughing. Ryan closed the picture and looked at the message again. It was from his sister. He thought that was odd as she didn't go out often, so how did she get this picture? If she had been there, she would have come over and made her presence known. Ryan replied to the text, 'We are just friends, so don't get too excited.' Then he hit send. He knew that wasn't going to cut it with his sister, but at least she would leave him alone for a while. Ryan put his phone back in his pocket and attempted to get back to work.

It was getting close to lunchtime, and he still couldn't find much motivation. He did pause for a moment to consider his options for lunch. Would he risk another incident and go to the café to see Hannah, or would he just avoid the situation altogether and just go to the burger place in the other direction? Ryan took a deep breath, considered his options, and made his choice.

Chapter 18

The clock ticked a quarter past twelve, and no Ryan. Hannah's heart sank, but at the same time, she was relieved; she felt her mood lift, and she started to relax. The next hour was crazy, but Hannah cruised through the shift; she smiled at every customer and laughed at their jokes. Hannah really felt at home and comfortable here. Lucy was amazing to work for, and the other staff were beginning to feel like family. When the lunch rush died down and the last remaining customers left, Lucy called the staff over to the big table. She grabbed a plate of unsold cakes and pastries and offered them around to the exhausted crew.

'I think', Lucy started with a coy look on her face, 'we should have a staff dinner party.' Everyone smiled, and excitement amongst the team was instant.

'When?' was asked by almost everyone at the same time. 'Where will we have it?'

As the staff eagerly chatted amongst themselves, Lucy looked over at Hannah to see she was the only one there who wasn't getting involved in the hype. She stepped behind the others and put her arm around Hannah and softly asked if she was OK. Hannah didn't want to bring the mood down, so she smiled at Lucy and assured her she was fine. Within the next ten minutes, it was decided that on Saturday next week, they would get together in the café for their dinner party. The chatter got louder as they all started talking over one another about what they were going to bring and if they should bring partners and what wine was going to go with all the amazing dishes they would all bring along.

But all Hannah could think about was if she was going to be able to find an excuse to leave the apartment on a Saturday night without Sean and actually have a great time with her new friends. Still standing at the back of the group, she just stood there and listened to the excitement that was buzzing. Watching the smiles and hearing the laughter were contagious. Without realising it, Hannah was smiling and laughing; and most of all, she was really looking forward to spending an evening with these wonderful people.

By two thirty, the tables were cleared, the floor mopped, and the café packed away, ready for the next day. Hannah stepped out the front doors and into the sunshine. She stopped for a moment and just breathed in the day. With a smile, she turned back, waved at Lucy, and started the walk back home. She wasn't in any hurry, so she took the time to take it all in—the houses and the pretty flowers all in bloom, the other people scurrying around in a mindless daze, the traffic moving in perfect sync.

Not far from home, Hannah stopped at the corner to cross the street when someone caught her eye. It was from a distance, and she wasn't sure, but it looked like Amy—the long brown hair, the short skirt, the attitude. Hannah stood at the corner for a moment and watched where Amy went. Without thinking, she started to follow her. She was no longer going in the direction to their home, but she didn't care. She just had to know who this girl was and where she was going. Was she going to her place? Would she now know where the other woman lived? Or was she going to meet Sean somewhere to continue the affair? Hannah's pace quickened so that she wasn't too far behind, but far enough she was hoping Amy wouldn't notice her. She followed for about five minutes when they reached a group of units. Amy reached into her bag and retrieved her keys. She went to the second unit in the row and opened the front door. Hannah got her phone and took a couple of pictures so she wouldn't forget the address. While looking at her phone, she became aware of the time and turned back in the direction she just came; and with a sense of urgency, she hurried home. Hannah couldn't risk Sean arriving home before her. That would lead to a whole lot of questions she wasn't prepared to answer right now, especially when she had a list of questions a mile long herself.

On the walk back home, Hannah's mind went into overdrive. How was she going to find out more about Amy? Where did she work?

Who was she friends with? Where did she go? What does she like and dislike? Hannah had convinced herself somehow she was going to become friends with Amy and find a way to destroy her. The more she thought about revenge, the angrier she got and the faster she walked. And the faster she walked, the more bad thoughts went through her head. She was going to do whatever it took to ruin this girl, and she wasn't concerned about the consequences.

Hannah rushed up the stairs to the apartment two steps at a time with a determination she had never known before. If Sean was going to cheat on her, he was going to find out just how far she would go to make sure he was punished. Once inside, she took a deep breath and held it in. Slowly exhaling, she regained her composure and smiled to herself. For the first time in a very long time, she had a goal, and nothing was going to stop her from achieving it—even if it meant giving up everything she knew. Hannah felt for sure she could do this; she could ruin this girl and make Sean regret meeting her. And if she had to, she would take Sean for everything he had. He had to pay for this. Hannah was not going to let him get away with making a fool of her.

Chapter 19

For the next week, life just happened; it was the same routine every day except for Wednesday, when Sean 'worked late'. Hannah got up, made Sean breakfast, Sean went to work, and so did Hannah. The only change was on the way home from work, Hannah would go past Amy's place. She would just sit at the bus stop over the road and spend fifteen or twenty minutes watching and waiting. On one of those days, Hannah crossed the road and went through Amy's mailbox when she noticed a letter only half in. She now had her full name and address; it was time to step it up a bit.

It was around eleven Saturday morning when Hannah heard Sean's phone buzz. She was reading the paper at the kitchen table, and he was watching the sports channel, getting ready for whatever game was going to be aired that afternoon. Hannah got up from the table and stood over at the far bench; from there, she could see Sean and watch his face as he read the message. He was smirking, so she knew who the text was from. When Sean looked up, Hannah smiled back. The smile was forced, and there was no happiness behind it. Hannah picked up an empty box from the counter and went to the bin. She pulled out the garbage bag to empty it; as Hannah walked past the lounge with the rubbish, she paused for a moment.

'All good?' she asked, smiling and in the best concerned tone she could put on.

'Yeah, the guys are going to Dave's to watch the game this afternoon and wanted to know if I was going.' He barely made eye contact with Hannah as he got up out of the chair. 'Think I am going to go. so I am just going to go shower and get ready.' As Sean walked past Hannah, he kissed her forehead and added, 'You'll be fine here on your own, won't you?'

'Of course, sweetheart,' Hannah answered with a sense of anger building in her. Her growing anger was mixed with a deep sadness as she saw her husband lie to her face. She knew their marriage wasn't special and hadn't been for a long time, but at least when they were fighting, he was home and paying attention to her; when he pushed her buttons, he was at least in the same room. She didn't understand why she preferred to be abused by him than have him out with another woman. She felt loneliness had taken over, and she wanted to cry. Hannah went to the front door with the rubbish and looked back. All she wanted to do right now was scream at Sean, telling him she knew everything that was going on, who the other woman was, where she lived, and all the other little facts she had learned this week. But she didn't. She just walked out the door and dumped the rubbish into the bin.

Hannah went back inside the apartment and sat at the kitchen table. She heard the bathroom door open and Sean humming to himself. It was time, she thought. Hannah was going to go to Amy's place and see Sean there. She needed to see this for herself—to confirm the story she had put together in her head. Her sadness went away, and she let her anger control her thoughts. Hannah knew if she was going to ruin the two of them, she couldn't confront them today; all she needed was some pictures of them together. She had a bigger plan in play, and she was going to let this affair continue until the very end.

Sean came out of the bedroom and went to the fridge to grab some beer. He pushed past Hannah, who was deliberately blocking the way. As he passed, she could smell the aftershave he had sprayed; it was her favourite, the one she always bought him for Christmas. Hannah stood up from the table and put her arms around his neck. She kissed him passionately, which took him by surprise, but he didn't pull away. 'Love you, Sean. Enjoy the afternoon at Adam's. What time should I expect you home so I can have dinner ready for you?'

For a moment, Sean looked down. Guilt maybe? Hannah wasn't sure.

'I should be back by ten, so don't wait for me to eat. I think there are two games on today, and I will probably watch both of them. Love you too, and I'm sorry.'

'For what?' Hannah was confused by the apology. 'Have you done something I should know about?' She laughed when she said this, trying to be funny; but at the same time, she thought for a moment he was about to confess. She held her breath.

'I don't know, I just am.' There was nothing further said, and Sean left.

Disheartened, Hannah sat back down, rethinking her plan to make Sean pay for his betrayal. Maybe he would go over there and break it off. With a glimpse of hope, Hannah grabbed her bag and hurriedly left the apartment to see if this was the case. In almost a jog, Hannah headed to Amy's. She didn't live too far, and before long, she was at the spot where she sat and watched. She got comfy and then noticed she couldn't see Sean's car anywhere. Her first thought was that maybe they were going to meet somewhere else, and now she had no idea what to do. Getting agitated and frustrated as she was now at a loss where to look for them, she looked up and saw Amy come out of her front door. She was carrying a bag and headed for the rubbish bins. *I'm back in business.* Hannah smirked to herself and got her phone from her bag. She clicked a couple of buttons and got the camera ready. Trying hard not to stand out, Hannah zoomed in and took a couple of pictures of Amy. She kind of felt bad for her as she didn't know Sean's lie about him being married, but still, she had to suffer too. Hannah was not going to let her off.

While Amy was still out the front of her place, Hannah saw a familiar sight. Sean was pulling up in his car. She could see the excitement on Amy's face at the sight of her new love, and Hannah took some more pictures. Sean looked happy too; he got out of the car and then leaned back in to get something from the front seat. It was his beer, Hannah figured, but she was wrong. He pulled a large bouquet of flowers out and presented them to Amy. Hannah could hear her squeal from the other side of the street. She took more photos and captured a very excited Amy throw herself at Sean. Sean pulled her in close and kissed her. It was that exact moment Hannah felt her heart break. He wasn't going to break up with her; he seemed to be in love. Hannah sadly took another photo of the two of them looking into each other's eyes and walking to Amy's front door. Hannah was shattered; the flowers explained why she got there before Sean, and that was something he had never done for

Hannah. He always told her they were a waste of money because they were going to die in a few days.

Hannah put her phone back in her bag and wandered towards home. As she felt the tears coming, she pushed them deep down inside; she was not going to let herself be the victim. She was in control, and she was going to make sure her revenge was served. Again, she let her anger control her. She started slipping into a dark, dark place. The sweet and innocent Hannah was gone; she knew she had to become something else. She needed to be strong, in control, and calculating. Manipulation wasn't something Hannah had much experience in, but she was willing to learn, and she needed to learn fast.

Chapter 20

Ryan was bored. It was Saturday afternoon, and he had nothing to do. He picked up his phone and called his sister; she was always up to something.

'Hey, Ryan,' his sister said, answering his call. 'What's up?'

'Hey, nothing much. Bored, so I thought I'd check in on you, see what you were up to today.'

'Well, actually, I have someone coming over.' Ryan's sister sounded a little mysterious. 'I suppose I should tell you that I have started seeing someone. We met through a friend a couple of weeks ago, and I just can't get enough of him.'

'Oh, OK then. If it gets serious, you know I am going to want to meet him and make sure he is good enough for you.' Ryan was happy for his sister, but a little jealous at the same time.

'Yeah, I know. I need to make sure my big brother approves and all that.' There was a distinct sarcasm in her tone, but nothing Ryan wasn't used to.

Ryan ended the call with his sister and now was completely lost at what to do. He sat back in the chair and started to think about Hannah. Although he didn't know her too well and he had no claims on her, he missed her. He missed her radiant smile, the way she got shy when she got a compliment, and, most of all, the way she looked in his eyes when she was talking to him. Sighing out loud, Ryan got up from the couch and went to have a shower; he decided he was going out anyway. He was sick of sitting around doing nothing while everyone around him seemed to be having a life.

After showering and changing into something nicer than a T-shirt and jeans, Ryan texted Alex. Laughing to himself, he knew this would shock the life out of his friend by asking if he could meet up and hang out for the night. Although Alex's stories didn't really interest him normally, he was still curious as to where he went and how he seemed to meet so many girls.

With a reply of 'WTF' from Alex, Ryan replied he was serious. This seemed to excite Alex, and plans started getting made. The first stop of the night was a bar down near the markets. Ryan had heard of it but had never been there. Ryan looked up the place on his tablet and went straight to the gallery. He figured this would give him an idea of what sort of girls would be there. After spending nearly ten minutes looking at the photos, Ryan had two thoughts: first, if these were the girls that were going to be there, then he was going to enjoy just watching them because he didn't even have the guts to actually talk to any of them; and the second thought was he now needed to go have a cold shower. These girls were hot, beautiful, scantily dressed, and appeared to enjoy drinking various coloured drinks. He was starting to understand why Alex was a frequent visitor to this place. Ryan looked at the time; it was only four o'clock, and he wasn't meeting up with Alex until eight.

Ryan thought about going down to the markets but figured that by the time he got there, most of the places would be shut. He needed to find somewhere to go as he really didn't want to sit around his place for the next few hours, and he was hungry. The downside to being a single male was that there never seemed to be any food in the house. Ryan grabbed his wallet and keys from the table next to the front door and left. He decided to go to the mall where the movie theatre was; he knew there was a restaurant there where he could go to get something to eat.

Arriving at the mall, he found a parking space almost right outside the door. Feeling pleased with his awesome parking efforts, Ryan got out of his car and stood for a second admiring the space he got. Chuckling to himself, he walked away from his car and into the restaurant. It wasn't a fancy place, but just one of those typical places you find on the outside of a mall where people come to eat before a movie. It was big and open, which made all the noise from the people talking echo. The loudness of the place made it feel busier than it really was. A young girl came over and greeted Ryan; she turned away and gestured for him to follow. She found a tiny table with two chairs in the back corner. Ryan didn't mind being away from the crowds, which at this time of the day was mostly families with young kids being very loud. Ryan watched the commotion from his corner and laughed at frazzled parents attempting to control the rambunctious little people and felt grateful he didn't have any kids. It wasn't that he didn't like kids, but he just hadn't met anyone who gave him the feeling that he wanted to settle down and have his own family; also, he liked sleeping a lot.

It was starting to feel like forever for his meal to be brought to him, and he was starting to get over the noise and the kids running around. To take his mind off his growing hunger, Ryan pulled his phone from his pocket and opened up his social media app. He soon became oblivious of the world around him, so he didn't notice someone standing at his table.

'Hey,' the voice said again, this time louder. Ryan didn't really look up but just assumed it was the waitress bringing him food. He sat up a bit and moved his glass to the side. When he didn't see a plate being placed in front of him, he turned his attention away from the article he was reading and looked up. Stunned for a second, he didn't say a word.

'Hi' finally left his mouth and broke the silence, which was becoming awkward.

'Are you here with someone, or can I join you?' Again, Ryan was speechless; he just looked up at Hannah, not knowing what to say.

'Ah . . . yeah, of course you can. Yeah, sit . . . Um . . . do you want me to go and get you a drink or order you some food?' Ryan shuffled in his chair and put his phone back in his pocket. 'Can I ask what you are doing here? Are you on your own again?'

Hannah sat on the chair opposite Ryan; she put her hands on her lap and took a deep breath. 'Yeah, I am on my own again.' Her voice was low, and there was a sadness to her words.

'Is everything OK? You seem really down. Let me go get you a drink, and then you talk, and I will listen.' Before Hannah could stop him, Ryan got up from the table, went to the bar, and got Hannah a glass of wine. He returned in only a few minutes and placed the wine in front of Hannah. Just as Ryan sat down again, the waitress brought him his long-awaited meal. It was only nachos, so he pushed the plate to the middle of the table so he could share with Hannah.

'So tell me what's got you so down tonight. You seem to be missing your beautiful smile, which, I'm telling you, is the highlight of my lunchtimes.' He smiled at Hannah, hoping that would make her smile back. Hannah lifted her gaze from the table and tried to smile; she really needed that compliment, and it was the only that was stopping her from crying.

'I've just found out my husband is having an affair. He doesn't know that I know, but I do, and I don't know what to do.' Her voice was becoming shaky, and she was barely holding it together; this was the first time she had said it out loud and to someone else.

'How do you know he is having an affair?' Ryan was stunned and didn't want to say the wrong thing.

'I've seen the text messages, and I saw them together this afternoon when he told me he was going to a friend's to watch the game.' Hannah's eyes became glassy, and a single tear rolled down her cheek.

'Oh my god, that's horrible! I am so sorry, Hannah. If you want to sit here all night and talk, then that's what we will do, OK?' Ryan reached over and put his hand on Hannah's arm. 'I'm here for you, Hannah. Anything you need, anytime—day or night—you don't ever need to worry about the time if you need something, all right?' Ryan moved his hand away from Hannah, and when doing so, his fingers brushed hers. He felt a rush of electricity run all the way through his body. Hannah looked Ryan in the eyes and smiled.

'Thank you, Ryan. You don't know how much hearing that means to me. Also, I owe you an apology for the other week in the supermarket. I was rude and out of line. I have no excuse for talking to you like that except I just found out about the affair.'

'Hey, look . . . Don't you worry about that, and you don't owe me anything.' Ryan was leaning forward on the table, and this time, he reached out and held her hand. Hannah didn't pull away, and she sat there, letting Ryan touch her; she no longer cared that it was wrong.

The two of them sat for about an hour talking. There wasn't any laughter like the last time they spent together; this time, it was a serious conversation. Feeling exhausted from telling someone how she was feeling for the first time, Hannah asked Ryan to drive her home. It wasn't a long walk, but she just didn't have the energy. Without a second thought, Ryan stood and offered his hand to Hannah to help her up. He let her walk in front through the maze of tables and out the front door.

'Nice park,' Hannah said, smiling.

'I know, right? How awesome is this! I never get a park near the door.' Ryan was still pleased with himself and appreciated the acknowledgement from Hannah.

The drive to Hannah's place seemed to take only a minute, and Ryan pulled up right out front. Hannah looked at the driveway and didn't see Sean's car. For a moment, she panicked in case he had come home early.

Hannah turned to Sean. 'Thank you so much for listening to me. I hope I didn't ruin your afternoon.'

'You're very welcome, and no, you didn't ruin anything. Now just remember the offer is there. Anytime you need me, you call me, OK?' Ryan found a scrap piece of paper, wrote his number down, and handed it to Hannah.

'OK,' Hannah replied and got out of the car.

Ryan waited and watched Hannah head towards the stairs; she never turned back, and he was disappointed that he didn't get to see her face one last time. *Please turn around, please turn around,* he said to himself in hopes of just a glance back over her shoulder. But she disappeared up the stairs, so Ryan drove away.

Chapter 21

It was almost six when Ryan got back to his place; he still had a couple of hours until he was to meet up with Alex. He had mixed feelings after his encounter with Hannah; he was sad for her and the hard time she was going through, and it was only going to get harder for her. But he was also finding himself more attracted to her. He saw her at her most vulnerable, and she trusted him. He suddenly felt very responsible for her, and he felt an overwhelming need to protect her from the hurt she was feeling, but he couldn't. It wasn't his place to interfere; all he could do was be there for her whenever she needed him. He knew it was very cliché, but what else could he do? Even if she were to leave her husband tonight, she still would need time to get over the relationship without having someone there waiting to swoop in. He also couldn't understand how someone could cheat on their spouse. Ryan was old-fashioned in the way; he believed that when you commit to someone, you see it through and not give in to temptation. All relationships go through bad times, and you will always meet new and interesting people, but there is no excuse for cheating. If you no longer want to be with someone, then have the guts to tell them and leave before you get together with someone new.

He also believed that you could have an affair with someone without getting physical with them. To spend time with someone and develop feelings was still cheating in his book. He got sick of reading articles and seeing news stories on people in relationships joining Internet dating sites just to sleep around. And he had one friend who left his wife and children, telling them there was nothing going on with anyone else, but within a few weeks, he was living with someone new. *How does that happen? How do you leave someone after ten years and suddenly be living with someone else and try to convince everyone that you weren't having an affair? Oh please,* Ryan thought angrily to himself. *It's not possible.* He was convinced, though, that if he became that friend she needed, eventually, when she was ready, she would see him for the man he was; and he would be everything she needed and more.

With time to kill before he was going out again, Ryan put on the telly and started flicking around, looking for something semi-entertaining to fill in some time. He settled on the comedy channel and soon found himself amused at the sitcom that he had seen several times before. Lost in his own little world, the sound of his phone buzzing at him brought him back to the time and realised that he needed to get his stuff together. He quickly checked the message still sitting on his screen. It was Alex checking in on him to make sure he wasn't going to back out as he has got a friend lined up for him. Ryan chuckled and texted back that he was just getting ready to leave. Ryan had decided he was going to drive and park in the multistorey car park a block from the bar so that if the night was bad, he could escape for home quickly; and if the night went well, he could leave the car there for the night. It was fairly secure, and he could get a cab back in the morning to pick up his car. Doing a last-minute check to make sure he was ready to leave, he received another message from Alex indicating his excitement that his friend was finally coming out on a Saturday night adventure with him.

Ryan left the building with a little enthusiasm and jumped in his car. He fussed with the keys until he found the right one and put it in the ignition. *Here we go,* Ryan thought to himself, sighing. He turned the key and nothing. *OK, let's try this again.* He turned the key, and still nothing. The radio made a weak attempt to come on and then silence again.

'No no no, you aren't going to let me down tonight!' Ryan angrily said aloud. 'I would never hear the end of this if I didn't turn up because you're being a bitch and won't start!' He pumped the gas pedal twice, took a big breath in, and turned the key one more time. This time, there appeared to be little life in the engine. He repeated what he just did, and this time, the engine turned over. It was struggling, but it was alive. He let it idle for a minute and then gave it a rev. She was running smoothly once again. 'Thank you,' Ryan said with relief. He decided to let her idle for just another minute before setting off on an adventure of unknown proportions. He didn't know if he was really ready for this, but it was now or never.

About halfway to his destination, Ryan pulled up at a set of lights. He looked over at the taxi next to him and saw four girls that looked to be in their mid-twenties giggling away at one another. The taxi driver appeared to be amused with ruckus, and when the girl in the front seat turned to face her friends, he seemed to be enjoying the view of her cleavage. Ryan found the situation funny; he looked back at the lights and waited for them to change. There was a good song on the radio, so he turned the volume up and started singing along. The increased noise got the attention of one of the girls, who turned her focus to Ryan. She wound her window all the way down and leaned out slightly.

'Hey there, where you off to tonight?' She winked at Ryan, who now also had the attention of all of her friends, who started blowing kisses and giggling at one another.

'I'm heading over to 1806 near the markets.' Ryan tried to say this in his coolest voice; he wasn't used to attention from girls like this, and to be honest, he wasn't hating it. 'Maybe I will see you beautiful ladies over there later.' He gave a little wave and slowly took off as the light had changed back to green. As he moved off slightly ahead of the taxi, he could hear the laughter and squealing of the girls. He had a good laugh to himself and let his ego remain boosted after the attention of four very beautiful girls.

The smile remained on his face all the way to the car park, which was only a couple of blocks from where he spoke with the girls; he parked on the first floor and took the stairs back down to the street. He crossed the road and entered bar 1806. He wasn't sure what to expect as he hadn't been here before, but it looked OK from first glance. Not too pretentious and in no way a nightclub. He felt more comfortable now and quickly scanned the room looking for Alex. He couldn't see him anywhere, so he made his way to the bar, found a seat, and waited for the bartender to come over.

'Hey, mate, what would you like?' The bartender was around his age and had a full beard, which seemed to be the new trend these days. Ryan hadn't considered joining the hairy blokes club as he was always told by his mother and sister that facial hair just didn't suit him. *Maybe if I don't shave for a few days, I could see what I look like*, he considered to himself while catching a glimpse of his reflection in the mirror behind the bar.

'I'll have a 150 lashes, thanks.' It was the trendiest beer he knew; and at eight dollars a glass, it had to be good, right? The bartender poured the beer and placed it on a paper coaster in front of Ryan. Ryan wasn't a big drinker but could hold his own when he had to, and he figured he needed a drink under his belt before Alex arrived, just to keep his enthusiasm for being here going. Twenty minutes later and one beer down, his friend still hadn't arrived. Ryan looked around again just to make sure he hadn't missed them hiding in one of many dark corners. He definitely couldn't see or hear him anywhere. He pulled his phone from his pocket and saw he had missed a message from Alex around ten minutes ago; he said he was on his way and for Ryan not to leave. This made Ryan feel better that he hadn't been forgotten, and he ordered another beer. Just as he took that first big sip of the fresh beer, he heard his friend enter the bar.

'There he is! Here's the man I've been telling you ladies about!' Alex walked over and slapped Ryan on the back of his shoulder. 'Glad to see you here, big fella! Now, ladies', Alex continued and gestured them over to a table just slightly away from the bar, 'what can we get you to drink? A little wine perhaps to get the evening started?' Ryan raised an eyebrow to just how gentlemanly Alex spoke to the ladies, almost condescending but in a fun way, and the girls just ate it up. Alex turned his back to the table and stepped back over to the bar. 'I was wondering if you were actually going to show, and I can tell you that you would never have lived it down if you bailed on me tonight, and boy, do I have just the perfect girl for you tonight! See the one in the blue dress? That is Haley, and she is all mine, OK? But her friend in the pink dress is Skye. And this, my friend, is my gift to you.' Alex suddenly came across in a creepy way. Ryan knew he was a womaniser and seemed to be able to charm his way with all the girls, but he also knew that he didn't care about them; they were just a bit of fun—toys for the weekend.

'A bottle of champagne, thanks, mate.' Alex leaned on the bar. 'And two more beers.' He gestured towards Ryan's glass. 'You ready for the night of your life?'

'Sure am!' Ryan tried to come across as enthusiastic but was starting to lose his want to be here. The drinks were put on the bar, and Alex grabbed the wine and glasses and left Ryan to bring the beer; they sat down at the table, and the appropriate introductions were made.

As the night went on and the more beer Ryan drank, his new friend, Skye, was becoming more interesting. She was giggly and flirty, and Ryan liked the attention. He had no real interest in the story she was telling, but he did like the way she smiled at him and kept rubbing his arm. It had just gone past midnight. Ryan was feeling quite drunk and wanted to leave. The bar was really noisy, and he was having trouble staying focused on any of the conversation that was happening between Alex and the girls. Ryan looked at his watch, exaggerated a stretch, and interrupted the endless flirting between the threesome.

'Thanks for a great time, everyone, but I am calling it a night. Ladies, it was a pleasure meeting you, and I look forward to seeing you both again sometime.' Ryan stood from the table a bit too quickly and felt a little light-headed; as he regained his composure, he saw Alex shoot Skye a look.

'Hey, Ryan, I was just thinking of leaving too. Would you mind if I shared a cab with you?'

'Uh . . . yeah, OK.' Ryan didn't know what else to say. If he said no, he would be the asshole who didn't help a drunk girl get home safely, and he wasn't that guy. He had no idea where she lived, but he didn't think it would be too far if she was friends with Alex. Ryan extended his hand and helped her up from her chair. Once to her feet, she hung on to his arm and led him towards the door. Ryan looked back at Alex, but he was already back to charming Haley, who was eating up every word. Ryan turned his attention back to walking, which was becoming a bit of a challenge; he seemed to have forgotten the basics of one foot in front of the other, and it was just as well he had Skye right by his side, steadying him along. Once out the front, Ryan looked lost; he did his best to scan the street for a taxi, but his vision seemed to be about as useful as his walking. He really started feeling the effects of just how much beer he had consumed. Skye was clearly amused at Ryan's state and ushered him up the street towards the market.

'Come on, honey. There is a taxi rank just up here. You don't need to worry about anything tonight. I'm going to take good care of you, OK?' And Ryan followed her like a puppy.

The taxi ride was a blur. Ryan only saw flashes of light from the street lamps and couldn't work out what direction they were headed; he could hear Skye giving the driver directions, but none of them made sense. He adjusted himself in the seat so he could see her better, and before he could speak, she leaned over and kissed him. Ryan felt himself get hot and aroused; it had been a very long time since he had kissed a woman, and he realised just how much he missed it. He closed his eyes and kissed her back. In his mind, he pictured Hannah, and the thought of being with her really got him excited. Skye pulled back from the kiss and smiled. 'We're here.' Ryan looked around and still had no idea where he was, but he paid the driver and got out of the car. He followed closely behind Skye and went into her apartment.

Chapter 22

I t was almost six o'clock when Hannah got home. She was exhausted.
The day had taken all of the emotional strength she had. In her
mind, she recapped the day: her husband lied right to her face about
going to hang out with mates, she had followed him to his lover's place
and seen first-hand the affair that was ripping her heart out, she had
bumped into Ryan and bared her soul, and now she was home again.
She felt lost. She still had this raging energy inside her that wanted to
confront Sean, and several times, she pictured herself punching him in
the face. She had a sadness for this girl Amy, who seemed to have no
idea that her new boyfriend was married and actively cheating on his
wife; she also felt a bit bad that Amy was needed as part of her plan to
punish her cheating husband. And then there were the feelings she had
for Ryan. It wasn't love, but there was certainly a deep connection that
she was starting to crave. She was beginning to feel infatuated with
him. She loved his smile, his laugh, and the way he looked at her with
genuine concern when she spoke. And the way he touched her hand
today. The thought of his hand holding hers sent tingles down her arm,
and she could swear she could still feel his touch, and this feeling had
her breathless.

Hannah stood for a moment just looking around the apartment in
silence. There seemed something different about the way everything
looked. They were the same pieces of furniture that had always been
there in the same place they were put when they moved there. She
moved into the kitchen and put the kettle on. While waiting for the
water to boil, Hannah went to the living room and pulled the lounge
away from the wall. She moved inch by inch to the middle of the

room and then went to the TV cabinet. She unplugged the cables and carefully manoeuvred the cabinet to where the lounge was. She stopped for a moment and looked over at the balcony doors. She stepped over the lounge and opened the doors both as far as they would go. In the doorway, she looked back at the new position of the TV. She looked back outside and projected where the sun would set and if this would impact the screen. Back over the lounge, she wiggled the cabinet down another foot and felt satisfied that there would be minimal glare from the sun. Hands on her hips, she started feeling good about mixing up the furniture. *A change is as good as a holiday*, she thought, although her actual motive was to see how Sean would react to this. He hated change, but even more than that, he hated change that he didn't get asked about. So let the fun begin. Hannah spent the next half hour moving every piece of furniture in the living room to a new spot; she even moved the pictures on the wall. When she was satisfied with where everything was, she proceeded back to the kitchen and made a cup of tea. She looked around at this small space and couldn't see where anything could be moved to, so she was going have to settle on the new look of the living room.

What's next? she wondered. *How about checking in on Sean and see how his night is going?* Hannah dug around in her bag for a minute and found her phone, which always had a way of burying itself at the very bottom, almost as if it never wanted to be found. She would send him a text rather than phone him just in case her mouth acted before her brain had time to stop her.

'Hey, Sean', she started, 'just checking to see how your night is going. Was just thinking about tea and wanted to see if you were coming home soon or staying out for a while longer. Say hi to everyone for me. Miss you.'

Satisfied with herself, Hannah put her phone down and went to the fridge to see what she could have for tea. She rummaged around for a while and saw a tray with a piece of steak.

'That will do nicely,' she said out loud to herself. 'And it's his favourite too. Such a pity he isn't here to enjoy it with me.' Hannah giggled to herself and wondered how he was going to react when he came home to the furniture being rearranged and no steak. 'Sucks to be you!' she said aloud. 'Not my fault you're not home, is it now?' She felt a real dark sarcasm come over her, and she started caring less and less that she consciously had a bad attitude.

The smell of meat cooking soon filled the apartment, and Hannah pretended to be TV chef explaining out loud everything she was doing, from making a salad to turning the meat. It wasn't long before she had a hot meal on the table and sat down to continue enjoying her own company. Halfway through her meal, her phone buzzed; it was Sean replying to her text. Hannah picked up her phone and opened the message.

'Sorry didn't see your text earlier, will be staying here for a while, not sure when I will be home don't wait up. Everyone says hi back.'

'Oh really? Everyone says hi, do they? I'm sure lover girl sends hugs and kisses too. Well, right back at you, honey.' Hannah made kissing noises at the phone while texting back.

'Ok sweetheart, thanks for letting me know, and you have fun tonight alright. You deserve it XX.' She wondered if he was getting the sarcasm—probably not; he never did get her humour very well.

Hannah sat in silence for the rest of her meal, wondering what he was really doing. Did he sneak off to answer her message, or did he pretend he was talking to someone else? She wondered how many other lies he was feeding her. Hannah cleared away her dishes and quickly cleaned the kitchen; she then went into the living room and decided to see what it was like watching the telly from a different angle. As she settled into her comfy chair, she got another text from her husband.

'Thanks babe, love you.'

Chapter 23

I t was early Sunday morning when Hannah was woken by the sun streaming into the bedroom. She rolled over and put the pillow over her head; she just wasn't ready to be awake yet. Now agitated from being awake too early, she took the pillow off her head and leaned up on her elbows. She looked over to the other side of the bed to see if Sean was stirring; she was hoping he was still fast asleep so she didn't have to start acting just yet. It took a few seconds before she realised he wasn't there. Now she was awake. Hannah jumped out of bed, pulled on her jeans that were crumpled on the floor next to the bed, and grabbed a T-shirt from the drawer. She slowly tiptoed into the kitchen in case he had fallen asleep on the couch when he got in last night, and she didn't want to wake him. She looked around, but he was nowhere to be seen. A dark rage started filling her head, and she could feel anger spreading like wildfire through her whole body. *How dare he spend the night with her! How dare he cheat and lie, and now he isn't coming home! He will pay for this, and he will suffer!* But how was she going to make him suffer for this betrayal? Hannah put water in the kettle and flicked the switch; she needed coffee in her system and quick. While waiting for the kettle, she went in search of her phone. She yanked it off the charger near the bed and unlocked the screen. There were no messages or missed calls. She drank her coffee and put on her shoes; she was going for a walk.

Hannah flew down the stairs and out into the street; trying to suppress her anger, she found herself almost running. In no time at all, she was at her spot over the road from Amy's. His car was still there parked out the front in the same spot she saw it yesterday. She took out her phone and snapped a few pictures. She had no idea what the pictures were for, but she just needed to take them—kind of like proof to herself that she wasn't making the whole thing up in her head. She must have sat there for about ten minutes just staring at the front door, hoping he would come out so she could see them together again, but nothing. She got up and started walking home. She need time to think. She needed to work out the next part to her revenge. She needed an outlet for all of her anger. Most of all, she wanted to cry. The mood swings between anger and sadness were exhausting; most of the time, she didn't know if she wanted to yell at someone or curl up in a corner and cry. Hannah went home.

It was around eleven when Hannah got the following message: 'OMG I am so sorry, had a few too many beers and crashed on the couch. On my way home see you soon.'

She replied, 'I figured as much, see you in a few minutes.' She had nothing else to say. She now only had a few minutes to put her game face on. She went to the bathroom and wet her face; she was hoping some cold water would take the redness from her skin. She brushed her hair and sprayed a little perfume. She stared at her reflection and smiled. *That's better,* she thought. *Let's keep our emotions in check, and he will be none the wiser.*

She went back to the kitchen and waited. She didn't have to wait long when she heard his heavy steps nearing the front door. She sat up straight and put her best smile back on.

'Hey there, stranger.' She smiled at Sean as he entered the kitchen. 'So how was your night? You look tired. Would you like me to make you a cuppa and something to eat?' She got up from the table and went to the fridge before he had a chance to answer.

'Yeah, that would be great, thank you. What you doing here?' He pointed to the photos scattered over the table.

'I was looking for something last night in the wardrobe, and I found a box of photos from when we were first together and our wedding album.' She came to Sean's side and put her arm over his shoulder. 'Look how handsome you were the day we got married.' She sighed and kissed his arm. 'We were so young and stupidly in love.' She went back to making his coffee and let him look at the photos for a moment in silence. She turned to watch him looking at the photos; his back was to her, but she could see him moving them around with his finger. But she couldn't read his reaction. 'Coffee's ready, hun.' She just had to break the silence and let him move away from the wedding photos. He came over to get his cup and kissed Hannah softly on the lips; he never said anything and couldn't make eye contact with her. He took his cup and went to the living room. Hannah followed him, she needed to see his reaction to the furniture as he didn't comment when he first came in. Maybe he walked in too quickly out of guilt that he didn't really pay any attention to his surroundings.

'What do you think?' Hannah asked. 'I know we don't have enough to refurnish the place, so I thought if I moved it all around and maybe went and got a few new blankets or something to cover the old couch, it would be as if it was all new.'

Sean looked around, and his first instinct was to get angry as he wasn't consulted on the changes, but he stopped and smiled at Hannah. 'If this makes you happy, then I am OK with it. Maybe I could look at getting some overtime, and we could update a few things.' He sat on the couch and nodded at Hannah as if his word was the final sentence on this matter.

'That would be amazing, Sean, thank you. But please don't feel like you have to work back at night. I barely see you as it is.'

'It's OK, babe. I don't mind doing extra hours. The place could use some attention. Will give you a project to work on. You look at the catalogues when they come in next week and work out how much you might need, and I will see about working late a few nights to get you the money.' Sean picked up the remote and turned on the TV; now that meant the conversation was really over.

Hannah went back to the kitchen and packed away the photos. She had now given Sean permission to work late, and she knew exactly what that meant.

Chapter 24

Ryan felt guilty. He knew he didn't need to as he and Hannah weren't actually a thing; but he still felt bad going out, drinking far too much, and going home with some girl he met that night. He was still having flashbacks from Saturday night, from the taxi ride back to Skye's place right through until lunchtime Sunday; it was blurry at best. Even now, on Monday morning, he still was feeling like crap. The headache seemed to have disappeared, but he still wasn't hungry and just wanted to go back to bed. He contemplated for a while calling in sick but then couldn't be bothered having to arrange a sick certificate from his doctor. Reluctantly, Ryan got out of bed and stumbled to the shower. He stood under the water for around ten minutes without moving except for gulping in big mouthfuls of water. How he hated feeling like this and couldn't remember the last time he drank so much. He was really starting to regret going out on Saturday night, and he was dreading having to face Alex this morning at work. He knew he hadn't done anything to embarrass himself; well, at least he didn't think so, but he knew he was going to get quizzed about the events after he left the bar. No doubt Alex had already spoken to Skye, but he would still want to hear it first-hand from Ryan.

Once again, he thought seriously about not going to work. Ryan stepped out of the shower, and his conscience talked him into going. *Better to get it over with than putting it off another day,* he told himself. *Let Alex have his fun, and then he will get bored and move on to someone or something else.*

Ryan drove to work and quietly made his way to his desk; he even brought coffee and water on the way to avoid the kitchen for as long as he could. The office was quiet that morning, and Ryan was very grateful. He took another couple of painkillers and found a task that didn't require much thought. The morning dragged, and with every passing minute, Ryan became irritated. He still felt like crap and would do anything to be able to curl up somewhere and sleep, but on the positive, his appetite was coming back. He scanned the office and still hadn't seen or heard Alex. He checked the time; it was ten past eleven. Now all he wanted was the next fifty minutes to go quickly so he could sneak out and go and have lunch on his own. He was going to go to the café and see Hannah. He missed her when he knew he shouldn't, but he really did. He needed to see her, hear the sound of her voice, and somehow have just a little body contact. He would settle for a brush of her arm as she walked past or a touch of her hand when she brought him his order; he would settle for any contact he could get from her. For a brief moment, the guilt from his one-night stand came back. He was sure she wouldn't care, but he couldn't tell her in case she did. What would she think of him, getting wasted and sleeping with someone he just met? It happens all the time, but not to him, and he desperately wanted her to think he was different from all the other guys out there.

It was time for a quick bathroom break before going to lunch. Ryan quickly made his way past the break room when he heard Alex. He couldn't see him, so he was taking the chance that Alex didn't see him either. He made it around the corner unnoticed and almost felt proud of his achievement. On the way back to his desk, he wasn't so lucky.

'Ryan. Hey, Ryan! Been meaning to come and see you this morning. Feedback I've been getting is you're quite the man. So now I want hear all the good stuff from you—you know, the bits girls won't talk about.'

Before Ryan could say anything, his phone rang in his pocket; he pulled it out and gave a little hand gesture to Alex like he would be back after taking the call and walked away, answering the call. Out of earshot, he sighed.

'Oh, thank you for calling, sis. You just got me out of a conversation I have been avoiding all morning.'

'Sounds interesting.' His sister giggled at him. 'Sounds like you now owe me lunch today. I'm going to be near you at lunchtime and thought it's been ages since we spoke last, and I did turn you down on Saturday. Sorry for that. So how about lunch today?'

She always had a way of talking that could convince anyone to do anything; she came across so innocent and sweet that you just couldn't say no to her.

'You know what? That sounds great. I was going to go to a little café round the corner from here. Not sure if you know, but I will text you the details. Is twelve OK?'

'Sure, twelve is good. See you soon.' She ended the call sounding really excited and had Ryan puzzled as to why she suddenly wanted to have lunch on a Monday. He was grateful for the fact he now had a reason to avoid Alex at lunchtime. He would catch up with him tomorrow when, he was praying, he felt better and could tolerate the twenty questions. Ryan relaxed a bit now; he sent Alex a message that he was seeing his sister for lunch and suggested for Alex to fill him in on all the details tomorrow. He got a reply almost instantly, which was on the abusive side, but Ryan knew his friend well enough to know he wasn't serious. Back to the mundane tasks to fill in time until he would go and see his sister.

The next forty minutes went fast, and right on twelve o'clock, Ryan was out the front door. It was only a few minutes' walk to the café, and he saw his sister waiting out the front for him. She ran up to her big brother and hugged him. She was grinning from ear to ear and clung on to his arm as they entered the café. Ryan looked around and saw Hannah in the far corner of the dining area setting the last of the tables. He headed to his usual table and gestured to his sister to sit. Ryan took his time sitting as he wanted to wait until Hannah turned around so he could say hello; he was craving her smile, and it was almost painful waiting. As Ryan finally sat, Hannah finished what she was doing and turned around. There was that big smile he had been waiting for. Hannah walked over on her way back to the counter. She stopped at the table and quickly lost her smile when she looked at his sister. Ryan raised an eyebrow as he wasn't sure what to make of the look and then introduced them.

'Hannah, this is my sister.'

Chapter 25

Not much was said between Hannah and Sean the rest of the night. They sat silently watching a movie, and when it was finished, they silently got up and went to bed.

The alarm went off at the usual time on Monday morning, and Sean got up without hitting snooze. Hannah was already awake too, so she got up a minute after him. While Sean was in the shower, Hannah went and put the kettle on and put bread in the toaster. After only a few minutes, she heard the water being turned off, and that was her cue to pour the hot water and to butter the toast. Sean came into the kitchen and sat at the table, and not saying a word, he ate his breakfast. When finished, he got up and grabbed his wallet, phone, and keys; then he walked out. Hannah was left in the kitchen in silence.

It took a few minutes for Hannah to figure out which was worse: her husband looking her in the eye and lying, or him not saying a single word. She almost felt that if the lies were better, at least then he was speaking to her and pretending to be there. The silence was horrible, and Hannah burst into tears; she abandoned her toast and coffee and went to the bathroom. She stared at her reflection, and the tired image stared back at her. She ran her fingers over her face, stretching out the fine wrinkles that looked like canyons to her. She dropped her robe and took off her top. She looked down at her breasts and squeezed them. Negative thoughts kept going through her mind. Maybe he was having an affair because she was looking old and wrinkly. What if she had bigger boobs? Maybe she was too fat for him now. What had she done wrong? Staring at herself and at a loss for why he was doing this to her, she felt hot and angry again. Hannah stopped feeling sorry for herself and again focused on how she would punish him. Then she showered and dressed for work.

She had some spare time before she needed to leave. She set her laptop up on the kitchen table and started looking for revenge stories. It wasn't long before she came across a site that was full of stories written by bitter exes about how they sought revenge on cheating partners. Hannah was surprised to read how many women cheat; she was always under the impression that men were the worst. She made a fresh cup of coffee and kept reading. The revenge acts varied and were filling her head with so many ideas. Some of her favourites were billboards and signs outside of the workplace of the cheater as well as painting messages on cars. None of that would do for Hannah, though; she wanted her revenge to be different and something people would talk about for ages. And nothing gross like hiding fish somewhere that the smell became unbearable. It would be classy—well, as classy as revenge could be. In a twisted way, Hannah felt better after reading the stories of others; she felt less alone as she had accepted that she wasn't the only person going through this. And from what she had read, everyone survives, many with scars and baggage, but still here and with some great stories to tell.

Feeling better and having passed enough time, Hannah got herself ready to leave for work. She looked out the window; it looked a little overcast, so she grabbed a jacket just in case. She felt good now and ready to go to work, ready to have a great day with her new family. It was the one thing she loved most about being a working woman; she loved the other people and the social interactions. They were kind to her and genuinely wanted to know things about her. They made her laugh, and Lucy made her feel important. Lucy was always saying that it's the little things that count—the smile when you talk, the 'pleases' and 'thank yous', the way you look someone in the eye when they are talking to you. If you get all those things right, everything else just happens.

Hannah arrived at work right on time as always; she had no excuse to be late, and being on time showed respect. Lucy appreciated Hannah's punctuality; she never made a big deal about it, but it was a nod here or a gentle touch on her shoulder as she walked in. Hannah had been working here for about six weeks now and no longer needed to ask what she needed to do. She grabbed the tray with the condiments and started setting the tables. She was always sure to wipe the tables first; even though they were cleaned at pack up each afternoon, she still liked to wipe them again anyway. While preparing the tables, Hannah noticed a song that she loved come on the radio. She started singing out loud and wiggling her hips. She looked up when she heard two others join in the chorus and saw them waving their arms around and jumping up and down. Without a second thought, Hannah joined in; and within seconds, all five staff were dancing around, singing at the top of their lungs. There were fits of laughter when the song was over, and one of the girls hugged Hannah so forcefully they both nearly ended up on the ground; this caused a second round of laughter and hysterics. Hannah had never had so much fun in all her life. She had caught herself wondering on a few occasions why she hadn't got a job earlier; there was so much of her life that just passed her by while she was stuck in that apartment like Rapunzel.

'OK, everyone, as much fun as that was—and I do believe that a few of you should stick to your day jobs—we are about to open. So let's keep the singing for Saturday night, all right? Oh, Hannah, you're the only one who hasn't confirmed if you are coming to our staff dinner party. Can you please let me know soon?'

Oh crap. Hannah had forgotten about this Saturday night. She so desperately wanted to come along, but how was she going to get out for the night? She was going to have to put some thought into this. 'I will definitely be here, Lucy. Wouldn't miss it for anything!' There was a cheer from the rest of the staff, and they opened the door for business.

Hannah quickly began setting the few tables at the back that she missed while messing around and didn't notice Ryan walk in. When she finished the last table, she stood up straight and, with self-satisfaction, put her hands on her hips. Hannah picked up the empty tray in one hand and turned to head to the counter. As she looked around the tables to get a feel for how many people just walked in, she saw Ryan in his usual spot. There was a girl with him, which was unusual; but with the great, big smile he was sending her way, she knew the other girl wasn't anyone she should be worried about. She quickly corrected herself and reminded herself that Ryan wasn't hers and that he was free to date whomever he wanted. Curious as to who the mystery woman was, she walked casually over to the table to say hello and suss out the competition. She got to the table and looked at the girl, and before any words could come out, she felt the ground move under her feet. She quickly looked at Ryan, who had an odd look on his face; he raised an eyebrow at her.

'Hannah, this is my sister. Amy, this is Hannah.'

His sister! What is going on? How could the person who was stealing her husband be Ryan's sister? *No no no*, Hannah said to herself. She needed to say something out loud now before the silence became even more awkward.

'Your sister? Hey, well . . . hello . . . Amy.' It took everything she had to say her name. 'You know the drill, Ryan. Come to the counter when you're ready to order, OK?'

Without waiting for a response, Hannah walked back to the counter as casually as she could. She quickly ducked into the kitchen to compose herself. She took a deep breath in and stopped to think for a moment; maybe this could work in her favour. Maybe getting to know her through Ryan could be just the advantage she had been waiting for. This made Hannah feel better. She didn't think twice to any possible consequences; she just knew she now had a new direction. She put on her biggest smile and went back to the counter to start serving customers. From the till, she had a great view of Ryan and Amy; and every now and then, he would glance over at her. She smiled coyly back and kept serving customers. When there was no one at the counter, Hannah helped take the food from the kitchen. She heard the bell and turned to see Ryan's order was ready. One of the other girls came to collect the food, but Hannah stopped them.

'I got this one,' Hannah insisted; the co-worker smiled and moved to the side. Everyone who worked at the café saw the flirting that went on between Hannah and Ryan.

'I have one schnitzel here. Let me guess. Ryan, that is yours.' It was more a statement than a question. 'And for you, Amy, the chicken salad. Is there anything else I can get for you?' Hannah looked at Amy for a response all the while never losing her smile.

'No, thank you. This looks delicious.' Amy smiled back at Hannah. Hannah turned to Ryan and waited for his response.

'Nope, this looks great as always. Thanks, Hannah!'

'You both are very welcome and enjoy!' Leaving them to eat their lunch, Hannah wandered past a couple of tables, collecting dirty dishes as she went. The café wasn't too busy today, which Hannah was grateful for; it gave her plenty of time to watch Ryan and his sister. She wondered what they were talking about. As she watched the two of them interact, she momentarily forgot that Amy was the enemy; she knew she didn't know, and now that she had seen her up close and spoken to her, she didn't seem so horrible. And how could she be horrible? With a brother like Ryan, you had to come from a good family. Hannah waited about five minutes after they both finished eating before going and collecting the plates. She didn't want to come across as nosey, so she waited a little while. When she saw Ryan check the time, she took that as a cue to go over.

'So how was everything?' Again, she made eye contact with Amy first; she needed her to feel comfortable and important in this moment.

'Great, thanks. That was really nice.' Amy seemed to be genuine with her reply and leaned back in her chair. 'I'm full now.'

'It was great as always. Thanks, Hannah. Please let the kitchen know they do a great job.' Ryan also leaned back in his chair and rubbed at his stomach. 'Won't be needing tea tonight after all that.'

'Excellent! Thanks, guys, and I will pass your comments to the kitchen.' As Hannah was clearing the plates, Lucy came over, clearly intrigued by who was with Ryan.

'Well, there's my favourite customer. How are you, Ryan?'

'Great, thank you, Lucy! The food is so good here that I thought I'd bring my little sister here so she can see for herself why I eat here all the time. Amy, this is the wonderful Lucy, and this is her place.'

'It's a pleasure, Amy. And flattery, my dear, will get you everywhere. How about a coffee each on the house to finish off your lunch?'

'Wow, that sounds awesome! Thank you, Lucy.' Amy gave Lucy a big smile, and from the kitchen, Hannah finally saw the attraction with her. She was polite, beautiful, young, and seemingly innocent. For a moment, Hannah became agitated but quickly took control of her emotions.

Hannah emerged from the kitchen and took her place behind the counter once more; it was time for the one o'clock diners to start coming in. Before long, Hannah was busier than ever and no longer had time to watch Ryan and Amy. Busy serving at the counter and clearing tables, Hannah didn't notice them leave. When she did look up and realised they were gone, her heart sank a little; she wanted to say goodbye and have one more look into Ryan's eyes. Lucy caught Hannah looking around and pointed at the door.

'They only just left a second ago. If you're quick, you will catch them.'

Hannah didn't need to be told twice; she quickly went out the front door and saw Ryan talking to his sister. Ryan looked up at Hannah and smiled.

'Thought you could leave without saying goodbye, huh?' Hannah jokingly raised an eyebrow and had her hands on her hips. Ryan walked back over to Hannah and bowed his head like a naughty child.

'Sorry, Hannah.' He smirked and looked up again.

'You're forgiven,' she laughed and put her hand on his arm. 'Have a great afternoon, and I will see you again soon. Bye, Amy, have a good afternoon.' Hannah waved at Amy, who in turn waved back, smiling.

Ryan smiled at Hannah and started to walk away. 'See you tomorrow!'

Yes, you will, Hannah thought to herself and walked back into the café to complete her shift. She felt so different around Ryan; it was like he really wanted to be near her. There was no obligation or commitment, and she wanted to be near him. She was starting to miss him when he wasn't around. *Another time and place*, she continued to think, *and things would be different.*

Chapter 26

'Where the hell have you been?' Sean yelled at Hannah as she walked in the door. 'I come home early expecting you to be here because you know you're my wife and this is where you belong.' He left the kitchen and started walking towards her. 'I get home, and you're nowhere to be found. I ring your mobile—you know, that funny little black thing I have told you to have on you at all times! And you don't answer.' Hannah grabbed her phone from her bag and saw thirty missed calls from Sean starting at around one o'clock. 'So I'm going to ask one more time where you were.' Hannah was still near the front door with her bag in one hand and her keys in the other. She was startled by the ambush and a little scared of the tone in his voice.

'I went to the library and stopped for a coffee on the way back.' Hannah couldn't make eye contact with Sean. He walked right up to Hannah, gripped her chin with his hand, and lifted her head so he could look into her eyes. He was angry. Hannah hadn't seen him this angry in a long time. He leaned right into her face, and she could feel his short sharp breath.

'You're a goddamned liar. I see it all over you.' His tone was low, and he gritted his teeth when he spoke. 'One thing about you . . .' He pushed her back against the door, still holding her face; now he was squeezing harder. 'Is you're a bad liar.' He lowered his grip from Hannah's face to the side of her throat, his thumb pushing into the middle of her throat and his fingers behind her neck. Hannah felt pain in her neck; he wasn't squeezing hard enough to stop her breathing, but it was starting to hurt. He stood like this for what seemed like an hour, but in reality, Hannah knew it was only a minute. She didn't dare say anything to avoid angering him further. She needed to let him calm down and back away from her before she said anything else. Sean eventually stepped back, letting her throat go.

Just when Hannah thought he was going to walk away, he turned suddenly and grabbed her arm and started dragging her. As he neared the kitchen, he pulled her so violently that she lost her balance and fell over a lounge chair; as she fell, he kept his grip on her arm, and it twisted behind her. Hannah let out a painful yelp. Sean stopped and glared at her, all the time keeping his grip on her arm. He pulled her arm up as if he was trying to help her to her feet, but all it did was twist her arm more. She let out a louder cry of pain; this time, he let her go and get herself to her feet. As she stood, she cradled her arm as the pain subsided slightly. He walked over to her, grabbed the back of her neck, and pushed her into the kitchen.

'So I guess you're going to tell me that the library pays you to read now? Well, if getting paid was that easy, what the hell have I been doing all these years working my guts out on a building site paying for your cushy lifestyle? Maybe I should go to the library and ask for a job too.' Hannah was confused at what he was yelling about until she looked over at the table and saw he had opened a bank statement from her secret account. Hannah felt the blood rush around her body like a dam that had burst, and she was lost for words. She started to stammer when Ryan grabbed the back of her neck again and pushed her forward towards the table; he held her head a couple of inches from the tabletop so that she was staring right at the bank statement. After a few seconds, he gave her neck a little shove and let go. He stepped back a pace and let Hannah stand up. She turned to look at Sean and was terrified. As she went to say something, Sean backhanded her across the face. 'The next thing that comes out of that mouth of yours better be the truth, or so help me God, you will regret the day you crossed me.'

With tears rolling down her face, Hannah sat at one of the kitchen chairs. Her shoulder was in agony, and her face started to ache. In a voice that was barely audible, Hannah started to talk.

'About six weeks ago, when I was on my way to the library, I saw a "Help Wanted" sign in a café about ten minutes from here. I went in, not expecting anything out of it, and the owner gave me a job. It's only three hours a day, and all I do is take orders and clean tables. It doesn't pay much, but it gives me something to do. I haven't spent any of the money. You can see that from the statement.' Hannah gestured towards the piece of paper. 'I just needed something to do as I was going crazy with boredom.'

'Were you ever going to tell me about this? Or do you enjoy having a secret from me?' Sean was speaking again rather than yelling. 'It's not so much that you went and got a job without my permission—it's that you lied to me. Right to my face, day after day for the past six weeks you lied to me.' Sean walked around the table and stood right behind Hannah. She couldn't see him, but she could feel his domineering presence hovering over her. She was afraid to turn around. 'Now what you are going to do is ring this boss of yours and quit. This is not a negotiation. You are my wife, and you belong here. If I wanted a working wife, I would have married someone with a brain, not you!' Sean backed away from Hannah again.

'No.'

There was a cold deafening silence. Hannah stood up from the table and turned to face her husband. 'I will not quit my job. It's three hours a day and still leaves me plenty of time to be here looking after you.'

'I said this was not a negotiation!' Sean was back to yelling. He walked right up to Hannah again, and his face was less than an inch from hers. 'You WILL quit your job, and you WILL do as I tell you!'

'No.' It just came out. Hannah regretted it the instant the word left her lips.

Sean grabbed both of her arms and pulled her away from the table. He was pushing her backwards towards the bedroom. When she was almost in the doorway, Sean pushed her hard and let go. The force knocked her off her feet, and she landed with a thud on the floor. She scrambled backwards but had nowhere to go as the bed was right behind her. He leaned over again, grabbed her arms, and pulled her to her feet. She saw a look in his eyes she hadn't seen before; she was truly frightened of him. He turned her around and pushed her face down on the bed. He put one hand in the middle of her back to stop her from getting up, and with the other hand, he put it under her belly and undid the button on her pants.

'Sean, stop!' Hannah pleaded. He hit her in the back of the head and continued yanking at her pants.

'You're my wife, and you're here to do whatever I want whenever I want it! Clearly, you had forgotten that, so I think it is time I reminded you of who is in charge.'

He leaned over, put his arm under her stomach, lifted her slightly, and pushed her further onto the bed. With one last tug, he got her pants off one leg. He parted her legs with his knees, and with a loveless thrust, he entered her. When she tried to move, he put his hand in between her shoulder blades and pushed down with all his weight. With his pressure on her like that, she struggled to breathe. He pounded at her with such relentless force. She stopped fighting him and let him finish. She closed her eyes and just focused on breathing. She tuned out the grunting noises he was making and tried to sing her favourite song to herself until it was over. It took approximately ten minutes for the ordeal to finish. When he was done, he lay completely on her and buried his face in her neck. He was breathing hard right in her ear. He lifted one arm and gently moved the hair from that side of her neck and face so he could kiss her skin. It took every ounce of strength she had not to cry; she just wanted to be still and hope he would get off her. He kissed her ear and pushed on her to get up. Without saying a word, he went to the bathroom and showered.

The moment Hannah heard the water running she lost control and cried. She cried so hard her stomach hurt. She pulled at the leg of her pants that was still on her and threw them hard onto the ground. She pulled her underwear back on and went to the cupboard to find something soft to put on. Her whole body now ached, from her shoulder that got twisted to her face that was hit and now from the waist down burned. She found a soft pair of pyjamas to wear. Gingerly, Hannah went back to the kitchen. She fussed around in her bag for a bottle of painkillers. She took out four and swallowed them in a single gulp of water. When she heard the shower stop, Hannah picked up the kettle and filled it with water. When Sean came back into the kitchen, she handed him a cup of coffee. He sat at the table and stared at her. She was terrified to move, so she just stood leaning back against the bench, waiting for Sean to say something. He leaned back in the chair and crossed his arms.

'I've decided that I will come and check out this place you have been working at. If I think it is acceptable, then you can continue to work there.'

Hannah mustered up a smile; it was fake, but she needed him to think that she was grateful for his permission.

'Now come over here.' He patted to his lap. 'Tell me about the place. What's your boss's name?' And like an obedient wife, Hannah went and sat on his knee and told him about Lucy and the café and the other people that worked there.

The atmosphere was dismal that night. Hannah only spoke when asked a direct question, and Sean moved around the apartment like he was the king that would be obeyed. It wasn't long into the evening movie when Sean looked at Hannah; he told her that she looked tired and that she should go to bed. Hannah jumped at the chance not to be in the same room as him anymore. As she walked past him, he grabbed her wrist. She looked down at him, and he turned his cheek and raised his eyebrow. She knew he was gesturing for a kiss. Hannah leaned over and kissed Sean on the cheek. He smiled at her and released his grip. Hannah left the room and never turned back. She climbed into bed and cried herself to sleep.

Chapter 27

The night seemed to last forever. Hannah couldn't sleep; the pain was keeping her awake. She got up twice to take more painkillers. The second time, she sat in the kitchen for a while. She sat there in the dark at the table, just staring into space. She hated her husband right now. She never knew rage like that before; he scared her beyond belief—and all over a part-time job she had got to fill in her day and give her a purpose. For a while, she sat there thinking about leaving him but came up with too many reasons why she should stay. Where would she live? How would she support herself? The café didn't pay enough for her to rent somewhere on her own. She would have to share with someone. Maybe she could move back in with her parents' for a while, just until she sorted herself out.

Her thoughts took her back to wanting to punish him for cheating on her, and now she didn't care; after what happened tonight, she just wanted out. He could have his fling, and he could have this apartment all to himself. She no longer wanted anything from him. Tomorrow she would call her parents and talk to them, and she prayed they would understand and help her move back. Who would have thought at her age she would still need her parents to rescue her? But she did. Hannah didn't know how to do this on her own; the thought of moving out was daunting. This was all she had known for such a long time. What would people think of her running away from her marriage?

When the pain reduced to a dull ache, Hannah went back to bed. She climbed in quietly so as not to wake Sean. She still couldn't sleep, and so she lay there once again listening to him breathing and imagining her life without him.

At long last, sunlight began creeping in. Hannah didn't wait for the alarm to go off; she got up, dressed, and went to the kitchen. She put on the kettle the same as she did every morning. While waiting for the water to boil, she went into the lounge and turned on the telly. She flicked through a few channels and settled on the morning news. When she heard the click of the kettle turning itself off, Hannah went back to the kitchen and made a cup of tea. She looked up at the clock and knew she had about fifteen more minutes before Sean would get up. Taking her cuppa out onto the balcony, Hannah watched as the world began to wake to another day. The sun was up, but it seemed cold today; there was still a chill from the night in the air. Holding her mug between both of her hands for warmth, Hannah stayed out on the balcony and watched the street as people began to emerge from their homes. She could hear the garbage truck a few streets away and saw a man over the road quickly dash outside in his boxers, taking the bin to the kerb. This made Hannah smile, seeing someone out in the early morning in their underwear panicking over trash. How his life from a distance seemed uncomplicated and the biggest issue of his day was rubbish. She knew that there was probably more to the man than this; there are always parts of people's lives that are secret and hidden behind the front door. She turned and looked the other way up the street and watched a young girl jogging, with earphones on and seemingly not a care in the world. Hannah was lost in her own little world people gazing that she never heard Sean come up behind her.

'Hey. What you doing out here? It's cold this morning.' Sean's voice was calm and soft. Hannah turned to face him. She didn't say anything for a few seconds as she really didn't know what to say to him. She was about to speak when he cut her off.

'I'm sorry about last night. I don't know what came over me. Please forgive me.' He seemed genuine and stepped closer to Hannah. He took one of her hands in his and brought it up to his lips. He kissed her hand softly and held it to his cheek. He opened his eyes and looked at her again. She saw remorse in his eyes, and her heart softened.

'I forgive you,' she whispered. Sean moved right over to her, put his arms around her neck, and pulled her close. He held her for a minute. As he released her from his embrace, he kissed her behind her ear and whispered, 'If you want to keep your job, you can. But I still want to come and meet the people you are working with. I just want to know that it is a nice place, and they are good to you.' Sean stepped back from Hannah and walked back inside; she knew that he wasn't asking permission from her to check out where she worked. He would just randomly turn up and make his presence known. But for now, she would take this as a win. She lost the urge to move out as she was convinced that what he did last night was a one-off. He had never hurt her like that before, so what was the chance he would do it again? And anyway, he knew her secret now; she had nothing else to hide. Nothing except Ryan and the feelings she had for him.

Hannah went back inside and waited for Sean to leave for work. She was exhausted and just wanted to go back to bed and sleep for a couple of hours before going to work. She set her alarm for two hours and was asleep before her head hit the pillow.

Chapter 28

The shift was hard today. Hannah was exhausted; although she slept for a couple of hours again before work, it just wasn't enough. Her shoulder still ached, and the pain between her legs was taking its toll. One thing she was relieved about was that her face didn't bruise; the other pain she could hide and took painkillers before her shift to get her through. At the end of the shift, Hannah made a quick exit. She checked her phone to make sure she hadn't missed any calls from Sean, which she hadn't; that gave her a little bit of relief. As she started home, she realised that she needed to go past the supermarket to get something for dinner. She changed directions and texted Sean her whereabouts. Better to tell him her every movement to make sure the previous night didn't repeat itself.

The afternoon was overcast, and Hannah started to regret not bringing a thicker jacket. She quickened her pace and made it to the supermarket in no time at all. As she walked through the front doors, she felt the warm air immediately; and as she thawed out, her mood lifted. Hannah grabbed a basket from the stack and wandered to the fruit and veg area. She felt her pocket buzz and saw Sean had made a request for dinner. Now that she had a menu in mind, she started looking around for the things she needed. As she scanned the vegetables, she saw Amy. Hannah stopped and stared for a moment just to make sure that it was her. Amy turned around and caught Hannah looking at her. Before Hannah could look away, Amy waved. Hannah waved back as she didn't know what else to do; she started to freak out inside when Amy started walking in her direction.

'Hey, Hannah! It is Hannah, right? I'm really bad with names, but you I need to remember since my brother seems to have a very big crush on you,' Amy said with a playful tone in her voice. Hannah smiled shyly back at Amy.

'You know there is nothing going on between me and your brother, right? We are just friends, and besides, I'm married.'

'Happily?' Amy raised an eyebrow, questioning Hannah's last statement. 'I see the way you look at each other, and there is definitely a connection. Any more obvious and it would be tattooed on your face.'

'Regardless of the happiness in my marriage, it doesn't change the fact that I am committed to someone else.' Hannah went to cross her arms in agitation at being questioned about her marriage when she let out a wince. The pain in her shoulder was coming back; the painkillers had worn off.

'Are you all right? That looked painful.' Amy moved closer to Hannah to comfort her when she saw the look in her eye. Hannah started feeling really hot, and embarrassment kicked in; she lowered her head, no longer able to make eye contact.

'I'm fine, really, I am.'

Amy looked at Hannah, unconvinced. 'I was going to go get a coffee before heading to work. How about you come and join me?'

'Oh no, really, I can't. I need to get things for tea and get home before . . .' She almost said his name. 'My . . . my husband.'

'Then let me help you, and then we can grab a coffee. What are you making?'

Hannah was confused; she had convinced herself to hate the woman sleeping with her husband, but now that they have met, she found herself liking her. She was kind and caring; she barely knew Hannah, yet she was taking a genuine interest in her well-being.

'Was going to make steak and veg, nothing exciting.' Hannah walked past Amy to the potatoes and started inspecting them. Amy grabbed a plastic bag and held it open. For the next few minutes, they walked around in silence. It wasn't an awkward silence by any means; it was almost peaceful, as if they could read each other and didn't need to force any conversation. Hannah started to relax and led Amy to the checkout; together, they both put the items on the counter and thanked the cashier. Outside the store, Hannah stopped and looked at Amy.

'So where is this coffee shop? I think a fresh coffee would be perfect right now.'

Amy smiled, and her face lit up. 'Just over there, past the post office.' Then she started walking almost with a skip in her step. The girls entered a little shop with only a handful of tables, and Hannah immediately picked a table at the back as far away from the door as she could get. She sat at the chair facing the door so she could see exactly who came in and out. She was feeling paranoid that somehow Sean would know she was here with his mistress and walk into this random little shop right at this exact moment. She saw Amy nod at the girl behind the counter. *They must be friends*, she thought, still feeling uncomfortable. Amy turned to Hannah.

'What would you like? My shout.'

'Cappuccino please.' Amy turned back to the girl behind the counter, and she could hear the high-pitched tone of the conversation between the two girls. Hannah never did understand why girls squealed when they got excited. Amy came back to the table and sat in the chair with a big sigh and still with a big smile. The smile was starting to annoy Hannah. *How can someone be so happy all of the time? Surely it's not possible.*

'OK, so I'm just going to come out and ask. Don't see any point in dancing around and making small talk. I can be pretty direct, and I don't mean to offend, but it's just the way I am.' Amy had lost her smile and was leaning in on the table like she was about to interrogate Hannah. 'So this is my observation. You and my brother have a connection. You are married so won't act on the feelings you have for him, and my brother is too much of a gentleman and would never cross that line either. You look miserable when you say you are married, and you are in pain. So my two questions for now are why do you stay in a relationship when you are unhappy, and did he hurt you?'

Hannah's breathing quickened, and she felt the tears building. She looked down at the table, took a few deep breaths, and fought back the tears. She had never spoken to anyone before about her marriage or the abuse. She suddenly felt ashamed. With one more deep breath, she looked up.

'I stay because a long time ago, I made a commitment. And besides, where would I go? I have no money except for the few dollars I make at the café, and that is not enough to live on.' Hannah paused before answering the second question; she needed to find the right words. 'Yes, he hurt my shoulder. It was an accident. I tripped over a chair, and he went to grab me to try to stop me falling. So please don't think there is anything bad going on 'cause there's not.' Her breathing quickened again, and she tried to keep eye contact, hoping her story was convincing.

Amy leaned further in and whispered, 'I'm not buying your story, but I won't push the issue. Can you please just do one thing for me?' Amy opened her bag, looking for something; she pulled out a pen and an envelope. She tore a piece off, wrote something down, and then slid it over to Hannah. 'It's my number, and I want you to ring me when you're ready to talk.'

Hannah looked at the piece of paper when a tear escaped and dripped onto the note. She quickly wiped it away and put the paper in her purse. In a voice that was not quite a whisper, she thanked Amy. A minute passed with neither of the girls saying a word. Hannah took the last sip of her coffee and looked up at Amy again.

'You said you were on your way to work. What do you do?'

'I work reception at the local medical centre, and because it's open from early in the morning to late at night, we all work on a rotating roster. So two weeks, I work afternoons and evenings. And two weeks, I work mornings into the afternoon. I enjoy the change as every couple of weeks, I get the time during the day to do things.' Amy laughed to herself and then added. 'I think my new boyfriend likes it too as I'm not one of those needy girls who wants him to come over every night. I actually like only having him part-time so I can still do all the things I like to do on my own and then get to hang out with him and then get me time again. I think in the long run, our relationship will be better for it.'

Hannah was shocked by what Amy just told her; she was now having a conversation with her about her 'boyfriend', who was Hannah's husband. She was lost for words but knew she had to say something quick. 'So where did you meet him?' *Oh crap*, she thought as the words left her mouth.

'Funny story, really. I had some friends over, and we were having a few drinks when a friend of one of my friends' boyfriend—and I use that term loosely—texted me asking to come over. I think they were under the impression I was having a party or something. I already had a bit to drink, so I said come over without really thinking about it. The boys came over and stayed. I wish it was a more exciting romantic story for you, but it was just a drunk weekend. He's not like the usual guys I go for. He's a boys' boy and just likes to come over and get takeaway and watch a movie. I'm used to guys that want to go out all the time, and they are exhausting. So the change of pace is nice. He's not a big talker, so we just cuddle on the couch and watch TV. Mind you, I find myself starting to watch a bit of sport so I can try to have a conversation with him. He bought me a big bunch of flowers last week, which was so sweet. And I know that's not his style, which made it even sweeter.' Amy suddenly stopped talking. 'Oh my god, here I am going on about how wonderful my boyfriend is when your husband is not so great. I am so sorry. I hope I didn't upset you at all.' The look on Amy's face was priceless, and all Hannah could do was laugh out loud; she couldn't control it, and then Amy started laughing. Hannah leaned over and held her hand.

'It's fine, don't apologise. Thank you for today. It was really nice, but I do need to get home before I get into trouble.' Hannah stood up and grabbed her shopping. 'Next time, I will buy the coffee.'

Amy stood up, and as Hannah went to pass, Amy hugged her. 'Don't forget to call me, OK?' Hannah smiled, nodded, and left.

Chapter 29

Sean came home to the smell of food cooking. He walked through the front door and yelled out to Hannah, 'Something smells great!' He continued through the apartment and to the bedroom. Hannah stopped what she was doing and turned, expecting him to come over and give her a kiss, but he didn't even look at her. With a big sigh, she turned back and continued what she was doing. She waited until she heard him come back into the kitchen before speaking.

'So how was your day?' Again, she turned to look at him. There wasn't a lot of care in her voice; she was just asking as it was expected. Sean sat in the chair on the far side of the table so he could watch Hannah cook.

'You know, same shit, different day.' His response was predictable and gave away nothing. Hannah finished serving dinner and placed a plate in front of Sean, then proceeded to sit opposite him with her plate.

They sat in silence for a few minutes before Hannah had the courage to ask, 'Hey, I was wondering—if you didn't mind, of course—if I could go to a dinner at the café on Saturday night. Lucy has invited the staff to come and share a meal together. It won't be a late night or anything. It's just dinner.' She held her breath, waiting to see what sort of reply she would get. The only reason she dared ask was that she was giving him an opportunity to go see Amy. As soon as the words left her mouth, Hannah remembered that Amy had mentioned today that she was on afternoon shift this weekend. She needed to quickly sell this as something Sean would benefit from. 'I know there is a big game on this Saturday night. This way, you could watch it here in peace and quiet. I wouldn't be too late, and I could make you your favourite snacks before

I go so you won't have to worry about tea.' There was a desperation in her voice this time; she longed to go and have a night out with friends—people who made her laugh and, for a short time, people who made her forget about what she would come home to.

Sean stared at her; his look gave her no answer on how he would react. But so far, he hadn't yelled or mocked her, so that was a good start. Another minute passed, and he still hadn't said anything and was still staring at her. Hannah was becoming uncomfortable and tried to finish her food. Her anxiety was building, and paranoia was taking over. 'It's OK if you don't want me to. I hadn't said if I was coming or not . . . just I was invited, so I wanted to ask you.' Hannah got up from the table and took her plate to the sink. 'Don't worry about it. I will tell Lucy tomorrow that we have other plans. It's all good.' Hannah smiled at Sean. 'Forget I said anything.' She turned back to the sink and started filling it with water to wash the dishes. Behind her, she could hear the clink of the cutlery being put down on the plate and the scraping of the chair on the floor. Hannah put a plate in the water and went to turn to go and get the dishes from the table. She jumped with fright as Sean was standing right behind her. He handed her his plate but didn't move. Hannah took the plate from him.

'You can go to this dinner of yours, but there are conditions. One, I will drop you off and come and meet these people. And if I think everything is legit, I will leave you to it. Two, you come home when I tell you to. You will order a cab and stay on the phone with me until it gets there. Three, you have your phone handy the entire time, and you will answer the phone the moment I ring or text. These are my conditions, and if you don't like any of them, then you can just stay here with me Saturday night.' He was neither aggressive or kind with the way he spoke; he was to the point and calm. Hannah smiled and kissed Sean in gratitude; excitement was building within her, but she didn't show any as she knew this was a very unique situation. Never had he allowed her to go out without him before, not even to family events, and this dinner was with a complete group of strangers to him. Sean left the room quietly, and Hannah finished the dishes. She was rather pleased with herself at convincing Sean to let her go with no arguing or hostilities; this had been quite a big day for her. Even the pain she had been experiencing for most of the day seemed to have almost gone. But she knew she wasn't to say another word to Sean about this; she wouldn't risk anything that would cause him to change his mind, and she knew she had to be walking on eggshells for the rest of the week. She remembered it was only Monday night; this was going to be one very long week.

Chapter 30

The week seemed to take forever to finish. Hannah tried to keep it as uneventful as she could, at least with the things she could control. She made all of his favourite meals, ensured all of the housework was done, and smiled and spoke as politely as she could without coming across as condescending.

One of the things she couldn't control was what happened during the day when he was at work. On Wednesday, he came home in a foul mood, stomping around the apartment and barely saying a word. Hannah kept quiet and tried to predict what he would want; she made him coffee after dinner, and he responded kindly. She sat on the couch and offered to rub his feet; he responded by falling asleep on the couch. Satisfied with her efforts, she reached over his legs and slipped the remote out from under him; and while he slept, she watched the TV shows of her choice. When he stirred, she continued rubbing his feet, and he settled back into slumber. When she saw it was his usual bedtime, she ever so gently stirred him; and while he was still half-asleep, she helped him to bed, where he instantly went back to sleep. Thursday morning, he was in a much better mood and gave Hannah a passionate kiss before leaving for work, and the next forty-eight hours went smoothly.

Saturday finally arrived, and Hannah was quietly excited. She had made a list of snacks for Sean to choose from for his night in watching the game, and when he was eating his breakfast, she started going through the options. She made her list and headed out to the markets. Hannah always preferred to shop fresh at the local market rather than the supermarket, and it had been a few weeks since she had been. Every time she walked in, the atmosphere almost took her breath away.

She stood for a moment and soaked it all in before heading off to her favourite stalls. This was the best Hannah had felt in a long time; having no more secret to hide removed a lot of stress she had on herself. And every time she thought about going to the dinner that night and knowing she was allowed to go, her excitement grew. Letting herself fall into her own little world, Hannah didn't notice Ryan at the counter of the fruit stand; it wasn't until she almost tripped over him that she came back to reality.

'Oh crap, sorry,' she laughed. 'I wasn't watching where I was going.' She put her hand on Ryan's arm to steady herself. He looked down at her and smiled.

'It's all good, Hannah. Nice to see you.' His eyes were mesmerising, and Hannah found it way too easy to get lost in them. 'So what's on the menu tonight?'

'Just making snacks for the game tonight, and I am making a dish to take to a staff dinner Lucy is putting on. Do you have big plans tonight?' Hannah always found herself curious at what other people did on a Saturday night; it stemmed from the countless Saturday nights she spent in the apartment and many of them alone while Sean went out with his mates.

'Actually, I have a family thing to go to, and it seems my sister has got out of it. So my mum would be shattered if we both didn't turn up. It seems no matter how old you get, you always still have to answer to your mother.' Ryan had a little chuckle to himself. 'But at least I get to fill up on her amazing cooking, which will guarantee that I will be full for days.' And he gave another chuckle; he seemed to be amusing himself with this conversation, which made Hannah laugh.

'Sounds like you have it all worked out. Well, I'd better get going. I have a big day in the kitchen.' Hannah slowly walked away. 'Enjoy your mum's cooking!' She gave a little wave goodbye and pretended to check her list, but all she really wanted to do was stay there and talk to him some more. She often thought about that Saturday they spent together, cooking and having coffee and then drinks into the evening. It felt so long ago, and she wished for just one more perfect day with him—one more perfect day for her to feel that way again. It saddened her heart knowing that she would never have that day, and the best she would ever get was to make it up in her head as she lay in bed, waiting to go to sleep. She liked the dreams she came up with, imagining faraway places and endless money so they would never have to come back here. She had found herself going to bed a little earlier these days when she wasn't quite ready to go to sleep so she could have that time dreaming about this perfect life she had created in her mind.

Hannah stopped and turned around; she didn't really know why, but she just wanted to see him again—just from a distance, just a little fix to get her through the weekend until she would see him again during his lunch breaks. He was nowhere to be seen. Hannah became agitated as disappointment kicked in. *Where is he? How did he disappear so quickly?* She turned the other way but still couldn't see him anywhere. *Where are you?* she repeated over and over while scanning the market in every direction. She must have wasted three or four minutes looking for him when her phone buzzed. It was Sean checking up on her. She replied she was done at the market and on her way home. Disappointed, she headed for the exit and started for home. Before leaving the car park, Hannah let her eyes adjust to the daylight after the dim markets. Ryan snuck up behind Hannah and, reaching around her, offered her a single rose.

'A beautiful flower for a beautiful girl.' Hannah took the rose and spun around, almost in tears at the romantic gesture.

'Oh my gosh, thank you! Thank you so much! It's beautiful. Thank you.' She didn't know what else to say.

'You're very welcome. I saw it and thought you must have it. I know it's probably inappropriate for me to give it to you, but I just wanted you to have it.'

'I don't know what to say. It's the nicest thing anyone has ever done for me, so all I can say is thank you a million times.'

'Again, you are very welcome, and I will let you go now as I know you have a lot to do. I will see you next week.' This time, Ryan walked away; he looked back over his shoulder and winked, and Hannah nearly melted right where she stood. She looked down at the flower, and she felt like a princess who had just been saved by her knight in shining armour. The walk home was too short; she didn't want this feeling to end, and she knew as soon as she saw or heard Sean, that moment would be over forever. She sighed as she looked up the stairs to the apartment and let the feeling go; she was back to her unhappy married self.

Chapter 31

Hannah entered the apartment to find Sean gone. In a way, she was relieved, but she was also curious as to where he was. Her first thought was that he had gone to go see Amy for a quickie. The thought of this just made her laugh—Sean just turning up and getting it over with as quickly as he could so he could get home to his wife again. How special Amy must feel if this was the case, the poor, naïve little girl. Her boyfriend just popping in for a two-minute piece of heaven. For a moment, she almost felt sorry for her; and as quickly as the feeling entered her head, it left again. And then she remembered that Amy had wanted Hannah to text her and handed over her phone number. Hannah went to her bag and fumbled around until she found it. She picked up her phone and started creating a new contact when her phone prompted her that she already had the number stored. Hannah had completely forgotten that she had taken her number from Sean's phone when she first found out about the affair. She cancelled out of the new contact and went into the contact she had made that day months ago. She had put the number under a different name; she edited the contact and renamed it 'Amy from work'. Sean wouldn't know the difference if he saw it as Hannah had a few contacts like that already, including 'Lucy from work'.

Hannah walked from the kitchen through the lounge and opened up the balcony door; she looked outside at the car park, and the space for Sean's car was still empty. She opened up a new message and thought for a moment what to write. *Just keep it simple.*

'Hi Amy, just wanted to say thank you for the coffee earlier this week. It was really nice having someone to talk to and you really are as lovely as your brother says you are. Hope you have a great weekend.'

There, that wasn't so hard. A quick thank you, and that's that. Hannah heard Sean's car coming up the road, so she went back inside to the kitchen and got to work on cooking his snacks for the game. She wasn't sure if he was having some of his mates over or not, so she thought she would make plenty just in case. Hannah heard the front door open at the same time she heard the message beep on her phone. She immediately snatched it up, went to the toilet, and locked the door. She heard Sean call out for her, and she called back that she would be out in just a second. Hannah opened the message.

'Hey there Hannah, you're very welcome and we should catch up again soon. If you have some time next week I am still on late afternoons so could meet you after your shift at the café that's of course if you want to?'

Hannah responded, 'Sounds great, how does Monday sound?'

Hannah put her phone on silent and pushed it deep into her pocket, flushed the toilet for effect, and unlocked the door. She went to the bathroom to wash her hands when Sean came and stood in the doorway.

'What time do you want me to drop you off tonight? Can we get there early so I can meet this Lucy chick before everyone else gets there? I really don't want to meet all of them, just Lucy.'

'Yeah, of course. She said to everyone six, so if we get there at ten to then, we should be the first ones there. The drive will be at most ten minutes, so five forty. I've started cooking for you so you and the guys will have plenty to eat while I'm gone.' She turned to the side and squeezed past Sean, who was still standing in the doorway. 'Who have you got coming over? Just so I can make sure there is enough.'

Like a puppy, Sean followed Hannah back to the kitchen. 'Just Dave and Jason are coming over, and we will probably get pizza delivered. So don't go overboard—unless you're making sausage rolls. Then you can make as many as you like. There is never any of those left over.'

Hannah looked at Sean and smiled. 'I will make an extra tray for you.'

Sean came up close to Hannah and stood towering over her, like he needed to remind her who was in charge. 'Thank you. Oh, and I don't want you drinking tonight. I'm not going to be there to keep an eye on you, and you don't know how to handle your drink.'

Of course I don't know how to handle my drink, Hannah thought to herself. *You never let me drink, even when we are celebrating something— not that we celebrate anything anymore.* 'OK, honey, I wasn't planning on drinking anyway. Best to stay sober around workpeople. I wouldn't want them to think that I am that kind of girl who goes out without her husband and uses it as an excuse to get drunk.' There was a hint of sarcasm in her voice, and she was hoping that Sean wouldn't pick up on it; she really didn't want to argue just a few hours before she was allowed to go out to dinner without him at her side, or was it *her* at *his* side? That's the way it usually was; he walked in first, and she followed like a well-trained pet. She didn't speak unless spoken to, and she certainly didn't ever give her opinion about anything.

Sean looked at her almost with contempt. 'Good. I'm going to watch TV while you cook. Let me know when stuff is ready to taste.' He walked out of the kitchen, and she watched him take his place on the couch. Remote in one hand and beer in the other. She had to look twice; she didn't recall there being beer in the fridge when she went out this morning. Oh, so that's where he was when she got back and he wasn't home. *He must have gone to the pub to get beer for tonight.* Hannah opened the fridge and saw a shelf full of beer. *Yep, that's where he went.* Feeling relieved (she wasn't sure why relief, but it was) that he hadn't gone to see Amy, she went back to cooking.

With her creations cooking in the oven, she leaned in on the lounge doorway and waited until Sean gave her the look that she could speak. 'I'm going to have a shower now. I have three trays in the oven. I should be back before the timer, but if you hear it, can you please come and tell me so it doesn't burn?' Again, she waited for his approval before leaving the conversation, with a nod of his head, and she knew it was in his best interest to listen out for the timer.

She went to the bathroom and showered. She didn't fuss with washing her hair or anything time-consuming or anything that might give the impression that she was dressing up for someone else. Just a quick wash. Then she brushed her teeth. She threw on her dressing gown and went back to the kitchen to check on the oven. She was back with a minute to spare. Staring into the oven for that last minute seemed to get her excited about going out again. With the trays now

THE DARKEST PLACE

cooling on racks, she walked back to the bedroom to get dressed. She was thinking of wearing jeans and a T-shirt but wondered if that was too casual. Maybe a dress would be more appropriate. She didn't have a lot of clothes to choose from, so she settled for an old dress that gave away no cleavage and came to her knee. Sean couldn't possibly complain about her going out in that. Just to be sure, she went to the lounge and asked if she looked OK. She got a disinterested yes, and that was good enough for her.

Hannah looked at the kitchen clock and grinned; it was five thirty, and soon, she would be free for a few wonderful hours to be around people who wanted her there—people who would talk to her and ask for her opinions on things. For the first time since high school, she had friends, and it gave her a feeling of warmth and belonging.

'All right then, let's go. I want to be back before six.' Hannah didn't need to be told twice; she grabbed her bag and headed to the door like an excited child knowing they were going somewhere fun.

Chapter 32

There wasn't much of a conversation between Hannah and Sean in the car. Hannah gave directions, and Sean said nothing, not even a sigh or a grunt. They pulled up right in front of the café. Sean turned off the motor and just sat there. Hannah looked over, worried that he might be about to change his mind about letting her be there tonight and make her go home again.

'Everything OK, Sean?' Hannah made sure her voice was soft and concerned; she looked inside and saw only Lucy setting up a big table in the middle of the room. She could see candles, fancy-looking napkins, and wine glasses. The lights were dimmed, and it looked like a romantic restaurant scene from a movie. Hannah sighed quietly; she had always dreamed of eating in a place that looked just like this, having a romantic dinner with a handsome movie star and all the other girls in the room wishing they were her. She stopped herself from giggling out loud and turned back to Sean. 'Lucy is in there on her own. We are the first ones here.'

Sean unfastened his seat belt and got out of the car. Hannah quickly undid her seat belt too and opened her door. By the time she got out of the car, Sean was already standing next to her. Uncharacteristically, he offered her his hand to help her up from the seat. She took it, and hand in hand, they walked to the front door. Hannah could tell that he was nervous. Sean hated meeting new people unless he absolutely had to. She took a step in front of him and opened the front door. She held it open and ushered Sean in.

Lucy looked up from what she was doing. With her famous big smile, she came around the table and gave Hannah a hug. 'Now why am I not surprised that you are the first one here! Come, come, and look at the table and tell me what you think.' She led Hannah away from Sean and moved her towards the fancy table. Lucy turned back and stepped over to where Sean was standing. 'Now let me guess . . . You must be Sean.' She held out her hand, and Sean shook it softly; he had been told on many occasions that he squeezed far too hard and would break someone's hand one day. 'Well, you are far more handsome in person. Hannah showed me a picture of you the other day when I asked about you, and it didn't do you justice.' Sean didn't know what to say; he hadn't ever met anyone like Lucy before, and he got why Hannah spoke so highly of her.

'Thank you. What picture did she show you?' He was curious now and looked at Hannah with a raised eyebrow. Hannah took out her phone and jolted when she saw a message from Amy sitting there on the front screen. All it said was 'Perfect'. For an instant, she had totally forgotten about texting her earlier. Hannah quickly cleared the message and opened the photo gallery to bring up the photo of Sean she had shown Lucy earlier that week. It was a nice picture, but Lucy was right; he was much better looking in person. She had never stopped thinking that he was a very handsome man; pity his personality didn't match his looks. Sean handed Hannah back her phone and took her hand.

'So, Lucy, what time do you think this will be finished? I need Hannah to get a cab home as I won't be able to come and get her again.' He didn't take his eyes off his wife; he was giving her the 'you know the rules' look.

'Don't you worry, Sean. I will take good care of her. And I will drop her home, I would say, around eleven. I'm not a drinker or a late-night person, so those who want to party on after can head to the pub up the road, but not me. I will be ready for bed well and truly by then'

Sean looked at Lucy and nodded in agreement and let Hannah's hand go. He said nothing further and left. Hannah let out the biggest sigh of relief. Lucy looked at her and laughed. Hannah laughed too; she could finally relax for a while.

Chapter 33

The night was over, and Hannah felt exhilarated. The night was more fun than she ever had imagined. Her ears still rang from the laughter. One of the kitchen hands was a natural comedian, and by the end of the evening, everything he said had the entire table in fits of laughter; one girl even pulled a muscle from laughing so much. Hannah was in the car with Lucy, who had kindly offered to take her home; it was a little before eleven, right on time for curfew. Because the café was in walking distance, the ride home took less than ten minutes; at this time of night, there was minimal traffic, so there wasn't even enough time for a conversation. Lucy pulled up outside of the apartment, and Hannah could see the light of the lounge room was on. She thanked Lucy for the lift and collected her bag of leftovers all the others insisted she take with her. Everyone else was going to continue the night at the pub down the road. Lucy said it was only her at home, so she would never get through all the extra food; and besides, if her husband had mates over watching the game, then by this time of night, they probably would all be starving and welcome the late-night snack. Hannah didn't put up any argument and graciously accepted the offer. As she lifted the bag from the back seat to the front, all the smells came up from the bag, and it filled her with joy of an amazing night—her first amazing night out with her new friends.

Hannah quietly opened the front door; she was cautious not to make a big deal of being out as she didn't want to set Sean into a bad mood. She could tell he was already struggling to let her go out as it was. She was surprised to see only Sean sitting on the couch; there were a couple of empty beer bottles on the coffee table and an empty tray.

He looked up at her, with his eyebrows slightly furrowed and no hint of a smile. She thought he might at least be a bit happy to see her home on time. She quickly walked past him and put the bag of food on the table. Hannah went back into the lounge to see if he was hungry, a peace offering of sorts.

'Hey, I have plenty of leftovers if you're hungry?' She spoke softly and without any excitement in her voice even though all she wanted to do was tell him all about the night, the funny conversations, and how great everyone was; but she didn't. She spoke to him as if she had been home all night. Again, he looked up at her almost with contempt this time; with the light from the kitchen on his face, she could see he had drunk a lot. His cheeks were rosy, his eyes glassy, and his body sort of slumped in the chair. He still didn't say anything, but he stood up; and with a slight stumble, he walked in her direction. She backed up into the kitchen and started taking containers from the bag so she could show him what was left. She heard his shuffling footsteps come closer, and when she lifted her head to look at him, he smacked her hard across her face. The force and the surprise of the hit were enough for Hannah to lose her balance and fall back onto the table. She barely had time to process what just happened when he grabbed her arm and pulled her back to standing, and with a fierce look, he pulled her like a rag doll and pinned her up against the wall. He had hold of both her arms between her elbow and shoulder and pressed his weight onto her with a vice-like grip. He looked her straight in the eye with a piercing stare that instilled an instant fear into her, and suddenly, her breathing sped up to short sharp breaths, and she could feel a numbness taking over.

He finally spoke; his voice was soft but had an angry growl to it. 'What makes you think you can just waltz on in here after being out all night and feed me your leftovers like I'm a dog waiting for its owner to come home? Is that what you think I am? Your dog you can just throw food at and expect me to dance around your feet in gratitude for your scraps and happy you came home?' He still had her pinned hard against the wall, and she knew better than to say anything right now. It was only a few seconds; but she held her breath, stayed quiet and still, and prayed that he would back off. He took a step back but didn't release his grip on her. With a forceful movement, he threw her to the ground, and she slid uncontrollably into the leg of the table. She felt a sharp sting in her side where the corner of the table leg was now digging into her. Sean stepped to the table and picked up one of the containers of food and removed its lid. He looked inside and even sniffed at the food; he looked down at his wife, who was still on the floor and tipped the food on her head.

'How about you remember your place? You're the dog who will eat my scraps.' He picked up a second container and a third one and dumped the contents on her. 'Go on, dog, eat the scraps.' His voice was getting louder and angrier. Hannah was frozen in fear and didn't move; she stared at the floor, with food dripping from her head. 'I said eat!' And without warning, he kicked Hannah in the stomach. He crouched over her and pulled her head back by her hair, grabbed a handful of food from the floor, and forced it into her mouth. Hannah started to choke and cough and cry. Sean let her hair go and stepped back a few paces. 'Clean this goddamned mess up and stay out of my sight.' Still looking at the floor, she watched his feet walk back to the lounge room and heard the huff as he sat heavily back onto the couch.

As soon as he had left the kitchen, she curled up into a ball on the kitchen floor and sobbed. She was lying there in intense pain and covered in food. She tried hard to control her crying so as not to make any noise and prayed hard that he would fall asleep on the couch and stay there until the morning. When she regained control of herself, she got herself to her knees and reached up to the table. The table was hard to grip with her sticky hands, but she held on enough to be able to pull herself to her feet. She gingerly walked to the sink and ran the hot water tap. As she leaned over the sink (it was too painful to stand straight), small pieces of food started running down her hair and fall off. She slowly started to wash the filth off her hands and arms and then ran her fingers through her hair to try to get any large chunks out. She washed her face and then unzipped her dress. She let it fall almost gracefully off her shoulders and onto the floor. She stepped out of the crumpled material at her feet and twisted to see if there was bruising on her side where she hit the table. The bruising was already there, and it was black and was right on her ribs. Now breathing just seemed to be the most painful action she was doing. She turned away from the sink and looked over at the table and to the floor, where there was a pile of food waiting for her, Sean's dog, to clean up. There were a couple of containers unopened on the table, so she put them in the fridge; she didn't want to waste anything else. Then with a roll of paper towel and a bottle of cleaner, she set to work. When the kitchen was back to an acceptable state, she picked up her dress and went to the bathroom to shower. As she walked past the lounge, she heard the familiar sound of her husband's snoring and felt an overwhelming sense of relief; with him asleep, she would be left alone for the rest of the night.

Hannah took longer than usual in the shower. She felt the need to shampoo her hair four times; every time she rinsed, the smell of food got fainter until she couldn't smell it anymore. She was exhausted; it was late for her anyway, but physically, she felt like she didn't have the energy to get from the bathroom to the bedroom. And the feeling like she just wanted to vomit was overpowering. Wrapped in a towel, she used her last bit of energy to open the bathroom door. She jumped back and almost slipped over, and the adrenalin surged through her. Sean was just standing there on the other side of the door, not moving or saying anything. Her heart pounded and felt as if it was in the back of her throat, and she just stared back.

'Let's go to bed.' His voice was calm and had a sleepy undertone. Hannah followed him to the bedroom. Sean undressed an slipped into bed, rolled onto his side, and went back to sleep. Hannah breathed again; her hair was wet, but she turned off the hall light and climbed into bed. She lay as close to the edge as she could and let herself fall asleep.

Chapter 34

I t was lunchtime Sunday, and Ryan was going to meet Amy for lunch. It had been nearly a week since he had spoken to her and was very protective of his little sister. The last time they spoke was last Monday, when they had lunch at the café and she met Hannah. His thoughts drifted back to that day; seeing Hannah and his sister together made him happy. If only it could be different, and they spent time together with Hannah as his girlfriend and not the married waitress where he ate lunch. He wondered what Amy thought of her; even though he knew they would never be together, he still wanted Amy to like Hannah and for Hannah to like Amy.

Ryan looked at the time again and started getting impatient that Amy was late; she was meant to be here at twelve fifteen so they could go in the same car to the pub for lunch. It was nearly twelve thirty, and she wasn't here. He sat back down on the couch, which gave Bruce instant permission to jump up on his lap. He was such a needy cat, always wanting to be pet and cuddled. He lifted Bruce right up to his face and stared into his yellow eyes.

'Bloody women, hey, mate? They are never on time. Why is that?' Bruce just stared back and then wiggled to get down, digging his back claw into Ryan's arm, drawing blood. Ryan dropped Bruce with a thud and swiped at him while holding his scratched arm up. 'Far out, cat, get outta here!' He got up out of the chair and went to get a tissue to wipe the blood away; at the same time, he heard a knock at the door.

'About time you got here!' he snapped at his sister. 'Why are you always late?'

'Wow, all right. If I'd known you were going to be an ass, I wouldn't have come today. Let me know if you are going to be like this all afternoon, and I will go home again.'

Ryan threw the bloodied tissue into the bin, gave his sister a sad look, and pointed to his arm. 'Sorry, Aims, Bruce clawed at me just as you turned up. Jesus, it stings!' He stared down at Bruce, who was pacing back and forth, rubbing himself up against Amy's legs. Amy bent over and picked up the fluffy cat, turned him over, and cuddled him like a baby. She snuggled her face into the cat's face.

'Are you being a big old meanie?' She put on a voice like she was talking to a naughty child. Bruce put his front paws up to stop her from getting close to his face again and started to struggle. Amy pushed her face past his paws and started kissing his face. She giggled at him and put him down. 'You're such a wuss, Ryan. Seriously, you're all grumpy 'cause a cat scratched you? Man up!' she stood there all matter of fact with her hands on her hips, mocking her brother.

'Oh, ha ha. You had enough yet? Can we please go and get lunch? I'm too hungry to argue with you anymore.' Ryan started for the door and jokingly pushed Amy towards the door too.

It was a cold day, and the tables outside at the pub weren't under any shelter. Ryan knew not to even ask if Amy wanted to sit outside. He knew Amy would scrunch up her face, shake her head, and then complain that she spent ages doing her hair and didn't want it to get all messy by sitting outside. He spotted a table in the corner at the back away from the salad bar (he hated sitting close as people would constantly walk past the table, bumping into his chair), and he caught the eye of the girl at the bar who indicated they could sit there. They weaved through the tables and dodged kids running from frustrated parents to the kids' corner and sat at the small table tucked away at the back. They had eaten here enough times to know where the good tables were.

'I will go and get us a drink and order lunch. Do you want the usual?' He always took charge; he was funny about letting his sister go up to the bar and order him a drink. He knew it was silly as she was well and truly old enough to go up to a bar, but he still liked to do the things he thought good men should. He still opened doors for women, let people in on queues at the supermarket if they only had a few things in their hands, and protected his sister like she was his responsibility.

He returned to the table a few minutes later and sat down opposite his sister, ready to quiz her about everything going on in her life.

'OK, so what's going on with you? How's work?'

Amy took a sip of her wine, answers already to go. 'Work is great. I have today and tomorrow off, and then I am back on mornings for two weeks, which means I should be able to spend some time with the new guy I started seeing a few weeks ago. We talk on the phone most days for a little bit, but it's just not the same as spending time with them in person. If it is still going well, I would like you to meet him in a few weeks and see what you think of him.' Ryan nodded; he had been waiting for the invitation to meet this man just to make sure he was right for his little sister. 'Oh, and guess who I had coffee with earlier this week! Tuesday, I reckon it was.' She raised an eyebrow and grinned. Ryan sat back in his chair and thought for a moment; he could just respond with 'I don't know' as she would push him to guess anyway.

'Well, it wasn't family as they would have said something last night when I was there. Oh, everyone says hi, and they all miss you. So that would make it a friend and, from the grin, someone I would find interesting. So I'm going to guess it was Maddie, the chick who used to live next door to you who always popped over whenever I was there— you know, the one you constantly tried to set me up with.'

Amy laughed at the thought of her and her neighbour scheming to get Ryan to go out with her; it became a game until Maddie moved. 'Nope, not Maddie. Actually, I haven't thought about her in ages. Maybe I should give her a call. She was always loads of fun. Want to have another guess, or should I just tell you?'

'Just tell me. You have me intrigued now.' Ryan always played along with Amy's games, and he just wanted to know now.

'Hannah.' She had a very proud look on her face.

'Hannah? Hannah who? Oh no, you don't mean my Hannah? Not that she's mine or anything, but you know what I mean.'

'Yep, *your* Hannah.' Amy leaned forward on the table and clasped her hands, looking very pleased with herself. 'We had a very interesting conversation indeed. I see why you like her. She has a gentle soul. Pity she's married, hey?'

Ryan looked at his sister with a hint of disappointment. 'It is what it is. Maybe one day she won't be married, you never know. People get divorced all the time.'

Amy started to fidget, not saying anything, but her body language was off. Ryan watched his sister fiddle with the salt and pepper shakers almost nervous like. She was bad at keeping secrets, and as she wasn't grinning at him, it wasn't a good secret. He wasn't going to probe her just yet; if he waited long enough, she wouldn't be able to help herself, and she would blurt it out. Amy looked up and saw Ryan watching her, which made her even more fidgety; she knew he always seemed to know when she wanted to say something. He was the one person she could never lie to or keep things from. But this, she wasn't ready to tell him; she knew he would get angry and potentially do something he may or may not regret. Before she could say anything, their lunch arrived and gave her the perfect distraction.

After two trips to the salad bar and what seemed to be a piece of meat big enough to feed a family, Ryan finally stopped eating; it never ceased to amaze Amy just how much one person could eat.

'I won't need to eat for a day or two now,' Ryan declared, rubbing his belly. 'That was a mighty fine meal.' Amy laughed at him; he was such a dag at times.

'It was pretty good. I do like coming here.'

Ryan shifted in his seat and suddenly appeared all serious, which was not normal. He sat up straight and looked at Amy; he went to speak but stopped himself. He made a strange face, trying to look for the right words.

'OK, so just before the food came out, you looked like you had something to say. I'm guessing it is about Hannah, and it's not something I want to hear. I'm going to ask you to please tell me what it is. What did you two talk about that you think I can't handle?'

Amy took a deep breath and hesitated a little. 'OK, so you need to promise that you won't overreact.' She waited for a nod before continuing. 'Hannah's husband hurts her. When I first saw her, we were in the supermarket, and she looked really tired. But when we started talking, I could see she was in all sorts of pain. I couldn't see any bruising, but you would have to be an idiot not see she was in pain. I asked her straight out—'

Ryan cut her off. 'You did what? Amy, you can't just ask someone you barely know something like that!'

'Please, Ryan, I didn't ask her in the middle of the fruit and veg section. I did wait until we were having coffee where no one could hear me. I'm not that insensitive.' She shot him a look to let her brother know that she was insulted by his comments. 'Anyway, if I can continue. I asked her if he hurt her. She denied it, of course, saying she tripped and he grabbed her to stop her from falling. But the look in her eyes told me a whole other story. I told her I didn't believe her but wouldn't push the issue. I did however give her my number so she can stay in touch, and she texted me yesterday to thank me for the chat. So I did the only thing I know how and invited her to catch up again. And do you know what she said to me?' Now Amy was looking all smug at Ryan, and before he could say anything, Amy said, 'She said yes. So there, I have another date with your dream girl.' Amy now had Ryan's full attention. 'Tomorrow around two thirty at the little coffee place next to the supermarket—you know, just in case you were interested.'

Ryan felt a sadness building; he remembered seeing Hannah last Tuesday and didn't really notice her in pain. She looked tired, but he didn't notice what she was hiding. The more Ryan thought about it, the more the sadness turned to anger. Amy could see him deep in thought and could almost read his mind.

'Stop thinking about it. You would never have known. Some people are really good at hiding bad things from the rest of the world, so stop punishing yourself for not seeing it. Just remember where I work. We are trained to look for things like this. You might think I only answer the phones, but we are trained to look at people when they come in and watch out for signs, things like overprotective partners, fear, odd-looking injuries. And then we send a note to the doctor if we see something strange so they can do what they need to do.'

'How can I sit here and do nothing if he is hurting her? Do you really expect me to do nothing at all?' There was a desperation in his voice.

'Ryan, you need to listen to me very carefully now. Do not go over to her place or anything stupid like that. You might be trying to help, but you might just make it worse. Let me talk to her again tomorrow when we catch up. She might not feel comfortable talking to you about it, so please put yourself in her shoes before you do or say anything, OK? Please?'

Ryan agreed to Amy's reasoning; he didn't like this sudden feeling of helplessness. He wanted to go straight over to Hannah's place and rescue her from the monster her husband had turned into. He would run up the stairs, kick the door open, scoop Hannah up into his arms, and carry her away. He would take her somewhere safe, somewhere he would protect her from all the bad things, somewhere no one would ever hurt her again. Amy stood up and grabbed her bag off the arm of the chair; her lunch with Ryan was over. There was no conversation that was going to make him forget about what she had told him. All she could do now was reassure him that she would speak with Hannah tomorrow and try to get her some help.

Chapter 35

Hiding bruises wasn't difficult; you just needed the right colour make-up and the right clothing. Today was going to be a bit more of a challenge than usual. In the past, Hannah didn't need to go to much effort as she didn't need to leave the apartment too often; she needed make-up only if she had a family event to attend, and the bruises were never on the face. Today was difficult; she had to cover as best as she could the mark he had left on her face. It wasn't too dark, but there was still some swelling on her cheekbone. Hannah considered calling in sick today in hopes that tomorrow would be easier; the swelling would be gone, and the bruises would be a little better. If she called Lucy, what would she say? She just saw her on Saturday and didn't show any signs of a cold, so would Lucy believe her? She could tell her that maybe her mother was ill, and she had to go and take care of her. But then there would be all the follow-up questions, and Hannah wasn't confident in her ability to keep a story going and if she would remember what she had said. Hannah dropped her head and stared into the bathroom sink. She was tired; she had barely closed her eyes because she was too frightened to sleep. If she did call in sick today, at least she could go back to bed and sleep the day away. The pros were outweighing the cons.

Hannah stood up straight and looked at her reflection again in the mirror. She hated what she saw—a weak, beaten woman who let herself stay in this situation. She was disgusted at the woman looking back at her. She was angry at the person she had let herself become and wanted her to just go away. She wanted her husband dead. For a moment, the reflection smiled at her. When she thought about her husband dying and then becoming a widow, the reflection smiled again; when she pictured herself at her husband's funeral, the reflection really smiled. Hannah walked back to the bedroom and dressed for work. Sean walked into the room, about to say something but stopped.

'What are you smiling about?' he asked, surprised, and leaned against the doorway.

'Just thinking that today is going to be a great day.' Hannah didn't look up from what she was doing; she couldn't stand to look at him, and she started feeling nauseous having him so close to her.

'OK, whatever then.' He seemed disinterested in the answer. 'I will see you tonight after work. I might be late, though, as there is overtime on offer this week. So I am going to ask for some.' Sean walked away, and Hannah heard the front door close behind him; there was no goodbye hug or a 'Have a nice day'. All pleasantries had vanished together with any civil conversations.

Yesterday they might have said three words to each other all day. Maybe it would be better tonight after they have spent the day apart, and if Sean did overtime, then she would have until around eight before he would be home again. A sense of relief passed over Hannah, knowing that she wouldn't have to be near him for another twelve hours. She wandered from the bedroom to the kitchen to the lounge room without any real purpose; she stopped and stared at the empty apartment and listened to the silence. The lack of noise started to agitate her, and she knew she needed to go to work; she needed to be around people who were having fun and talking and laughing and who wanted her to be there. She went back to the bathroom and started covering the bruise on her face; little by little, it disappeared from sight, and she became confident to leave her home and go and join the outside world.

Chapter 36

There was no sunshine for the walk to work today. The clouds were black, and the street was wet from rain during the night, and there was an icy chill to the air. Hannah rugged up in a winter coat and scarf and some old gloves she had from years ago. She looked ominously up to the sky and hoped that the rain would hold off a little while longer so she could get to work dry. Hannah made a mental note to herself that she needed to buy a small umbrella next time she went to the supermarket. One thing about the cold was it made her walk faster, and she was almost at a jog when she arrived at work. She opened the door to the café and felt a rush of warm air greet her, and immediately, she felt OK again. She looked around and couldn't see anyone. She walked farther into the shop and then heard the familiar sound of Lucy's voice coming from the back of the kitchen. Hannah walked around the counter and into the kitchen. Lucy was standing at back with Sarah, who was the kitchen manager. There were three plates in front of them, and they were discussing the food that was on them. They hadn't seen Hannah come in.

'Morning, ladies. Something sure does smell wonderful in here already!' Hannah took a deep breath in, smelling the air that was filled with freshly cooked food; the smell was new, and Hannah wondered if they were making something new for the menu.

'Ah, Hannah, you're here already. And you are just the person we have been waiting for!' Lucy seemed genuinely excited to see Hannah and walked over to help her with her coat and scarf. 'Come over here and taste these new dishes Sarah has come up with. She has taken some of the ideas from the food from Saturday night. Did you enjoy our little get-together? I thought it wonderful, and everyone brought along so much great food!' Hannah laughed at Lucy and the way she always talked with her hands; she became very animated when she was excited about something. Hannah let Lucy take her coat and scarf and hang them on the coatrack tucked away in the corner of the kitchen, where Lucy had made a little nook for staff to put their belongings.

Sarah handed Hannah a fork and pushed plate number one towards her. Hannah was always told to eat with her eyes first, so she took her time looking at the food and making a comment on the presentation. She then closed her eyes and leaned over the plate so as to only get the aroma of this dish, and then she picked up some food with the fork and tasted it. It was sensational, and she felt a warmth in her belly that you only get when you eat something amazing. Lucy laughed and clapped her hands in excitement; it was the reaction she was hoping for. Hannah spent another ten minutes in the kitchen tasting the other dishes and discussing what should go on the specials board this week. She felt important to be included in this discussion and had a real sense of belonging here, and even though she had been in big trouble with Sean about working here, she believed that it still was the best decision she had made. When the menu was set, Hannah went about her normal routine of setting up the café ready for lunch.

━ ━ ━ ━ ━ ━ ━ ━ ━ ━ ━ ━ ━ ━ ━

Lucy watched Hannah closely; her movements were forced, and when she thought no one was watching, she lost her smile. Lucy was worried; this wasn't the first time she had noticed something peculiar about Hannah on a Monday. One of her favourite customers came in almost every day; she saw the connection between him and Hannah, and if Hannah wasn't married, she would have subtly encouraged the friendship. Hannah's mood always lifted when he came into the shop; she had a little extra skip in her step. Lucy liked this side of Hannah; but when he left, her enthusiasm dropped, not by much. And most other people probably would never had noticed, but Lucy did. People always commented on how perceptive Lucy was around strangers and how she just seemed to know things, and she always had a great sense of character and could spot a liar a mile away. That's why she knew something was wrong with Hannah; she felt it in her gut, but how to approach the issue was a whole other game. For today she would watch and take note, and tomorrow would be a whole new day.

~~~~~~~~~~~~~~~

Her shift was over, and Hannah was physically exhausted. Everything ached, and she just wanted to sit down and take off her shoes. She went into the kitchen, collected her coat and scarf, and saw Lucy putting away the last of the dishes.

'Hey, Lucy, I'm off now and look forward to doing it all again tomorrow.' Hannah barely had the strength to lift her arm and wave.

'Hannah, before you go, can I quickly steal a minute of your time?' Hannah forced a smile and nodded. 'Of course you can.'

'Come with me and sit down. You look like you're going to fall over if you stand a minute longer.' Lucy walked past Hannah and went into the dining area; she pulled out a chair for Hannah at the closest table. 'So I just wanted to check in with you to see how you are doing and how you are enjoying working here.'

Hannah smiled at Lucy. 'I love working here. Everyone is so wonderful, and I couldn't imagine not coming here every day. Have I done something wrong?'

Lucy laughed at Hannah, reached across the table, and patted her hand. 'No, you have done a great job since you started, and you are a real asset to me. I'm just making sure you are happy.' Just as Lucy finished talking, Hannah's phone buzzed. Not wanting to seem rude and open the message, Hannah quickly looked at the screen just to see who it was from.

'Oh crap, I forgot.' Hannah quickly stood up. 'I was meant to meet a friend soon, and I had totally forgotten.' She looked down at Lucy, not sure if she should excuse herself and leave or if she needed to wait until Lucy said she could go.

'It's all OK, Hannah. You get going so you're not late for your friend, and I will see you bright-eyed and bushy-tailed tomorrow.' Lucy stood up and put her arm around Hannah's shoulder. 'Thank you for your help this morning with the menu. I think we have some great new things to add to the next menu revamp.'

Hannah sighed; she was relieved she wasn't in any trouble. She left the café and headed towards the supermarket. She stopped momentarily to text Amy back that she was on her way. She was hoping Amy was cancelling their catch-up as she really wasn't in the mood to talk to anyone and just wanted to go home and sleep, but no, Amy was really looking forward to seeing her soon. The walk seemed to take a long time today; her feet hurt from standing, and her ribs were bruised and aching. She needed more painkillers just to get through the next hour. Before entering the little coffee shop, Hannah found a packet of painkillers at the bottom of her bag; she swallowed two, which was an effort without water, but she just needed them in her system. She just needed the pain to go away for a while. Mustering up her best smile, she walked through the door and saw Amy sitting at the same table they sat at last week, two mugs of coffee already made and a plate with a muffin cut in half. Amy looked up and waved at Hannah and had that bright smile she always seemed to wear. Hannah went and sat across from Amy and was grateful just to be sitting.

'Thank you for the coffee, Amy, but I'm pretty sure it was my shout this time.' Hannah wrapped both her hands around the mug; the warmth was instantly soothing, and she took a tiny sip of the coffee. It was the perfect temperature, so she took a second big sip. She put the mug down and looked up at Amy, who hadn't said a word. The smile was gone, and she had a sad yet concerned look on her face.

'So what happened this week?' There was no excitement in her voice; it was serious and almost accusing.

'Sorry? What do you mean?' Hannah was taken aback by the question and went on the defensive. Amy grabbed her bag off the chair next to her and found her compact; she clicked the button, held the mirror to Hannah, and pointed to her cheek. Hannah hadn't realised that through the course of the day, she must have rubbed at her make-up; and now if you looked hard enough, you could see the bruise on her cheek.

'It's nothing. Don't worry about it.' Hannah picked up her mug and started drinking again. Amy just sat there and stared back.

'How bad is it? I can see you have put on a fair covering of foundation. And I'm going to guess that you have other injuries. You looked like it was painful to sit. So where else is hurting?'

Hannah couldn't speak straight away; as the words were about to come out, she felt the tears building up, and she wasn't sure she was going to be able to stop them this time. She turned to the side and checked to see if anyone was watching them; she lifted the side of her T-shirt to show Amy her ribs. Amy gasped and covered her mouth, and Hannah saw the horror on her face. She didn't know why, but she trusted Amy; maybe it was because she was Ryan's sister, but she thought it was more than that—there was something about her that made it OK to show her the sins of her marriage. She pulled her shirt back down and straightened herself back in her chair and said nothing. What was she going to say? There were no words to defend her husband; this was no accident.

'Hannah, you can't stay. You know that, right? It's getting worse, and he's not going to stop. Please tell me you know that he won't ever change, no matter what he says. People always say they are going to change, but they never do. Please let me help you before . . . well, before it's too late.' Amy was close to tears, pleading with Hannah. Hannah looked at Amy and was heartbroken to see another person in pain over her and just wanted to reassure Amy that everything was going to be OK and that she didn't need to worry about her and that she was touched and truly grateful for her concern. But she still couldn't speak; her tears were still blocking her, and she just couldn't let them escape here. All she could manage was a whisper. 'Thank you.'

The two girls sat in silence drinking their coffee and sharing the muffin. It was choc chip and had been warmed in the microwave, so as they ate, they got little mouthfuls of melted chocolate. Hannah smiled at Amy; it was like the chocolate had a way of making everything better. Amy giggled back and picked up the mirror again so Hannah could see her reflection. Hannah laughed out loud when she saw a blob of chocolate smeared on her chin. It wasn't really funny, but both girls laughed and laughed. When the laughing stopped, Hannah checked the time and indicated she needed to go. She still wasn't sure if Sean was working late or if that was a cover so he could go and see Amy, but she needed to be home in case he came home as normal.

Outside, Amy gave Hannah a folded sheet of paper and told her to read it when she was at home alone. Hannah slipped it into her bag and assured Amy she would read it. The girls hugged goodbye, and Amy's phone buzzed; she looked at the text and raised an eyebrow.

'Looks like I have a date tonight.' She held Hannah's hand. 'Please read that sheet, and can we catch up soon?'

Hannah squeezed Amy's hand and then let go. 'Yes, I will read it. Now you go and have fun, and I want all the details next time, OK?'

'Of course, but you might just regret wanting ALL of the details. I might make you blush.' Amy made a silly shocked face and turned away from Hannah. *She's right*, Hannah thought. *I will probably regret wanting to hear the details of you and my husband.* She was becoming more conflicted about not telling Amy the truth about her and Sean. She just hoped that he was treating Amy better than she was being treated. If he was hurting her too, it would be her fault for not warning her about who he really was. Hannah went home and went to bed; she knew where Sean was and that he would be home late, so for now, she could sleep in peace.

Chapter 37

The café was closed for the day, but Lucy was still there. She sat in the little office at the back, away from main dining area. She had her laptop on and started googling. She didn't know how, but she knew she needed to help Hannah. Something was bad was happening to her; her gut told her that much, but without knowing exactly what it was, she wasn't sure where to start looking for help. Lucy knew domestic violence was a big social issue. She saw the articles in the paper, and there was ads from the government on the television, but she didn't recall ever meeting someone who might be a victim. Lucy sat for a moment and reflected. How could you tell if someone was being abused at home? It's not like they wear a sign promoting it. She assumed they would keep it to themselves; she knew she would. So now this made her mission to help Hannah that much harder. How do you try to help someone who doesn't ask for help? Lucy picked up her mug of hot tea and took a big sip; she was hoping the tea would help her find the answers. Two hours passed when Lucy called it a night. She had read multiple papers on domestic violence, and the statistics were scary. But she still didn't find the answer to the one question she had: how do you help someone if they don't ask for help?

\\\\\\\\\\\\\\\\\\\\\\\\\\\

Amy texted Ryan that afternoon after her catch-up with Hannah. 'Hey, just finished my date with Hannah and I think it is worse than I first thought. She didn't say anything but you would have to be blind not to see the injuries she had today. I have given her some information to read and hopefully that will prompt her to get help. I want to do more but I think if I come on too hard she will stop talking to me and then I won't be able to help. Will speak further to a friend at work who has experience in this area to see what we should do next. Talk soon.'

Amy felt sad; she had this strong urge to help Hannah out of this situation, but she was stuck on what to do next. Her colleague at work simply suggested to just keep being there for her and to try to open up the conversation and see if she could get her to talk about it. Once she could get her to talk, she could suggest some crisis care places who should be able to help her leave and become independent. Amy went to the kitchen and opened a bottle of wine; she poured a generous amount into a glass and sat on the bench. It wouldn't be long now, and her boyfriend would be here for tea. She missed him more than usual today, and she was getting impatient waiting for him to arrive. She gulped a big mouthful of wine and slid off the bench; she grabbed her glass and went to the front window to watch the car park and wait for him to arrive. She needed him now; she needed to feel his strong arms around her and to feel safe and secure. Her patience was rewarded, and earlier than expected, his car pulled up. She watched him get out of the car with a bottle of wine in one hand and flowers in the other. She felt her mood lift, and she put her glass down on the side table. She rushed to the front door and opened it before he had a chance to knock. He entered the room, and Amy threw her arms around his neck and kissed him long and passionately. When she released him from her hold, she felt a rush of emotion.

'I've missed you so much.' He put the wine and flowers down on the bench and came back to Amy; he kissed her and picked her up. She wrapped her legs around his waist, and he carried her to the bedroom, where they stayed for the next several hours.

\\\

Ryan read Amy's text and felt angry again. It was four o'clock, and he needed to leave work; he could no longer concentrate on any of the tasks he was meant to be doing. He scanned the office and noticed his boss was nowhere to be seen. He went over to the boss's assistant and enquired if she knew where he was. When he was told he was in a meeting with clients away from the office and wouldn't return until the morning, Ryan decided to leave. He convinced himself no one would notice he was gone for the last hour of the day. He collected his stuff and left. He had driven in that day; it wasn't often he was grateful for his morning laziness, but today he was. It took a few attempts to get the car started, which intensified his anger. The tyres screeched as he pulled away from his parking space, and he headed for the exit. He had no idea where he was going, but he didn't really care as long as he wasn't there anymore. He ended up at the markets; they were closed today, but this place had a special meaning to him. It was the place he first saw Hannah; it was several months ago now, but when he closed his eyes, he could still see her as if it had just happened. It was also the place they first spent any time together. He would never forget that day—the cooking class, the museum, and then watching her get tipsy and laughing so hard he thought she was going to fall off her chair. Then later when she did fall, he took her home and tended to her injury. He could still smell her perfume and hear her laugh and feel her hand on his arm as he helped her up. He was completely in love with her and would do anything to get her away from the monster that was hurting her. He opened his eyes again and thumped the steering wheel several times in anger. He needed to get her alone again so he could talk to her and make her see that she needed to leave. Deep down, he wanted to make her see that she should leave her husband for him. He would never hurt her; he just wanted to love her for the rest of her life. The air was becoming cold as the sun was beginning to set; the days were getting shorter as they headed into winter. Ryan started his car and put the heater on; frustrated and angry, he left the market car park and went home. Today he couldn't do anything to save her; maybe tomorrow would be the day.

Chapter 38

The sound of the front door shutting woke Hannah from her sleep. She slowly opened one eye and tried to look around the room. It was still dark outside, so she couldn't tell what time it was. She opened the other eye and sat up; her alarm clock read 11.20. She had been asleep since five in the afternoon, and now she was awake. She pulled back the covers and climbed out of bed; she found her dressing gown and went into the kitchen. Sean was sitting in the lounge in the dark with the TV on. He had kicked his shoes off and had his feet on the coffee table. He looked up as she walked into the room. Hannah rubbed her eyes and waited for him to say something. He didn't speak but motioned to the spot next to him on the sofa. Hannah walked around the coffee table and sat next to him; he raised his arm and again, without speaking, indicated for her to snuggle up against him. She shuffled over and leaned on his chest. She missed this part of their relationship and hoped maybe the rough patch was over. The thought of having his old self back made her feel warm and safe, and for now, the sense of fear vanished. As she got comfortable, she could smell Amy's perfume on his skin; it was like he wasn't even trying to hide it anymore, but still, she stayed snuggled under his arm in this familiar embrace. She closed her eyes and just let it be. Her brain wanted to start asking questions as to why he was home so late; she knew they never worked past eight when doing overtime, but she didn't. She couldn't stand the thought of hearing him lie to her, so she chose to ignore it.

After a few minutes, he started to wriggle and got her to sit up; he leaned over to the chair next to him and got the big cushion. He put it up against the arm of the sofa and turned his body so he was lying on the couch on his back; he dropped one leg off the sofa so Hannah could climb in and lie with her head on his stomach. It only took a minute, and she was fast asleep again. This was the most comfortable she had been in months, and the warmth of his body on hers and the movement of his breathing were enough to rock her to sleep. In this moment, she had forgotten that she hated him. For tonight, he was her loving husband, and they spent the night together, entwined on the sofa.

A distant beeping stirred both Hannah and Sean. Hannah pushed herself up away from the warm and safe space she had been nestled in and stretched. She stood up and wandered back to the bedroom, where she turned off the alarm. She went back to the kitchen and saw Sean's silhouette against the bright sun now pouring in through the balcony window; he still was a striking figure to her. He was in pretty good shape, which was due to the manual labour of his job. He stood for a second and stared back at her before walking over to her; he put one hand on her waist and pulled her close. He kissed her softly on her forehead and then went to the bathroom to shower and get ready for work. He still hadn't spoken a single word to her, but it was better than being yelled at.

Content with the past seven hours of peace and a kind of intimacy, Hannah set about getting Sean some breakfast. She put the kettle on and had decided on making scrambled eggs on toast. While making breakfast, Hannah heard Sean's phone vibrating on the kitchen table; she glanced over and saw Amy's name. The vibrating stopped, and a few seconds later, she heard the ding of a message being left. She was really curious at the content, but she dared not touch the phone; she knew the moment she picked it up would be the exact moment he would come back in, and she was not going to do anything to anger him. Less than a minute later, Sean appeared back in the kitchen, and she kept her back to the table. She made a little more noise than normal, hoping that when he picked up his phone, he would assume that with all the noise she was making, she would not have heard it ring. Hannah served up the eggs, and when she went to put it on the table, she noticed the phone was gone. Sean smiled at her and hungrily ate. Hannah giggled to herself that he must have really worked up an appetite last night. He stopped eating and raised an eyebrow at her as if to silently ask what was funny. She sat in the chair next to him and leaned on one elbow.

'You're eating like you haven't been fed in a while. Did you not stop to eat at all? Do you want me to make you some more?' Hannah was becoming good at pretending that she didn't know what was going on. With a half-chewed mouthful, Sean finally found his voice.

'Nope, didn't stop to eat last night. The new boss had me working like a Trojan. I would love some more. These eggs are amazing. Thanks, darling.'

Hannah leaned over and kissed Sean on the cheek. 'It will be only a few minutes, and I will have another serving ready for you.' She walked over to the fridge, opened the door, and turned back to him. 'Maybe you should get this new boss of yours to back off a little, no need to treat you like a slave.' She turned back and leaned over to get the carton of eggs. Sean must have found that last part amusing as he actually laughed out loud, something really rare for him to do unless he was surrounded by his mates and they were talking sleazy. When Sean laughed, Hannah laughed too; it was strange and slightly surreal for Hannah. There was no tension or angry words. He sounded happy, and she was happy to be near him. She felt her hatred of him completely disappear. And when she looked at him smiling, she fell back in love with him, and all seemed right with the world once more.

Hannah served up a second breakfast and made enough so she could sit with him and eat together. When Sean was finished, he cleared his plate and hers; and for a second time that day, he kissed her. This time, not on her head, but on her lips. It only lasted a second, but it happened. She sat there like a love-struck teenager smiling away as if the school's hottest boy picked her from the crowd, and they were to live happily ever after. Sean gathered up his stuff to leave for work and stopped before walking out the door; he stepped several paces backwards and leaned in on the kitchen door frame.

'If you like, I will pass on overtime tonight and come straight home. Maybe we can watch a movie or something and grab a pizza for tea. What do you think?'

Hannah gazed up at Sean and, with a contented sigh, replied, 'I think that sounds perfect. I can't wait.' Sean smiled back at her and blew her a kiss, then left the apartment for work.

Hannah leaned back on the chair and stretched her legs out under the table and felt very satisfied with herself. She knew if she just waited it out, the old Sean would come back, and they would be happy together again. As she pulled her legs back in, stood up, and twisted the wrong way, the bruising on her ribs sharply brought her back to the past few months. She winced and took a few deep breaths. She opened her dressing gown and lifted her top; her ribs were black and purple. She caught herself getting angry and quickly stopped herself mid-thought. *This was from the past, and we no longer need to worry about that behaviour anymore.* After last night and this morning, all of the bad stuff was behind them, and she was going to be happily married again. Hannah got to cleaning the breakfast dishes; and in her mind, she replayed the feeling she had when she was snuggled up in Sean's lap, so warm and safe. This was the feeling she was going to focus on and nothing else, and she was not going to let anyone ruin it now that she finally had it back.

Chapter 39

A few weeks passed without incident. Hannah was happy again. Sean still did overtime, and then Hannah would get a text from Amy telling her how wonderful and thoughtful her boyfriend was. Hannah would reply in a polite way and make a few jokes; their friendship was really becoming important to Hannah. She hadn't had a true friend in a long time, and she had forgotten what it felt like to have someone to confide in. They still met once a week for coffee and talked. Hannah told Amy about the special night and how things were getting back to normal. There was still no intimacy between them, but they did snuggle a lot on the couch, and they had started kissing again. Hannah was convinced the bad was over, and they were being given a second chance, and she was going to grab it with both hands and not let go. Amy would gush about how romantic her boyfriend was and how she really liked only seeing him occasionally as when they did get time together, it was special. There was even a giggle from Hannah when Amy suggested they go on a double date. Hannah said she would think about it.

And then there was Ryan; he still came into the café most days for lunch, and Hannah enjoyed talking with him. She pushed her feelings for him deep down inside, where they couldn't cause any trouble. There were a couple of times when she caught herself staring at him, and she had to tell herself off and go find a distraction.

It was a Wednesday night. Hannah was home after work and preparing dinner for Sean. Right on six o'clock, he walked through the front door and came straight into the kitchen. He came up behind Hannah, squeezed her gently, and kissed her cheek. She smiled to herself and let the embrace happen. Sean excused himself and went to the bedroom to get changed out of his work clothes. Hannah thought for a moment and grinned; she walked into the bedroom to see Sean sitting on the bed in just his underwear, getting into his trackpants. Slyly, Hannah leaned up against the door frame and smiled. Sean looked up and raised his eyebrow at his wife. Hannah took this as approval and shimmied over to him, one hand on her hip and attempted a seductive look. Sean laughed softly and pushed himself back onto the bed and let his wife try to seduce him. Trying not to laugh, Hannah stood in front of Sean and started taking off her shirt in the sexiest way she could think of. Sean lay back on the bed and enjoyed watching her; after a few minutes, he leaned on one side and reached out to ask for her hand. Hannah reached back and took his hand. Sean pulled, but she resisted and blew him a kiss. Sean pulled a little harder, and Hannah let herself lean forward. She let his hand go, climbed onto the bed, and straddled Sean. Sean put his arms behind his head and smiled approvingly at her. Hannah, on all fours, leaned over Sean and bent forward and started kissing his neck. He breathed in deep and let out a sigh. Hannah moved slowly down and started kissing his chest; she sat up and ran her fingers ever so softly over his skin and watched his skin get goosebumps. His whole body relaxed under her. Feeling a sense of control, Hannah wiggled down and started kissing his chest down to his stomach and firmly rubbed her hands down his side until she reached the band of his underwear. On each side, she tucked two fingers and gently pulled at the elastic. Sean let out a groan, and she knew she had him completely under her spell. She wiggled a little farther down and ran her tongue just under the edge of the elastic. She could feel the heat of his groin, which turned her on. She pulled a little more at the elastic and felt his body tense in anticipation when there was a loud and uninvited bang on the front door. Hannah stopped and sat up, Sean jumped and swore, and they both looked at each other with confusion and accusation as if one of them had invited a guest and forgot to tell the other. Hannah climbed off and swiped at her shirt that was on the floor.

'Who the hell is that?' she whispered angrily. Sean adjusted his underwear, which was halfway off, and grabbed her around the waist, nuzzling the small of her back.

'Damned if I know, but I will make them regret interrupting us.' He found his trackpants and yanked them on; before leaving the bedroom, he kissed Hannah and then leaned his forehead against hers. 'Just remember where you were at, OK?' Then stomped towards the front door. Disheartened, Hannah sat on the corner of the bed and listened for voices. She laughed when she heard the voice of Sean's best friend, and he was getting told off for interrupting. Then the front door closed, and she could hear more than one set of footsteps making their way to the kitchen. With a defeated sigh, Hannah got up and made her way to join the other two.

Dave looked at the floor and apologised to Hannah for interrupting. Hannah laughed and made eyes at Sean, which indicated they were not finished and it would continue once their guest had left.

'So . . . Dave, would you like to stay for dinner? There is plenty here and will only be about fifteen minutes.' Dave looked at Sean for approval. Sean rolled his eyes and pulled out a chair for his friend to sit down. Without saying anything, Hannah got an extra place setting ready and went back to cooking. She knew she was not to comment or actively participate in the conversation unless asked a direct question, but they couldn't stop her from listening.

'Why are you here?' Sean was always to the point with everyone; that was one of the things Hannah loved most about him. She never needed to guess how he was feeling.

'I entered a competition about a month back in one of the fishing magazines I get. And this morning, I got a random phone call from a private number, which I don't normally answer. So I don't know why I did today, but turns out it was the chick that was running the competition, and she was ringing me to tell me I won.' Dave sat at the table, looking very proud of himself. Hannah looked at Sean and laughed under her breath. Dave was one of those people who got easily excited over anything. Sean looked at Dave and waited to see if there was any more to the conversation; when it got to the point no one was talking, Sean broke the silence.

'Do we have to guess what you won, or are you going to tell us?'

'Oh, shit. Yeah, that would help, hey?' Dave chuckled at himself. 'I won a four-night trip away up the coast in a house for me and five friends with a fully catered fishing charter for Saturday.'

'What the . . . ! That's awesome!' Sean was almost speechless. Hannah stopped what she was doing and went to congratulate Dave but stopped herself; she finished plating dinner and placed the meals in front of the boys. She got her plate and sat quietly at the other end of the table.

'So you gotta come with me, right?' Dave questioned Sean. 'I mean, what's the point of going if you can't come, hey?'

'Hell yeah, I will be there! When is it for? And I will organise the time off work.' Hannah could see the excitement building in Sean; they never went on holidays, so small things like weekends away with the boys were a big deal. Hannah knew she wasn't going to be consulted, so there was no point in saying anything; she didn't want to start an argument. When the boys had finished eating, she cleared the plates and started filling the sink with hot water to start washing up. The boys moved into the living room and continued planning the pending weekend away. Hannah was OK with Sean going away; it gave her another chance to spend some time alone. Maybe she would go see another movie or see what the others from work were doing. Even better, she would see what Amy was doing. What could be better than when you husband is away, you hang out with his mistress? Hannah laughed at the thought. As she finished the dishes, she heard Dave yell bye from the front door and then the door close. Sean came back to the kitchen, smiling from ear to ear. He sat at the table and watched Hannah silently as she finished up and beckoned her over. She straddled his lap and put her hands behind his neck.

'That was a surprise. Imagine winning a prize like that!' She leaned in and kissed Sean gently. 'Do you know what weekend it is for so I can mark it on the calendar?' Hannah restrained from sounding too excited, but she really was looking forward to another weekend alone.

'It's in two weekends' time. I will get the Friday and Monday off. We will drive there late Thursday afternoon and be back around lunchtime Monday. You going to be OK on your own for that long? Last time was only two nights.' Sean genuinely looked at her with concern. Hannah hugged Sean and held on for a while; she sat back up and smiled.

'I will be OK. I will miss you like crazy. But you need a good break, and this sounds like a great place to go, and the fishing charter sounds amazing!'

Sean smiled back. He grabbed Hannah under her butt and stood up with her in his grip; he carried her to the bedroom and kicked the door shut behind him.

Chapter 40

Sitting alone at the bar, Ryan stared into his beer. It was Tuesday night. He didn't go out to bars very often, and it was rare that he would during the week, but he was feeling sorry for himself. It was his birthday next weekend, and he thought he might do something to celebrate, but his sister had turned him down. She had been invited away with this new boyfriend of hers to some place up the coast for a few days. So now his only other choice was to mention something to Alex and see if he wanted to go out. He knew he would because he went out every weekend looking for someone to drink with and picking up girls. Almost every week since the last time they went out, Alex insisted they did it again, but Ryan always found an excuse not to go. But he couldn't have the girl he wanted, who seemed to be doing really well the past few weeks, and his sister now had someone. So if he wanted to have birthday drinks, it was going to have to be with Alex. Sighing heavily, Ryan had a big gulp of his beer; it was going warm, so he sculled the rest of the glass. He acknowledged the bartender and ordered another one. He looked around to see only a handful of people and no one he knew. As the beer kicked in, Ryan started feeling even more sorry for himself and started questioning all of his choices. Why didn't he have a better job? Why didn't he have a girlfriend? When was life going to give him a break? He was so caught up in his self-pity that he didn't notice the woman who came and sat next to him.

'Why the long face, Ryan?' The voice was friendly and familiar. Ryan looked up and laughed; he gestured to the bartender and swivelled the bar stool so he was now facing the stool next to him.

'Hey, Lucy, let me buy you a drink. What would you like?' He had a slight slur. Lucy grinned and turned back to the bartender.

'Just a glass of your house white, please.' Ryan pulled cash out of his pocket and paid for Lucy's drink. Lucy climbed up onto the stool and raised her glass to Ryan. 'Thank you, my dear, very nice of you to buy an old lady a drink.' She took a big sip and placed her glass down gently on the bar. 'Now you look like someone who has had his toys taken away. What's going on?'

Ryan felt comfortable around Lucy; he had been eating at her shop for many years and had got to know her quite well, and she always seemed to know when he wasn't great. 'It's nothing too bad, Lucy, just feeling sorry for myself tonight. Was trying to plan birthday drinks with my sister, but she is going away with her new boyfriend next weekend, so that's the end of those plans. And I'm not sure if I am talking out of place here or not, but have you noticed something strange with Hannah recently? There's been a few times I thought she looked injured, not sure that's the right word or not. I have a gut feeling something bad has happened to her. Then all of a sudden, she's back to normal. It just doesn't seem right. And I know, before you say anything, it's none of my business. But she's such a nice person I would hate to see anything bad happen to her.'

Lucy put her hand on Ryan's arm in comfort. 'I was thinking exactly the same thing. You know, Ryan, there were a couple of times recently where she seemed to be in a fair bit of pain. And I'm sure I saw some bruises, but I can't be sure of how she got them. I met her husband. And he seemed off, like he didn't want to leave her when I had a staff dinner, but he did. He made it pretty clear, though, that she had to be home by a certain time. So I took her home to make sure she was on time. It's a tough one. I would hate to say something, and she get offended and quit. She's one of the best people I've had work for me, but I also would hate her to think I didn't take any notice or didn't care. So I really don't know what to do.'

Ryan and Lucy sat in silence thinking about Hannah and if they should say anything. Lucy turned back to Ryan with an idea.

'How about the next time either one of us sees her in pain or bruised, we both sit down somewhere away from the crowd and talk to her together? It might be better if we do it together so she knows we both see what's going on and we care. What do you think?'

'Sounds like a plan to me.' Ryan raised his glass to Lucy and then finished the beer in one gulp. Lucy too finished the rest of her wine in one go and then, in a most awkward way, got down off the bar stool. Ryan followed Lucy out of the bar and looked around for a taxi.

'Come on, Ryan. I will give you a lift home. I only had the one drink, so I am OK to drive. I assume you don't live too far from here?'

'Nah, only about five minutes. Thanks, Lucy.'

Ryan walked next to Lucy and put his arm over her shoulder. 'You're a good friend, Lucy.' Lucy chuckled and unlocked the car from a few steps away.

'She will be OK, Ryan. We will make sure of that.' Lucy drove Ryan home. As Ryan got out of the car, he turned back to Lucy; she could smell the beer on his breath.

'I think I love her.' He spoke in a way like the words were forbidden, but they needed to be said.

'I know, Ryan, and we will look out for her together, OK?'

'Yeah, we will.' He leaned back in and gave Lucy a kiss on the cheek, then shut the door a little too hard. He waved as Lucy drove off; he felt better knowing someone else saw what he did. But then it hit him—did he just confess his love for Hannah to Lucy? Now his feelings were real; he never quite knew what they were, but now that he had said it out loud, they just became reality. He really did love her, but she was not his to love. Now what was he to do? Feeling like crap again, Ryan went inside and went straight to bed.

Chapter 41

The countdown was on; only forty-eight hours to go, and Hannah would have a few days to herself again. She was going to meet Amy after work for their weekly catch-up. Hannah couldn't wait to tell her all about her weekend of freedom and to see what she was doing Saturday night; maybe they could go out to dinner or to a bar somewhere and have some fun. She never gave Amy specifics of Sean's trip away as he had probably told her about it, and she didn't want Amy to figure it out or get any crazy ideas about the two of them driving up there and surprising them. Sean had left her a list of things he wanted to take away with him and asked her to go to the shops for him. She picked up the list and scanned the requests—nothing out of the ordinary, just the usual snacks and a bottle of whisky. All easy enough for her to get from the supermarket next to the coffee shop where she had catch-ups with Amy. Hannah grabbed her bag and coat and left for work.

Hannah arrived first, which was nothing unusual, and helped Lucy set up. Lucy had the radio on and was humming away to the song that was playing. Hannah started swaying to the music and singing softly, which caught Lucy's eye. When the chorus came on, both women broke out into song at the top of their lungs and finished facing each other with arms in the air and laughing. It was twenty to twelve, and the rest of the shift arrived and got ready for the lunch crowd. Hannah stood behind the counter; the two older women went back into the kitchen and got all of the things from the fridge and prepared the kitchen for service. Lucy went back there to help. Then there were two others—a young guy in his early twenties, who was the resident barista, and a girl who had just turned eighteen, who was studying part-time; this shift helped fill in her day between lectures. The set-up worked really well. Hannah took the orders and sent them to the kitchen, the two older women did all the cooking, and Lucy jumped in if it became too busy. One person was banging out the coffee, and the young girl was taking out orders and clearing tables. Hannah would swap with her about halfway through the shift to give her a break.

As the first customers started coming in right on twelve, Lucy turned the radio down and set to work on greeting everyone as they came in. It was one of the reasons people came back time and time again. It was a place where you could get to know the regulars, and no one was treated like a number and rushed out.

Like clockwork, Ryan arrived at ten past and made his way to the same table he sat at every day. His friend Alex was with him today and was doing all of the talking. Hannah gave them a big smile as they walked past, and Ryan winked back. Within a minute after arriving, the boys were at the counter, ready to order. Hannah found it amusing that she knew several customers who ordered exactly the same thing every time. She liked the predictability.

'Schnitzels and Cokes?' Hannah was already entering it into the system, and the boys already had their cash ready, so the question was merely a formality. There was no one else waiting to be served, so Hannah took the opportunity to have a conversation with the two boys. 'What are the plans for the weekend, boys? Anything exciting?' Hannah leaned forward on the counter on one hand, eager to hear what they had planned. Alex answered first.

'Family wedding for me. My cousin is getting married, and his wife-to-be has some really hot friends, so I'm hoping to get me some bridesmaid action.' Alex stepped back, looking proud of himself.

'And you, Ryan, are you going as his plus one?' Hannah laughed as Alex gave her a look of disgust.

Ryan answered, laughing, 'No, I wouldn't want to show him up and have all the bridesmaids to myself.'

Alex punched Ryan in the arm and retorted, 'As if, dude, you couldn't land a bridesmaid even if I paid her to be with you!' Alex walked back to the table, but Ryan paused.

'Actually, it's my birthday on Saturday, and I was trying to organise drinks. But Alex is busy, and Amy is apparently going away with this new boyfriend of hers, some random weekend away up the coast. So looks like I will be home all alone on my birthday.' Ryan dropped his head and pouted at Hannah.

'Poor thing, all alone on your birthday, hey? Well, as it happens, I am on my own too this weekend. Now I can't have you spending your birthday alone, so how about we go see a movie or grab some dinner or something?' Hannah tried to smile, but underneath, she was seething. Sean had invited Amy to go away with him. *How dare he!* And Amy had not said a thing to her. Hannah breathed in deep and fought the urge to scream. The smile on Ryan's face was enough to calm anyone down, and for a second, Hannah forgot.

'That would be great, thank you. I guess I can stop feeling sorry for myself now. How about you look at what's showing and let me know tomorrow what you want to see and what time? Thanks, Hannah, you have made my day.' Ryan saw Lucy come out from the kitchen and waved at her. 'Thanks for the lift home last night, Lucy! Appreciated.' Lucy waved back, and as Hannah turned to look at Lucy to find out what that was about, Ryan went and sat down.

Lucy walked up behind Hannah and giggled. 'Just so you hear it from me and not from any gossip', Lucy couldn't help but laugh as she was talking, 'I had drinks with that young man last, and then I took him home.' She raised her eyes at Hannah, looking for a reaction; she was so comical with her expression that Hannah couldn't help but laugh at her.

'Oh really? Never pictured you for a cougar.'

Lucy laughed back, made some claws with her fingers, meowed at Hannah, and then walked off. The rest of the afternoon went quickly, and Lucy kept meowing whenever she walked past Hannah; and by the end of the shift, everyone was in on the joke. Hannah helped pack away the chairs at closing and then hurried off to meet Amy. She was still really angry that Amy had been invited by Sean to go away with him, but she wanted to see if Amy was going to tell her about it. Hannah knew she had organised to catch up with Ryan on Saturday out of spite and hurt feelings, and that was the wrong reason to want to see someone, but it was too late now, Ryan seemed really happy that she had offered, and it was his birthday after all. She knew all too well what it was like when no one celebrated with you or even seemed to care.

Hannah arrived a few minutes late, and Amy was waiting for her. As usual, coffee had been ordered, and a muffin was cut in half to share.

Hannah liked the predictability of their meetings. It made her feel at ease not ever having to guess what was going to happen. Hannah led the conversation today, which was unusual as Amy always had a million things to say.

'A little birdy told me that it is your brother's birthday this weekend.' Hannah smiled at Amy, hoping to open up the conversation about the trip to see if Amy would tell her all about it.

'Ha ha! Would that little birdy be the birthday boy himself?' Amy raised an eyebrow, knowing that Ryan loved celebrating his birthday or at least telling everyone it was his birthday.

'Yeah, it was,' Hannah replied. 'Seemed a bit down about it, though.'

'Let me guess . . . He is sulking because I am going away this weekend? He didn't seem impressed when I said I wasn't going to be available to go out with him Saturday night.'

Hannah sensed something wasn't right. Amy didn't at all seem happy and bursting at the seams like she imagined her to be when talking about going away for the weekend with her boyfriend.

'Yeah, he was disappointed, but I'm sure he will get over it. So tell me about the trip.'

Amy looked around the room, completely disinterested. She turned back and caught Hannah's eye. She looked down, leaned on the table, and put both hands around her cup; and with a sigh, she looked up again.

'Don't get me wrong, I am looking forward to going away. It will be nice having our first weekend away. But I had pictured it to be very different and not with five other people. Apparently, the deal is his mate won a four-night stay at a house up the coast and a fishing charter for the Saturday. So there will be my boyfriend, two of his mates, me, and the two other girlfriends. I can picture it now—the boys will be out all day fishing, and the girls will be sitting around the house, waiting for them to come back. Then the nights will be everyone sitting around, drinking and so on. Sounds OK, but I don't really know how much time we are going to get to be together alone, so I'm almost thinking that it's not really worth going, if you know what I mean. And I can't say anything as I know he would be disappointed if I don't go. What would you do?' Amy looked at Hannah, eagerly waiting for some friendly advice.

Hannah sat back in the chair and pondered the question; she picked up her cup and finished the contents. She placed the cup back on the table softly and spoke. 'If I were in your position, I would go for two reasons: First, you are making an assumption on how you think things are going to happen, and if he really does like you as much as you like him, he will find plenty of ways to get you alone. And why wouldn't you all be going on the charter? I think it would be a lot of fun. Second, how many opportunities are you going to get for a free holiday? Sounds like an amazing gift, and you should jump at the chance to go. Honestly, I think you would be stupid not to go.' Hannah heard the words leave her mouth and still couldn't believe that she was encouraging this woman to continue the affair with her husband. Upon receiving this advice, Amy's mood suddenly went through the roof, and the over-the-top, bubbly persona was in full swing. Hannah let herself get caught up in the newly found excitement, and it didn't take long for their catch-up to be over. Amy hugged Hannah as they left and thanked her several times for helping her with her dilemma.

The walk home gave Hannah time to reflect on her out-of-the-blue invitation to Ryan. How did she really think Saturday night was going to go? Was it a date, or was it going to be two friends just hanging out? Nervousness started to set in as she started to overthink how Ryan was feeling about the invitation. What if he thought it was a date, and what if he was going to expect date-like behaviour and want to take it to another level? Nervousness turned into panic; one part of her dreamt time and time again about dating Ryan and scenes of intimacy, and when she let her mind wander, she felt little flutters of excitement deep down in her belly. The other part of her, the sensible married part, knew she was just going to hang out with a friend on their birthday so they didn't need to spend it alone, and that's what a good friend does. Nothing more.

By the time she got home, she was more confused than ever. The only thing she was certain of was either way, as a date or as friends, she craved the idea of spending more time with Ryan; and she cared less and less if it was right or wrong. Hannah sat at the kitchen table once inside and immediately went to the local cinema's website to look to see what was showing. She then moved onto restaurants and bars in the same area and now had a plan of what Saturday night was going to look like, and it didn't feel wrong; in fact, the more she thought about it, the more she gave herself permission. She had started convincing herself that if it was OK for her husband to have a special friend on the side, then it was OK for her too. Maybe this was how she would get revenge on him; maybe it wasn't about confronting him about his affair and somehow humiliating him and ruining the reputation of his mistress. Maybe it was doing exactly the same thing that he was doing. The more she thought this way, the more it became OK, and no one would tell her otherwise. She closed down her laptop and quickly set about getting dinner started; she would now play the part of the perfect wife until he went away, and then she would set her plan in motion.

Chapter 42

Thursday afternoon came fast, and Hannah packed Sean's things so he could leave as soon as he arrived home from work. He arrived home a little early but soon left. Hannah sent Amy a text wishing her a wonderful weekend and that she looked forward to catching up the next week to hear all about it. Hannah had also seen Ryan at lunchtime and subtly found out what his plans were for the evening. With Sean out of the house and on his way up the coast with Amy, she knew she was going to be far out of his thoughts and was going to go out. She had it all planned; she would go to the same place as Ryan and appear surprised when she saw him. He would then invite her to join him, and her plan would be under way.

She went to the bedroom and started going through her clothes to find something to wear. She hated that she didn't have anything new in her collection. She always took notice of the younger girls that came into the café with beautiful outfits, and she wished she would one day be fortunate enough to have such wonderful things to wear. But for tonight it would be something from her vintage collection. After changing a number of times, she settled on a buttoned shirt; she could leave the top couple of buttons undone to give a hint of cleavage. She had a reasonable figure, so she picked a pair of jeans that were slim fitting and found an old pair of boots. She dusted them off and realised she had bought them not long after she first got married. She pulled her hair into a messy bun and tied an old piece of ribbon that was the same colour as her shirt around. She looked at herself in the mirror and thought her ensemble looked OK. Lastly, she put on a soft coloured lipstick and a spray of perfume, and she was ready to go.

She had the bus timetable out and rechecked the time. It would take her about twenty minutes to get to the other side of town to the bar Ryan said he would be at. She still had a few minutes until she needed to leave. She found her phone at the bottom of her bag and started going back over the photos she had taken months ago when she was doing her own PI work to find out who Amy was. She stopped on the one where Amy had come out the front of her place and was hugging Sean, who had brought her flowers. Hannah felt a pain in her heart as she remembered how she felt when she discovered the affair. It was the most painful humiliation she had ever experienced. And in that moment, she realised that the only man she ever had loved was loving someone else; and still to this day, she hadn't worked out what she had done wrong that forced him into the arms of another. Hannah felt the tears coming again, so she locked the screen and threw the phone back into her bag. She grabbed a tissue from the box on top of the fridge and dabbed at her eyes. She was going to take this pain and use it to get through this weekend. She put the tissue in the bin, put on her coat, and slung her bag over her shoulder. She was ready to go; she was ready to go and find Ryan.

The bus was right on time, and so far, everything was going according to plan. She got off a block away from the bar and walked quickly to the front door. She was a bundle of nerves mixed with a bit of fear. She pushed open the door and walked in. She let her eyes wander around the room and take in where everything was: The bar was to the back left with a few stools at the far end. A row of six booths was across the far side wall, and small round tables scattered with four and five chairs between the booths and the door where Hannah was standing. A sign above the door indicated the toilets at the back to the right, and there was what appeared to be a dance floor along the right side wall. It was nothing spectacular and was busier than she had thought for a Thursday night.

She moved in further and decided that she should make her way to the bar and have a drink in her before Ryan got there, for courage. She stood at the bar for about a minute until the bartender was free and came and served her. She hadn't put any thought into what she was going to drink and suddenly became flustered. Put on the spot, she glanced over at two girls sitting at the table, saw they had champagne, and quickly ordered the same. The bartender went to work pouring the drink and even put a sliced strawberry on the edge of the glass. Hannah found a table to sit at in the middle of the cluster and picked a chair that would allow her to watch the bar and the front door. She sipped at the champagne and waited. Fifteen minutes passed, and still no Ryan; her glass was empty, so she went back to the bar and ordered another. She sat back down in the same chair and continued to wait. The bubbles from the first drink started to make their way to her head, and she relaxed a little. She didn't drink often, but she always loved that feeling when the alcohol started to give her that warm and relaxed feeling. In the back of her mind, she knew she had to drink slow; otherwise, she would be a mess after three drinks, and she had a plan to action that didn't involve her being drunk on night number one.

Another fifteen minutes passed, and doubt was starting to dominate her thoughts. She got out her phone and started flicking through apps, looking for something to distract her. Another ten minutes went by, and she had finished her second drink. She was about to go for a third when an older-looking man put a drink down in front of her and then sat uninvited at one of the other chairs. Stunned, Hannah looked up at him.

'Um . . . thanks?' She questioned, not really sure what the protocol was when a stranger bought you a drink. The man picked up his glass and tilted it towards Hannah, waiting for the customary clinking of glasses.

'I couldn't have a beautiful lady sitting here all alone now. That just wouldn't be right.' Hannah picked up her glass and clinked it, then took a sip. The man continued talking. 'I'm Robert, and you are?' He seemed nice enough, not sleazy or trying to get into her personal space. And since Ryan hadn't shown up, she thought there was no harm in making conversation; after all, he did buy her a drink.

'Nice to meet you, Robert. I'm Hannah.' She took another sip and waited for her new friend to continue the conversation. He quickly took over the conversation, and Hannah just had to sit and listen, nodding and laughing on cue. This man bored her, but she was liking the attention; he offered her another drink, which she tried to turn down as she now had three glasses and was starting to get that tipsy feeling. Ignoring her declining, he went to the bar for another round. Hannah thanked him again when he returned, and this time, she was going to make sure she drank very slowly. Robert finished his drink quickly and went back to the bar for a third, Hannah was getting tired and had been here now for an hour and a half with Ryan being a no-show. She felt foolish thinking she could turn up and he would be here and everything would go to plan.

Robert came back to the table, and this time, he moved his chair so he was sitting right next to Hannah. She didn't like where this was going as she felt him rub his leg against hers. She excused herself and rushed to the toilet. She took this time to evaluate her situation and think of an exit strategy. She washed her hands and splashed a little cold water on her face. She would go back out there, finish her drink, and just tell him that she needed to leave as she had to start work early in the morning; she laughed a little at the excuse as she had heard that line in so many movies when someone was trying to escape a bad date, but it was the best she could come up with. Armed with a plan, she left the safety of the ladies' toilet. Head down and on a mission, she quickly went back to the table with an eager Robert waiting patiently for her. She took the opportunity to change seats and took a large sip of her drink to try to finish it quickly. She drank too fast and ended up inhaling bubbles, which started her coughing. The bubbles burned the back of her throat, and she couldn't stop. Being a gentleman, Robert dashed to the bar for a glass of water, which the bartender had ready for him as he had seen Hannah coughing. He passed her the glass, which she gulped down; the coughing stopped, and Robert sat back down in the other chair next to her. She thanked him for his help and took a few deep breaths. Once he was satisfied she was OK, he picked up right where he left off, telling her all about his life.

A few minutes of forcing herself to listen passed and Robert excused himself and went to the toilet. Hannah sighed and finished her drink; when he returned, she was going to thank him for the company and then leave. She put on her coat in anticipation and had her bag at the ready. She saw him making the return trip back to the table, and his face dropped when he saw she was ready to leave; in one last effort to keep her attention, he offered to take her home. She politely declined and started to walk away; he started following her out the door and asked if he could call her. Genuinely flattered, she made up a story about not being in the right space to be starting a new relationship but hoped she might bump into him again one night here. He accepted defeat and went back inside.

Feeling a little bad for him, Hannah looked up the street for a taxi. Nothing in sight, so she turned to look the other way; thinking her luck had changed, a taxi was pulling up over the road to let someone out, so she dashed across the street to jump in. As she rounded the back of the taxi, she stopped dead in her tracks—Ryan was getting out. It was like she was paralysed; she couldn't move, and no words were coming out. She had given up on seeing him tonight. He looked at her with surprise, and then a big smile took over.

'Well, of all the people, I know you would have to be the last person I was expecting to see here tonight. Don't tell me you are leaving now?'

Hannah found her voice. 'Yeah, I was on my way home. I had drinks with friends, but it was getting late, and I didn't want to drink much more, so I just left. Are you meeting someone?' She hadn't meant to be so forward, but she had four drinks under her belt and had forgotten any subtleties. Ryan leaned on the taxi with the door still open and shook his head. 'No, I was just coming to have a couple of beers and see if there was anyone here I knew. But seeing I haven't gone in yet, would you like to go somewhere else and have a drink with me?' Hannah blushed and nodded. Ryan moved to one side and let her get into the taxi. She shuffled across to the far seat, and Ryan got in after her. The taxi driver turned back towards them, waiting for instructions where to take them. Ryan looked at Hannah and asked, 'Got anywhere in mind?'

Without thinking, Hannah replied, 'How about your place?' Ryan didn't need to ask a second time and told the driver to take him back from where they just came.

Chapter 43

Hannah sat on the edge of Ryan's couch. A flurry of nerves had taken over, and she became fidgety. Ryan was in the kitchen getting Hannah a drink; she knew she'd already had enough, but now that she was here, she needed one more just to keep the nerves at bay. While she was waiting, she looked around the room. There wasn't a great deal of stuff, and she was impressed with how tidy and clean the place looked. Trying to appear more relaxed and like this was no big deal, Hannah sat back into the couch and tucked one leg under the other. She looked into the kitchen and watched as Ryan had a cloth and was polishing two wine glasses; watching him made her smile. He looked up and saw her watching, so he became animated, trying to get her to laugh. Hannah couldn't help but giggle at him, and then she really started to relax. Hearing voices, Bruce woke from his deep slumber from under the couch, stretched his front paws out, and grabbed at the back of Hannah's foot. Hannah jumped and let out a small squeal from fright. Ryan rushed over to see what was wrong.

'What happened? Are you OK?' He sat down next to Hannah and took one of her hands into his. Looking spooked, Hannah was swiping at the back of her leg.

'Something just ran up my leg. I don't know what it was or where it went.' Ryan got down on his knees and looked under the couch. He reached under, and Hannah could see him grabbing at something. She put both of her feet up on to the couch. Ryan looked up at her and started laughing.

'What's so funny?' Hannah demanded to know. 'Something really did go up my leg.' She looked back down at Ryan with an angry stare.

'I should have warned you. I keep a man-eating monster under my couch. He attacks anyone who dares sit down.' Ryan tried to sound scary and laughed again at Hannah. 'I call him Bruce!' And with that declaration, he pulled out the big fluffy cat and held him up like a prize. Hannah looked Bruce in the eye and then broke into laughter. She took Bruce off Ryan and cuddled him.

'Was that you attacking my leg then?' She nuzzled Bruce and then put him down. Bruce scampered away and sat in the kitchen doorway; he stared at Hannah for a moment and then began grooming himself. Ryan went back to the kitchen and poured two glasses of wine. He walked back slowly and never took his eyes off Hannah. Hannah smiled up at Ryan and again snuggled into the back of the couch, making herself comfortable. She reached up and took one of the glasses from Ryan. He sat down next to Hannah, not too close to make her feel uncomfortable, but close enough that he could easily touch her if and when the time was right.

'Do you want to watch something or listen to music?' Ryan ran his finger over her knee. Hannah felt her body temperature rise, and the nervous feeling she had under control was once again taking over.

'Music sounds good.' Hannah took a sip of her wine and shifted herself in the seat. Ryan got up and went over to the TV cabinet; he got his phone out of his pocket and connected it to his speakers. He spent a few minutes playing with the phone when music finally started playing. He put the phone down on top of the speakers and smiled at Hannah. He came back down and sat next to her. He picked up his wine and took two big sips. Hannah smiled back at Ryan, and they both laughed. She relaxed again. He turned in the seat so he was facing her and gave her a look that said he needed to ask her something. Hannah leaned forward and put her glass down on the table.

'So go ahead and ask.' She spoke softly and looked him in the eye. Ryan hesitated for a second, then put his glass down next to hers on the table. He sat back and took her left hand in his.

'Where's your wedding ring?' Hannah looked down at her hand and watched Ryan's finger rubbing the indent in her ring finger where her wedding band should have been. She looked up again and waited until he looked her in the eye.

'It's at home. My husband is away at the moment, and I found out that the woman he is sleeping with is also at the same place. I'm not stupid. I know there is more to their affair than just sex, so I have come to accept that my marriage as I once knew it is over, and it's only going to be a matter of time before he admits it too. So I've decided that I'm not going to sit around and wait to get my heart broken any more than it already is, so I am moving on. I figure if it's OK for him to move on before ending our relationship, then it's OK for me too.' Her words had a slight slur to them, and she finished her sentence with a matter-of-fact look. 'And I don't know if you have noticed, but I like spending time with you.' Those words came out before she could stop them, and now the wine had seemed to take over her mouth. 'I think about you a lot, and knowing that I am going to see you most days at lunchtime is why I get up in the morning.'

Hannah grabbed for her glass again and finished the wine in one gulp. Ryan took the glass from her and put it back on the table; he could see she was on the tipsier side of tipsy, so he didn't offer her a refill. If she was going to be here—and he had thought about this night many times—he wasn't going to take advantage of her if she had drunk too much. He looked at the time, and it was just after nine. Still plenty of time to enjoy her company and hopefully let her sober up a little. He leaned back on the couch when one of his favourite songs came on. 'Ah, this is one of my favourites! I haven't heard it in ages.'

Hannah clambered up from the couch in a less than graceful way and went to the other side of the table; she reached out her arm and beckoned him to come and join her. Ryan stood up and joined her in the space between the table and the TV. She took both his hands in hers and started dancing to the song. She moved in a little closer and put his hands on her hips and her hands around his neck. Together they moved to the music and said nothing. The song changed to a slower ballad. Ryan moved in closer again so their bodies were touching; his hands were all the way around her waist and hers were around his neck. She turned her head to the side and leaned against his chest. She could feel his heart beating, and the heat of his chest warmed her face. As the song was finishing, she lifted her head and looked up at him. Ryan looked down at Hannah, and his heart skipped a beat. She was the most beautiful woman he had ever known, and she was here now in his house, wanting to be with him. He took his hands from around her waist and cupped her face. He leaned down slowly and kissed her. He was soft and gentle and in no rush. Hannah put her hands under his arms and kissed him back. It wasn't a long kiss, but it was perfect. Hannah felt hot, and her breathing quickened; her heart started racing, and she felt her hands start to shake a little.

Ryan stayed close to her and whispered, 'I hope it was OK for me to do that.'

Hannah kept her eyes locked on to his stare and let the words linger for a moment. She pushed herself up on to her toes and leaned in, with her lips only millimetres from his, and whispered back, 'Yes.' He felt breathless and kissed her again—this time, harder and with passion. One hand held the back of her head, and the other was on her back between her shoulders. He held her tight and didn't stop the kiss. She put her hands behind him, pulled him close, and kissed him back with the same intensity. After a minute, he broke the kiss and breathed in deep several times; he put his forehead on hers and cupped her face again.

'I have wanted this to happen since the day I met you.' His voice was shaky, and she could tell he was nervous. 'Stay with me tonight.' Hannah didn't reply. She stepped back one step and took one of his hands; she looked around and saw a door leading to a passageway. She stepped towards the door, pulling Ryan in her direction; she looked at the door and back at Ryan, and without needing words, he knew where she wanted to go. He stepped past Hannah, still holding her hand, and opened the door. Hannah followed him into the darkness.

Chapter 44

The room was dimly lit by a small lamp in the corner near the bed. Hannah looked around and saw it was as neat as the rest of the place. Ryan quickly grabbed at a few things that were on the bed and put them in the corner of the room. He came back to Hannah and took both her hands. 'Are you sure you want to do this?' Hannah smiled up at Ryan and leaned up to kiss him. 'OK then, just wait here one sec.' He walked quickly out of the room, and she heard the music go off in the lounge room, and then the lights were turned off. She could hear him fussing with something in the kitchen and became curious as to what he was doing. Ryan came back in with his phone and a small speaker, which was playing something softly, and he had two wine glasses half filled. He handed her a glass, put his down on top of his tallboy, and then set the speaker down. He turned the volume up a little and picked up his glass. He came back to where Hannah was standing and clinked his glass gently on hers. They both drank, and Hannah put her glass on the table next to the bed. Ryan finished his drink and put his glass next to the speaker.

He stepped back to Hannah and immediately kissed her again. This time, there was a sense of urgency, and it was harder. Hannah kissed him back and ran her hands up his chest under his shirt and started lifting his shirt up. He stopped kissing her, removed his shirt, and dropped it on the floor. Hannah gasped a little; his body was better than she imagined. He wasn't ripped like a gym junkie, but he had the beginnings of some abs and just a little hair on his chest. His arms were defined, and he had a small tattoo on his ribs. She couldn't make out what it was of, but she would ask about that later. Hannah unbuttoned her shirt and let it fall to the ground. Ryan ran his fingers over the top of her shoulder, which gave her goosebumps. She shyly looked away from him and sat on the edge of the bed; she knew there was no sexy way to get her boots off and didn't want to risk falling over if she tried to take them off standing up. With a bit of effort, she got them off. She stood up again, and Ryan came over to her. He undid the button on her jeans, and putting his fingers under the edge, he started manoeuvring them down. They were a little tight-fitting, so as he was having trouble, she giggled and finished taking them off. While she was doing that, Ryan undid his jeans, and they fell without too much effort.

Hannah felt a little self-conscious being in her underwear in front of someone else and put her arms across her stomach. Ryan gently lifted her fingers on one hand and pulled her towards him. He ran his fingers softly up and down the top of her arms, and she let him look at her. She blushed when she saw through his underwear that he liked what he saw, and she wasn't sure where to look, so she sat back on the bed and pushed herself backwards until she was in the middle. Ryan knelt on the bed over her, and she lay back. He lowered his body onto hers, and they kissed. Hannah reached behind her back and undid her bra. She reached out and dropped it on the floor. She then removed her knickers and kicked them off the bed. She was now completely naked and at her most vulnerable. Ryan lay on the bed next to her and rubbed his hand up her side while kissing her. She ran her hand down his back and flicked at the elastic of his boxers. He removed them and then lay on her again. They kissed some more, and then he stopped.

He rolled to one side of her and reached into his drawer. He looked slightly embarrassed. 'Sorry, mood killer, I know.' She looked over his shoulder and saw what he was doing. She hadn't actually thought of protection as she had been with just one man her whole life, and she was a little fascinated at watching what he was doing. He rolled back towards her and continued touching her. She let him move her body to where he wanted it, and when he entered her, she gasped with pleasure. She had never felt desire as much as she was feeling right now. With every move and every kiss, she lost herself a little more into the moment until she let her body take over and just went with it. When it was over, she was breathless, and her body felt heavy. Her toes tingled, and she was exhausted. Ryan collapsed next to her and lifted his arm so she could snuggle into him. Neither said another word for the rest of the night, and they slept in each other's arms until the sun came up.

Chapter 45

H e lay awake for some time with her in his arms. He didn't want to wake her and for this moment to be over. He had imagined many times what it would be like to have her in his bed with him, and the events of last night did not disappoint. He was still concerned over the fact that she was technically married, and she had told him it was over, but he still worried about that part. He looked at the time and knew his alarm was about to go off and tried to reach for his phone without disturbing her. He wanted just a few more minutes. As he picked up his phone, it slipped and fell on to the ground. He swore under his breath and reached as far as he could from his current position to get it. He touched it with his fingertips but couldn't get a hold of it. Desperately trying to beat the alarm, he stretched a little further and was able to slide it slightly closer to him, but he was too late. The alarm went off and was at full volume. Hannah jumped and lifted her body up off his arm. Ryan was able to reach further now, picked up the phone, and turned off the alarm. When he lay back down, Hannah was on her stomach, leaning up on her arms. She had a lock of hair coming down over her face, and Ryan carefully moved it behind her ear. She leaned over and kissed him.

'Good morning,' she said in a husky morning voice and turned over to lie on her back next to him. Ryan turned to his side and leaned up on his elbow so he could see her better.

'Yes, it is.' He smiled cheekily. 'In fact, I couldn't think of a more perfect morning except that I have to get up to go to work.'

Hannah looked up at Ryan and felt her stomach flip; he was everything she wanted. 'Well, how about I go make some coffee why you shower? And then I will leave when you do. Would you like me to get breakfast ready for you too?' Ryan leaned down and kissed her.

'You don't need to make me breakfast. Thank you anyway. I only usually have cereal, but please help yourself to whatever you can find.' Ryan sat up and found his underwear on the floor. He put them on and went towards the door; he turned back over his shoulder. 'Feel free to stay in bed all day if you want.' He winked and left the room. Hannah stretched out in the bed and took it all in. She was happy, really truly deep down happy, and she didn't want to leave. She heard the water running and got dressed; she wanted to have coffee ready for him when he came out.

Hannah stood in the kitchen and quickly looked around. She found the kettle and turned it on; then she opened a few cupboards to see where everything was kept. He was very organised, and all seemed to be where she would have kept things. It didn't take her long before she had coffee ready and set two places at the breakfast bar with bowls and spoons for cereal. Hannah opened the pantry and found the only box of cereal, and she put that next to the place settings. She sat on the couch and picked up her phone. She had no missed calls or any text messages. Bruce walked over to her and rubbed up against her legs. Hannah reached down, picked him up, and put him on her lap. Bruce made himself at home and lapped up the scratches under his chin. At first, she was angry that Sean hadn't given her a second thought and even checked in on her; but when she heard Ryan come out of the bathroom, she got over it. She glanced up and saw him walk back to the bedroom with just a towel wrapped around his waist and his hair all wet and messy. Her stomached tingled again, and she wanted to follow him back to the bedroom and steal his towel. Hannah was brought back to reality when Bruce dug his claws into her knee when trying to rearrange himself.

'Ouch! Your claws are like needles!' She tried to pull his claws off her knee, which made him hold on tighter. 'Come on, let go of my knee!' Her knee was stinging now, and she tried to lift him off, but he wasn't having any part of it. He eventually retracted his claws and purred really loud, and she cuddled him to her chest. 'It's just as well you are so cute!' She plonked him on the ground and went back to the kitchen to re-boil the kettle so the coffee was nice and hot. Ryan emerged from the bedroom and sat at one of the places Hannah had set.

'If you're going to treat me this well, I might just have to keep you.' He opened the cereal box and filled his bowl; he pointed to the other bowl, and Hannah nodded. She brought two hot cups over and sat next to Ryan. They didn't say much while they ate but kept looking over at each other and smiling. Breakfast was over, and Ryan stood up; he looked at his watch and kissed Hannah on the cheek.

'I have to leave in five, but don't you feel any rush to go. You stay and make yourself at home.'

Hannah cleared the dishes and stood right in front of Ryan.

'I have to go too. I need to go home and change for work. But if you have no plans for tonight . . .' She looked down shyly to her feet. 'Maybe I could come back again tonight?' She took a big breath in and was almost waiting for rejection. Ryan lifted her chin and kissed her softly.

'I would love for you to come back again tonight. I get home around five thirty. So whenever you want to get here after that, you just turn up, OK?' Hannah smiled and nodded. She went over to the coffee table, picked up her bag, and walked to the front door. She opened the door, and Ryan came up behind her. She stopped so she could hug him one last time before leaving. She walked down the path to the road and looked around. She suddenly had the realisation that she had no idea where she was. Out with her phone and she opened her map app and waited until it found her. Relieved that she was only a few streets back off the main road where her bus ran, she headed off.

Hannah only waited a minute for a bus to turn up, and in around fifteen minutes, she was home again. Just as she entered her apartment, her phone was dinging. She looked down and saw it was Sean. She opened the message and read, 'Having fun here. Bloody cold tho. Place is great. U OK?'

Hannah laughed out loud and spoke to herself. 'Yeah, I bet you are having fun.' She typed back, 'I'm fine thanks. Glad you're having fun. Stay warm. Love you.'

Within a minute, she got another message. 'Love you too.'

Really, you do? she thought and again said out loud to herself, 'You sure have a funny way of showing it!' Hannah went to the bedroom and put the phone on the charger, stripped off, and went to take a shower. From the bathroom, she heard it ding again but ignored it. Whatever he wanted, she didn't care right now. She stepped under the water, stood for a minute, and let the warmth flood over her. She opened her eyes again and started her routine of washing her hair, shaving her legs (she giggled knowing she had a reason for this tonight), and washed everywhere twice with body wash. Satisfied that she was clean and date ready, she turned off the taps and stood on the bath mat to get dry.

She heard her phone ding again, and out of annoyance, she went back to the bedroom. She was surprised to see the messages were from Amy. Now she was curious and opened them. The first one was a picture of the beach from the balcony, and the second was an essay of how glad she was that Hannah had convinced her to go and how much fun she was having. Hannah was happy for her in a strange way. She replied that she was glad she was having fun and looked forward to hearing about in next week. Hannah put the phone back down and dressed for work. The phone dinged again, and Hannah snatched the phone up again. She opened the message from Amy, and it was another photo. Hannah threw the phone hard onto the bed and stormed to the kitchen. She paced for a few minutes while calming herself down. She put on the kettle and made a cup of tea; although it was still early in the morning, she found the biscuit tin and grabbed three sweet biscuits. She dunked each one in the tea and gobbled them up before they became soggy and fell into the cup. Feeling better after some sugar, Hannah went back to the bedroom and opened her phone again. The photo that made her angry was still on the screen. She looked at it again and let a tear roll down her face. The pain she felt seeing a selfie of Amy and Sean all cuddled up together was horrible, and she wanted to scream. She closed the message and went back to the bathroom to wash her face. Her eyes stung, and her cheeks were burning up. She splashed cold water several times on her face and felt the heat subside. She dried her face and stared at herself in the mirror. She hated the way she looked when her eyes were puffy and red.

She looked away and decided to go through her wardrobe to look for something to wear back to Ryan's tonight. She wanted something sexy, but not trashy, and she found a V-neck dress that was fitted at the bust but dropped at the waist. It did not show too much cleavage and finished just above the knee. It was teal in colour and looked good with flats and a plain black cardigan. She was going to have her hair down tonight. She smelled a couple of her body sprays and picked a soft musk. Having her outfit planned for tonight put her back in a good mood as she let he mind wander back to the night before and how amazing

Ryan made her feel. Ready for work and organised for tonight, Hannah left her apartment. She rugged up in a thick winter coat and scarf and walked a quick pace all the way to the café.

Early as normal, she walked in and felt the warmth of the heater on her face. Lucy was in the kitchen doing her daily stocktake of fresh produce, ready for the biggest day of the week. There was around 50 per cent more customers on a Friday, and Lucy always made sure she had more than enough stock. Now that the weather had turned cold, her homemade soups were a huge success. Hannah could smell the deliciousness the moment she opened the door. She went around the counter and took off her coat.

'Smells amazing again, Lucy.' Hannah hung up her coat and scarf and went to the stove to take in the aromas. Lucy looked up from what she was doing and took a bow. Both women giggled, and Hannah applauded in appreciation. 'Maybe one day you could teach me to cook like you.' Lucy packed away the last of the stock back into the fridge and put her fingers on her chin in a thinking pose.

'Yes, I see it now,' she started. 'Lucy's school of cooking . . . and you, my dear, would be my star student.'

Hannah clasped her hands in front of her chest and animated her face with surprise. 'Yes, you could teach me how to be a chef to the rich and famous!'

Lucy clapped and laughed. 'And when you're highly sought after, just remember where you started, all right?' Lucy walked past Hannah and patted her on the shoulder. Hannah followed Lucy out to the dining room and started setting the tables.

'Of course. How could I ever forget this place and the wonderful boss I had here.' Hannah blew Lucy a kiss.

'Flattery will get you everywhere.' Lucy pretended to catch the kiss and put it in her pocket. 'I'm going to make a coffee before we open. Would you like one?'

'Oh, yes please! You make great coffee.'

The two women sat down to drink their coffee when the other staff started arriving, and Lucy offered each and every one a hot drink to warm them up. Hannah sat back and admired Lucy; she was so thoughtful and cared for everyone who worked here, and in return, everyone gave their all every shift.

Chapter 46

Hannah looked at herself in the mirror, and she liked what she saw. She felt good about herself today. Her make-up looked good, she liked her dress, and her hair was behaving. She let it dry without brushing it too much so a few curls would remain. Hannah had come straight home after finishing work so she would have plenty of time to get ready and head back to Ryan's. She had planned to get there around a quarter to six so as not to be waiting on the doorstep when he got home from work; she didn't want to appear needy or clingy.

She had it all planned; she would head out soon and go to the mall before it would close. She had remembered earlier in the day Ryan had mentioned it was his birthday on Saturday, and she wanted to make sure she had a small gift for him. She had no idea what she was going to get, but she just felt it important that she got something for him. From the mall, she would take a taxi to Ryan's house as it would be too dark to get the bus or walk, and she didn't want to get lost. This was the part about winter she hated; it was dark at five thirty in the afternoon. One last check of her hair and make-up and Hannah was ready to go. Back on with her winter coat, and she was off.

The air was icy cold, and she could smell the rain coming. Hannah quickened her pace to try to get to the mall before the rain came. She was a bit over halfway when the first drops fell. Almost at a jog, Hannah made it to the front entrance when the sky opened up, and down it came. She smiled to herself, thinking she had a win against Mother Nature; an older lady who hadn't been so lucky ran in the door and cursed under her breath. Hannah gave her a sympathetic look and walked away before she laughed out loud; another thirty seconds and that would have been her.

The mall appeared quiet this afternoon, so Hannah could wander from shop to shop without the frustration of having to navigate through crowds of people. She knew it would get busier in an hour when the nine-to-fivers finished work and headed here for their late-night shopping. After walking out of the fourth shop and still clueless as to what she wanted, frustration was starting to creep in. She was conscious of the time and had everything mapped out in her mind of when she needed to leave to be at Ryan's at the time she had decided on. Across the mall, she saw a tobacconist, which also sold gifts; she was running out of options, so she told herself she had to pick something from there no matter what it was.

The shop was a treasure trove of gift ideas. Hannah was mesmerised by all the different and shiny things they sold. There were adult games, which she had never seen before. There were framed rock band pictures, glassware, and trinkets of all shapes and sizes. She picked up a highball whisky glass that had 'Happy Birthday' etched into it. It sat in a velvet-lined wooden box. She thought it was perfect, not too personal since she was really just getting to know him and not straight-off-the-shelf generic. They also sold cards, so she was able to get everything she needed. At the counter, while the young girl was gift-wrapping the box for her, Hannah wrote in the card,

Happy Birthday Ryan
I hope you have a wonderful day
And get everything your heart desires
From Hannah xxx

She paused and read the card again; happy with her choice of words, she put the card in the envelope and waited for the girl to finish. Another check of the time and she was back on schedule. She sent a quick 'hope you're having a good day' to Sean and put her phone away. Back at the front of the mall, she could see a couple of taxis in the waiting bay. She went to walk over to the front car but stopped suddenly. She never wrote down Ryan's address. She quickly opened up her map app and moved it around to follow her bus route. She kind of knew which stop she got on at, but became confused from which side streets she walked down to get there. She started to freak out as her perfectly planned night was starting to fall apart. Maybe if she got the taxi driver to the bus stop, she would recognise the area. She looked up again, and the darkness had crept up on her.

She could feel herself starting to lose it when she frantically scrolled through her contacts, looking for Ryan's phone number. She rang his number, and there was no answer. So she tried again. Nothing. She sat down on the bench seat outside the front door and stared at her phone. She was at a loss as to what she was going to do. With tears welling up and her emotions taking over, she decided to get in the taxi anyway and have a go at trying to find his house. She got in the front seat and showed the driver the map and where she had got on the bus that morning. The driver nodded and pulled out of the bay. Once on the main road, he looked over at Hannah and tried to make conversation. Hannah politely answered his questions but didn't show too much interest. The driver pulled over to the side of the road next to the bus stop. Hannah looked around, but in the dark, she didn't see anything she recognised. About to admit defeat and give the driver her own address, she was startled by her annoying ringtone. She sighed in relief and answered the call.

'Oh my god, am I glad you called just now!' Hannah blurted out.

'I just saw your two missed calls. Sorry, I had my phone in my coat pocket and forgot to take it out, and when you hadn't arrived yet, I was starting to think you weren't coming.'

Hannah laughed into the phone. 'I am in a taxi near your place, but I never wrote down the address, so I have no idea which way to go next.'

Ryan laughed back. 'I will text it to you so you have it. How far away did you say you were?'

'Just on the main road where the bus goes, so probably in a minute.'

'OK then, I can stop worrying now. I will hang up and text you the details.'

Hannah turned to the driver, who was trying not to laugh at her; she smiled politely and showed him the address when the message came though. Two side streets and less than a minute, she was at Ryan's house again. The front light was on, and Ryan was in the doorway, awaiting her arrival. Hannah paid the driver and exited the taxi. She walked sheepishly towards Ryan, and when she was a few feet away, they both broke into laughter. He put his arm around her and guided her in through the front door. Once inside, Ryan took Hannah's coat from her and hung it on a hook on the back of the door. The house was warm and inviting. Ryan had a glass of wine waiting for her and an array of takeaway menus for her to choose from.

'I thought because it is so cold out tonight, we could stay in and order food to be delivered. There are a few movies to choose from on the telly. That's if you want, of course. I'm happy to do whatever you want. Oh, and you look beautiful, by the way.'

Hannah blushed and looked away for a moment. She wasn't used to hearing compliments like that. She looked around for Bruce, who was sitting like an ornament on the coffee table. She walked over, picked him up, and sat on the couch. She put her feet up and looked up at Ryan. 'Staying in sounds perfect to me.' She snuggled the cat, who lapped up the attention. Ryan smiled from ear to ear.

'So just continue making yourself at home.' He passed her a glass of wine. 'And I will wait on you. You just let me know anytime you want something, and I will get it for you.' Ryan bowed at Hannah and then picked up his glass. They clinked glasses, and Hannah took a big sip. The wine was delicious, and she felt very relaxed.

Time passed quickly, food arrived and was eaten, one movie down, and the second only minutes away from starting. Hannah had her feet on Ryan's lap, and he was gently rubbing them for her. She reached over for her glass and made a sad face when she realised it was empty. Ryan lifted her feet and went to get up when she stopped him.

'It's OK. You don't actually need to do everything for me tonight. How about I refill the glasses and you sit and relax?' She picked up the empty glasses and shimmied past Ryan, who smacked her on the bum.

'Well, all right then, if you insist. And you will need to open another bottle. There are a couple to choose from in the cupboard above the fridge.'

Hannah turned back to see Ryan stretched out, feet on the coffee table and arms behind his head. She put the glasses on the counter and looked up at the cupboard. She could reach high enough to open the doors, but not to get another bottle down. She looked around for something to stand on when Ryan came into the kitchen.

'Out the way, shorty. I will get one for you.' Hannah poked her tongue out at him and stepped back. Ryan selected a bottle and put it on the counter next to the glasses.

'Why, thank you, sir.' Hannah mocked.

'You know my services come at a fee?' He raised an eyebrow at her.

'Oh really? And what do you require for payment?' Hannah felt butterflies in her stomach as Ryan came closer to her. He put his arms around her neck and kissed her.

'That will do for starters.' He spoke softly and then kissed her again.

Hannah reciprocated and kissed him back with a little more intensity. She liked the feeling she got when she kissed him. She felt warm all over and slightly light-headed and tickly in the pit of her stomach. When his fingers touched her skin, she found it hard to breathe. And when he looked deep in her eyes, she was lost forever. It was that kiss, that exact moment she realised she was in love with him, and she never wanted to be apart from him again. It was that night her life was going to change forever.

Chapter 47

Although it was raining outside, Ryan couldn't think of a better way to start his birthday. It was a Saturday, and he had the woman he loved in his bed for a second night in a row. It was too early to get up, so he lay there watching Hannah sleep. She looked so peaceful, and she lay so still that he checked twice to see if she was breathing. Trying to deny to himself that he needed to go to the toilet, he changed positions again. He didn't want to get up and risk disturbing her, but no matter how he lay now, he could not hold it in any longer. He pulled back the cover ever so slightly and slipped his feet out onto the cold floor. He tiptoed to the toilet and shut the door carefully. It felt strange to shut the door as he had lived by himself for so long; it didn't matter if the door was open. He flushed the toilet and waited to open the door until the cistern had refilled, and he tiptoed back to the bedroom. He slipped back into bed and tried to warm up his hands again. Hannah was still asleep and hadn't noticed him leave and come back. Proud of his stealthy efforts, he closed his eyes and hoped to drift back off to sleep. It didn't take long for him to find a comfy position and fell sleepy again. He was almost back to the land of nod when he heard a giggle and whisper. He opened one eye and saw Bruce standing on Hannah, who was scratching under his chin. Annoyed that the cat had woken his sleeping beauty, Ryan swiped at him, pushing him onto the floor. Hannah looked over at Ryan and made a sad face.

'I'm so sorry he woke you up.'

Hannah rolled onto her side and faced Ryan. 'It's all right.' She wiggled closer so they were nose to nose, and she kissed him. 'I'd rather be awake when I'm with you anyway.' Ryan grinned at Hannah. She leaned up onto her elbow and lay her head on her hand so she was looking down. 'So what does the birthday boy want to do today?'

Ryan turned to lie on his back and slipped one arm in the gap of Hannah's arm and pulled her down onto him. 'I want to stay here in bed all day with you.' Before she could respond, Ryan kissed her and turned her over so he was now on top.

Hannah ran her hands over his chest and down to his hips and pulled him closer. 'Well, if that's what the birthday boy wants, who am I to deny it?'

And for the third time, they made love. Hannah quickly picked up on how he moved and found it easy to adapt to his rhythm. It was becoming more comfortable, and she was less nervous about him touching her. He liked to kiss her neck, and when he kissed her just behind her ear, she felt it tingle all the way to her toes. It was less than ten minutes, and it was over.

Ryan apologised. 'I'm so sorry, but you are so beautiful that I just can't stop it from happening so fast.' He lay next to Hannah, looking up at the ceiling with his arms behind his head. He struggled to make eye contact; he didn't want to see the disappointment in her eyes. Hannah sat up, then climbed on top of Ryan to make him look at her.

'You have nothing to apologise for. Really, you don't. I'd rather quality over quantity, and the way you make me feel is incredible. Oh, before I forget, I have something for you.' Hannah climbed off Ryan and hurried to the lounge room to get her bag. She came back into the bedroom and sat on the edge of the bed. She pulled out a gift and the card and handed it to Ryan. Excitedly, Ryan sat up, holding the box; and with a stunned look, he opened the envelope. He smiled as he read the message and then, like a child, ripped the paper off the box and tossed it to one side. He carefully lifted the lid. His eyes lit up.

'Thank you so much. When did you go shopping? I wasn't even sure if you remembered me mentioning my birthday the other day.'

Hannah looked very proud of herself. 'Never you mind when I went shopping, and I'd like to think I am good at remembering the important things like birthdays. Addresses not so much, but definitely birthdays.'

Ryan laughed as he remembered her sad voice on the phone the previous night when she thought she wasn't going to find him again.

'I trust you saved my address so you will always know where to find me?'

Hannah sat up straight and nodded like a child receiving praise. 'I sure did. Now why don't you go jump in the shower, and I will go and get some breakfast started?' Hannah stood up and then started searching the floor for her clothes. She remembered Ryan undressing her, and he was kissing her last night while making their way from the lounge room to the bedroom, and her recollection of the exact location of her dress was vague. She walked naked back to the lounge and found her dress crumpled near the kitchen. She picked it up and started feeding it in on itself, trying to get it from being inside out. Ryan went to the bathroom and turned on the shower; before she could get dressed, he came back and pulled her by the arm.

'I'm not the only one who needs a shower, you know.' Hannah dropped her dress again and allowed herself to be taken to the bathroom. She stopped behind Ryan as he was checking the water temperature and checked out his body from behind. She definitely liked what she saw and couldn't resist pinching him on the bum.

'Hey!' Ryan looked over his shoulder and then stepped into the shower. Hannah followed. The shower was tiny, and they struggled to be in there together. Every few seconds, they turned so the other person could get some hot water on them. Hannah attempted to soap up Ryan in some sort of attempt to be sexy, but with very little elbow room, it wasn't a success. Instead, they both laughed and decided that his shower was only ever going to be a one-man show. Hannah turned off the water, and Ryan got out first. He grabbed his towel of the rail and then realised that he didn't have a towel for Hannah. He quickly wrapped the towel around his waist and left the bathroom with Hannah dripping wet and getting cold in the shower. He madly went through his linen cupboard, trying to find a nice soft towel that wasn't frayed. He spotted one at the back, and when he pulled at it, the entire contents of the shelf came tumbling to the floor. He heard Hannah laughing and turned to see her head poking out of the doorway. He rolled his eyes and stepped back to hand her the towel. He saw her shivering, and her skin was covered in goosebumps. She quickly wrapped herself in the towel, and Ryan rubbed her arms, trying to warm her up.

'Let me go put the heater on so I can warm you up again.' Hannah watched from the bathroom doorway as he went to the lounge and fiddled with the remote that controlled the air conditioner. As he jogged back towards the bathroom, the towel that was wrapped around his waist came loose and fell to the ground. Hannah laughed really loud.

'Oh, you think that is funny, do you?' Hannah nodded and ran to the bedroom. Ryan plucked his towel from the floor, chased after her, and caught her by the bed. The fell onto the bed; instantly, their want for each other took over, and they stayed in bed until lunchtime.

Chapter 48

'Move in with me.'

Hannah stopped mid-sip of her coffee and blankly stared at Ryan.

'I'm sorry, what?' Her eyes widened as she still wasn't sure if she had heard him correctly. 'You want me to move in with you?' She raised one eyebrow and tilted her head slightly; she held the mug tight between both hands and pondered the question.

'Yes! I want you to move in with me. You said your marriage was over, and why wait until he's had enough and potentially cop more abuse? You deserve a better life than that. I love you, Hannah, and I want you to be here with me.'

Hannah was stunned; she sat there staring at Ryan, wondering if her brain was making this up. She put the mug down and made a weird thinking face. She leaned back in the chair and bit on her bottom lip.

'OK.'

Ryan's face lit up, and as he stood up from the table, he knocked his chair over; he stepped to the side and stood the chair back up. He came around the table and reached out to take Hannah's hand. He pulled at her arm gently to get her to stand up, and as she got to her feet, he put his arms around her waist and picked her up. He went to walk while holding her but caught his foot on the leg of the table and just about dropped her. She landed hard on her feet but managed to stay upright. She was laughing at his enthusiasm and how animated he was being. 'So how do you want to do this? When do you want me to move in?'

Ryan grabbed her hand and twirled her around like a ballerina and then caught her as she faced him. He had one arm around her waist, and the other held her hand tight; he brought it to his lips, closed his eyes, and kissed her fingers. He slowly opened his eyes and for a moment gave her a gentle gaze. 'How does today sound? We can head over to your place now and pack all of your things. You won't need to bring any furniture or things unless there is something special you want, and we will find the perfect place for it here. I wouldn't think we would need more than one trip. That way, you won't need to see your husband again. You will be safe here. I will protect you.' His voice was soft, but deep, and there was a soothing undertone that made Hannah go weak in the knees. She felt dizzy, and she fought to keep her breathing under control. She had never felt this before; she was completely and utterly under his spell, and she wanted to stay like this forever. She looked up at Ryan and held eye contact for a few seconds and then leaned up to him and kissed him. She felt a wave of heat surge through her body, and when she stepped back, she felt so surreal.

'Let me go put my shoes on, and we will go. He's not expected back until tomorrow afternoon, so I will make sure I take everything I want today so I don't have to go back there again.' As she turned to walk away, she stopped, almost frozen to the spot; and without turning back, she asked in a very calm voice, 'Are you 100 per cent sure this is what you want? It's not too late if you suddenly regret the words coming out of your mouth.'

She couldn't bring herself to turn around just in case he said he changed his mind. The seconds felt like minutes while she waited for Ryan to respond. He said nothing. She felt tears building inside when from behind, she felt his warm breath on her neck. Goosebumps ran all the way down her back, and her head was dizzy; she leaned her head forward and to the side and allowed Ryan to kiss the back of her neck. The first two or three kisses were so soft she barely felt them, and then they got a little firmer; she put her hands behind her and rubbed his legs and then twisted her body in between kisses so she was facing him again. She looked in his eyes and didn't need his verbal response. She walked away and put on her shoes; she picked up her bag and stood by the door. Ryan found his keys on the counter and followed Hannah to the front door.

The drive to Hannah's place was quiet, but it wasn't uncomfortable. Every now and then, they looked at each other and smiled. It felt right. Hannah felt relieved her old life was about to be over and a peaceful one was about to start. There was moment when she stopped to think how Sean was going to take it, to come and find her gone. He would be angry, but from the messages she was getting from Amy, he was happy with her. So she figured he wouldn't take long to get over it, and maybe it would be for the best for him. Clearly, he wasn't happy in the marriage as he needed to find love in another, so this was an easy out for him. Hannah had convinced herself she was actually doing him a favour by leaving; now he could get on with his relationship with Amy and not have to come home and lie. He would no longer be a cheater, and his life would be better.

They pulled up to Hannah's place, and Ryan grabbed a couple of boxes he had in the boot of his car. She looked around and couldn't see Sean's car in the driveway, so she proceeded up the stairs to the apartment. She fussed in her bag for her keys and cautiously opened the door. Paranoia was creeping in, and for the first time, she felt sneaky and underhanded. She stopped just inside the doorway and listened for a moment. Nothing. The apartment was silent. When she was satisfied there was no one inside, she walked straight through and to the bedroom. Ryan put the boxes on the bed, and Hannah immediately set to work on emptying her dresser drawers. When the two boxes were full, she went to the kitchen and got a roll of garbage bags from the bottom drawer. Back to the bedroom, she yanked her clothes off the hangers in the wardrobe and stuffed them into the garbage bags. It was a quick job getting her things together as she never went shopping, and she didn't have a lot of stuff. She had a quick look around the bathroom and only took her toothbrush. In the kitchen, there was nothing special that she wanted. She had a bookshelf in the lounge, which housed her small library, and these were definitely coming with her.

In less than an hour, her life was in two boxes and three garbage bags. So sad that at her age, she really had nothing to show for her life—a few measly possessions and that's it. If she were to die tomorrow, what would people say about her? Failed marriage, no kids, no career, not exactly the most loving daughter that ever existed, no great moments in life. She had never done anything great that anyone could speak about. But this was all about to change. She was now in a loving relationship, and she would contribute the best she could. She was going to work out what she loved doing and see if she could find a job doing that. She wasn't too old to start a family. A family, kids of her own, the thought of her and Ryan having a baby brought a rush of emotion to the surface. She longed for many years to have a family, but Sean was never interested; and the way he treated her, she was glad they never did. No child should have to grow up in a home with arguing that often resulted in a physical ending.

Ryan made three trips to the car while she wandered from room to room, double-checking she wasn't leaving anything behind, a bit like the way you leave a hotel after you have stayed a few days. When Ryan picked up the last bag, she smiled; her heart was full of hope for the future. She walked to the front door and pulled it shut behind her. She never looked back as she walked down the stairs and to Ryan's car.

As he pulled away from the kerb, Hannah laughed, a deep 'all the way from her belly' laugh. Ryan reached over and held her hand. She was free, and she never ever wanted to go back to that dark place. A place where she lived in fear. A place where she felt worthless and invisible. A place so dark that she might as well not even have existed.

Chapter 49

As quickly as she had packed up her life into bags, she was unpacked in her new home. Ryan was just like her and didn't have a need for a lot of material things, so finding space in the bedroom for her clothes was easy. While she was sorting through her things, Ryan was in the kitchen cooking dinner. It was Sunday night, and there was an unusual feel about this Sunday night. Hannah felt at ease and was under no pressure to have had all her chores completed by dinner time; that was one of Sean's rules if she wanted to keep her job. He told her the minute she slacked off around the apartment, if just one chore went undone, she was to give up the job. Hannah sat on the end of the bed when she was done and took a moment to take it all in. On a whim, she changed her entire life, and she wasn't scared. She felt comfortable here; she felt positive about what lay ahead for her. She picked up the empty garbage bags and started neatly folding them so they could be put away and reused. She folded the boxes back down and carried them out to the kitchen.

In the kitchen, Ryan was dishing up dinner. Hannah sat at the table and waited to be served. He placed a plate in front of her and then sat in the chair next to her. He placed his hand on her knee and kissed her on the cheek.

'Are you doing OK?' He looked at her seriously but spoke softly. 'This was a really major thing you have done, so it's OK to have lots of thoughts running around your head, and it's also OK to just let them out whenever you need to. I want you to feel like this is your home, and we are partners in this together. So please don't ever be worried to talk to me about anything and everything.'

Hannah picked up her fork and took a bite of her food. It tasted amazing, and she let out a little groan of delight.

'This is delicious. Thank you so much for cooking. You're right, I do have a hundred things running through my brain right now, and it's probably going to take a few days to start sorting them out. I was thinking when I was putting my stuff away that the first place he will come and look for me is the café. So tomorrow I need to go and talk to Lucy about taking the rest of the week off. I'm going to ask her to lie for me as I don't want to quit, but I need her to tell him that I did. I'm really hoping she will do this for me, and then if I'm not there for the rest of the week and he pops in, he will hopefully believe her that I'm gone. And another thing I am worried about is I don't know that I make enough money to pay my fair share to live here with you. I don't want to take advantage of your generosity or for you to ever feel like I'm not contributing. So can you please tell me how much per week I need to give you to cover my half of everything?'

Hannah let out a huge sigh and felt instant relief that she was able to tell someone what was bouncing around her head and not get laughed at or dismissed. She took another mouthful of her dinner and waited anxiously for a response.

'I think talking to Lucy is a great idea. I know she has been worried about you for a long time, so she will have no issues helping you. And I will think of an amount for you towards the bills. The mortgage is in my name, so I don't expect anything towards that, just a nominal amount for utilities, and we will split the shopping. And don't ever worry about money. You pay what you can afford and make sure you have plenty left over to have some fun with.'

Hannah found it hard right now to comprehend everything that had happened in the last few days; it was like a dream. As she continued to eat her dinner, she watched Ryan. He fascinated her; he was strong yet gentle, in control yet wanted to make sure she was OK. It almost confused her as she couldn't predict him. Sean was so different. Just quiet and angry most of the time, and if she stood her ground, she was punished. As she watched Ryan, she tried to imagine him angry; and no matter what quick scenario she came up with, she just couldn't see him raising his voice at her. She did giggle to herself when she pictured his disappointed face; she could just see his big puppy dog eyes looking at her. It then hit her; he could so easily be hurt. He trusted her after such a short time, and he had opened up his heart and his home to her; and when he said he would protect her, she knew he truly meant every word. She looked around the room and let her imagination take her to cold winter nights snuggled under a blanket together watching a movie and Sunday mornings cooking breakfast and being lazy. She wondered what was out the back; she hadn't yet seen what was beyond the back door and what treasures she might find. Completely lost in a dream, she hadn't noticed Ryan smirking at her.

'So you want to share what's going on in your head? You are so deep in thought that I am curious to know what is making you tick.'

Hannah looked back at him and blushed a little; she hadn't realised just how deep in thought she had been.

'Was just looking around and picturing what life will look like from today, and also what's out the back? I haven't made it that far yet.'

'Come on and let me show you.'

Hannah quickly shovelled the last couple of bites of her dinner into her mouth and stood up still chewing. Her bulging cheeks made Ryan chuckle, and he led the way to the back door. He flicked a light switch and unlatched the door; he pushed it open and let Hannah go out first. She looked around, taking it all in; her eyes lit up when Ryan turned on another switch, and rows of fairy lights came on. The yard wasn't very big, just a small courtyard size. It was all paved with some oversized pots in the corner, which had some palm trees growing. There was a large wooden table in the middle with chairs and a large BBQ to one side. Smaller pots with ferns were around the edge of the garden, giving a tropical feel to the space. Over the top of the yard, running from the house wall to the rear fence, were rows of fairy lights. Hannah took it all in.

'Come with me.' Ryan took her hand and led her to the back fence. 'Wait here.' He walked back towards the house and turned on one more switch. To one side of where she was standing, she heard the trickling of water; she turned in the direction of the sound and saw water coming out of what she thought was just a statue. Ryan took his phone out of his pocket and took a photo of Hannah under the lights. She looked perfect. He put his phone in the middle of the table, turned up the volume, and let the music fill the night air. He walked back to Hannah and took her hand; he held her close, and they danced under the lights.

In a whisper just loud enough for Hannah to hear, Ryan said, 'Welcome home.'

Chapter 50

Hannah was nervous and waited impatiently to leave for work. It was a little farther to walk now, but she needed that time to calm her nerves before speaking with Lucy. She had a plan of what she was going to say and just hoped that Lucy would help her. Ryan had left for work already, and she hated sitting there by herself. He had such a calming influence on her, and now that he had gone, she was a mess. She paced around, picked up things, washed the couple of dishes in the sink, and rearranged her clothes in the wardrobe for a third time. As Hannah was putting on her shoes to leave, she heard her phone ding. She leaned over the couch to the side table and picked it up. It was a text message from Sean. She froze as now her decision to leave was about to become reality. She unlocked the screen and opened the message.

'Hey babe, packing up now and leaving soon. Will be home for tea.'

Hannah's heart raced, and a wave of nausea rushed over her. She felt a lump grow in her throat and tears building. She quickly replied 'OK' and threw the phone in her bag and left for work. The walk to the café seemed to take forever, and she became agitated and frustrated at everything from the dog that tried to sniff her as it walked past to the red light that just wasn't changing to green. When she arrived, she burst through the door like she was being chased. Lucy looked up from what she doing and hurried to her. She pulled out a chair for Hannah to sit and poured two glasses of water. She didn't say anything; she gave Hannah time to compose her words and waited. Hannah took several deep breaths, and as she opened her mouth to start talking, she started shaking uncontrollably. Lucy moved her chair closer to Hannah and put her hand on top of Hannah's. Still, she said nothing but comforted her until she was ready. Hannah looked into Lucy's eyes and let a tear or two roll down her, face and then she started to talk.

'I've left Sean, and I moved out yesterday. He is away with mates until this afternoon, and when a friend said I could stay at their place, I accepted the offer. So I packed all my stuff yesterday and left. I haven't told him, and I don't want to tell him or talk to him or see him. He is going to be so angry, and I'm scared of what he would do if I see him now.' Hannah paused for a moment and fought back the tears. 'Can I ask a favour please?' She looked up at Lucy and waited for a response. Lucy squeezed her hand and nodded in acceptance. Hannah continued, 'Sean will come here looking for me, and I'm sorry about that. Can you please tell him I quit and you have no idea where I am? I will send you a text message now to that effect, and if we can go back and forth a little so you can show it to him then to make it more believable. And if I could please have the rest of the week off to settle into my new place and also not to be here because I'm sure he will watch the place for a few days to see if I come back?'

Hannah finally took a breath and relaxed a little. Lucy stood up and beckoned Hannah to do the same, and she hugged her tight. When Lucy released Hannah from her grip, she wiped the tear from Hannah's cheek and smiled reassuringly.

'Of course I will do this for you. You have no idea what a relief this is to me and how long I have been concerned about you. Send me a message now, and we will get the story going. Do you want to stay for your shift?'

'Yes please, but if I can be gone as soon as the rush is over, I would really appreciate it.'

Over the next ten minutes, Hannah and Lucy exchanged text messages about Hannah's resignation. Hannah completed her shift, and Lucy let her leave without having to stay for clean-up. She promised to let her know if Sean turned up and what he said; she wished her luck and to enjoy the week off to get settled and to come back the following Monday refreshed.

Hannah walked slowly back to her new home but couldn't help but feel guilty. She had never asked someone to lie for her before, and she knew in her gut that he would turn up and make some trouble. Tonight was going to be hard. Sean would be home in a couple of hours and discover that she had gone. He would ring and text to find her, and she wasn't ready for that. She powered off her phone and continued the walk home. To her surprise, Ryan was home when she got there. He had taken the afternoon off to make sure she wasn't alone; he understood the next few days were going to be hard, and he wanted to be able to support her in any way he could. Hannah walked in, dropped her bag, and hugged him tight. She was terrified of what was going to happen if Sean found her, and she just wanted to hide from the world for a while. Ryan held her close and waited until she was ready to let go. When she looked up, he kissed her gently and smiled. She felt reassured she had made the right decision and was ready to let him go.

'Coffee?' he asked, walking towards the kitchen. 'Are you hungry at all?' Hannah followed him, sat up on the counter, and watched him make coffee.

'I'm starving actually,' she responded, holding her stomach. She wiggled off the counter and opened the fridge. She smiled and looked over her shoulder at Ryan. 'You've been busy today.' She looked back in the fridge to its overflowing contents to see what he had bought. She selected a container that she hadn't seen before and studied it. Ryan watched her looking at the container and carried the coffee mugs to the table.

'That's really yummy. It's from the organic store near where I work and is all made fresh on-site. I wasn't sure if you liked soup. But on a cold day like today, with some bread hot out the oven, it will be delicious. Comfort food.'

Hannah put the container back in the fridge and sat at the table with Ryan, who had opened a packet of biscuits. She grabbed one from the packet and dunked it in her coffee. 'Thank you so much for everything you are doing for me. I feel very spoilt right now.'

'I want you to take it easy over the next few days, so I thought if I shopped, you won't need to go out if you don't feel up to it. How did it go with Lucy?'

Hannah smiled gratefully at Ryan; she really appreciated the effort he had gone to, to make it easy for her to settle in.

'It went well. She understood why I asked her to help me, and she was totally OK with me taking the rest of the week off. I feel so blessed to be working for her. She really is an amazing and caring woman, and

I'm not sure what I would have done if she wasn't like that.' Hannah bit her bottom lip and took a second biscuit.

'Have you heard from him at all today?' Ryan hated asking, but he wanted to know everything so he could completely understand everything that she was going through as best he could. He wanted to know every time she received a bad text message or an abusive phone call. But he didn't want to come across as pushy or controlling either, so he was careful what and when to ask about him.

'I got a text this morning just saying he was packing up and would be home by dinner time. I've actually turned my phone off. And tell me if I'm being paranoid, but I was going to get a new number. What do you think?'

'I think that is a great idea. Let me know if you want me to drive you somewhere far from here so you can do that. Would hate for you to be at the mall over here and run into him.'

Hannah went, got her phone, and turned it back on. She waited with bated breath while it searched for a signal and beeped with new messages. Three messages. Hannah tentatively opened her phone. One from Sean saying he was leaving now; that was at one o'clock. It would be a three-hour drive, plus she knew he had to drop Amy home, so it would be at least five before he would get home. She looked at the time, and it was a little after three, so she could breathe for a little while longer. The second was from Amy telling her how wonderful the weekend was and that she couldn't wait to catch up tomorrow for their usual weekly coffee. Crap! She hadn't thought about that. She would think of a reason to cancel or pick somewhere in the complete opposite direction to meet. She decided not to respond while she knew she was in the car with Sean; she would do that from Ryan's phone later. The third message was from her mother, just checking in as she hadn't heard from her in a while. She quickly replied to her mother that everything was good and that she would come and see her on the weekend sometime. She was sure Ryan wouldn't mind at all.

While she had her phone on, she wrote down some important numbers so when she got a new number, she didn't need to turn her phone on again for a little while. Hannah showed Ryan the messages to give him comfort that nothing bad had happened yet. She looked at Ryan and powered off her phone again. She put it in her bag and told herself to forget it was there. She was now starving and offered to go and heat up the soup and bread. Ryan followed her to the kitchen just to make sure she really was OK.

'How about you go take a nice hot shower and change into something comfy and I heat up the soup?'

Hannah stopped what she was doing and hugged Ryan. She had no idea how she was ever going to repay him for all that he had done for her so far. She thought fairy tales were for children, but she seemed to be having her own right now, and he was her knight in shining armour who had rescued her from the monster. She needed to think of something special she could do for him, and since she had the rest of the week off, she would plan something amazing for the weekend.

Chapter 51

I t's been twenty-four hours since Hannah had turned off her phone. She sat in the chair staring at her reflection in the mirror. She was nervous about the outcome of today's unplanned decision as she listened to the young girl go on about some new show that aired last night while she painted Hannah's hair and wrapped the sections in foil. And it still didn't seem real that she had actually escaped the only life she knew. There would be no more yelling at her or being told she was stupid or any other derogatory phrases. She believed Ryan didn't have it in him to ever be angry like that, and even if something made him cross, he would sit down and rationally discuss things, and he would never lay an angry hand on her. Looking like something from a sci-fi movie, she giggled at her reflection with all the foil pieces sticking up from her head and wondered what Ryan would think of her now looking like this.

The young girl offered Hannah a drink while she waited for the next thirty minutes until the next stage of her transformation. Hannah accepted and then retrieved a box that was in her bag and opened it. A new phone and a new number to go with her new look and her new life. The girl was back in a jiffy with a mug of instant coffee for Hannah and offered to plug the charger in under the counter so she could start playing with her new toy. Hannah smiled and thanked the girl for her help and set about getting the new SIM card inserted, which not surprisingly was taking a long time. The young girl came past on the way to the counter and laughed at Hannah, who was having all sorts of issues. Hannah handed her the phone, and in a few seconds, the girl had it all sorted and plugged in for her. Hannah put her head in her hands and laughed along with the girl, who patted her on the shoulder and exclaimed her mother also had issues working out technology. Hannah instantly looked up at herself in the mirror and wondered if she looked old enough to have an adult child. She didn't think so.

Approximately thirty minutes later, Hannah had the few important contacts keyed in and sent a message to Ryan letting him know her new number. He quickly responded with a 'congrats' and was about to go in a team meeting for the rest of the afternoon, so he would talk to her tonight. The young girl—whose name was Jazz, Hannah thought it important to know this, seeing she was about to transform her into someone new—ushered her to the sink and started pulling the foil pieces from her hair. Jazz then washed her hair and massaged her scalp. Hannah let out a small groan of appreciation and let her eyes roll to the back of her head. Jazz laughed at her and asked if she liked that. Hannah was in heaven; she felt the tension just melt away under Jazz's fingertips. Massage over and her head wrapped in a towel, Hannah sat back in the seat in front of the mirror. Jazz smiled at her through the reflection in the mirror and asked if she was ready to see the colour. Hannah nodded, and Jazz removed the towel. It was amazing; she never pictured herself as anything other than a dark brunette. Jazz ruffled the towel over her hair and started brushing.

Then came the scary part; she picked up a pair of scissors and some clips and started sectioning off her hair, and she could hear the snip of the blades coming together. Hannah closed her eyes and let it happen. It didn't seem to take long for Jazz to work her magic with the scissors as she felt the hot air of the dryer on the back of her neck. Hannah slowly opened her eyes and stared at the stranger in the mirror. She did not recognise herself, and she was overwhelmed with the transformation. She was a new person and could not have asked for a better result. She thanked Jazz multiple times while leaving the salon and promised to be back in a few weeks for a trim.

Next, she went into a small clothing store a few shops down from the salon and picked something off the rack she never would have ordinarily worn. She tried it on and was surprised how it fit, so she immediately bought it before she changed her mind.

Hannah was tired; it had been a big few days for her, and she knew she was emotionally drained. She jumped in a cab and went home. She opened the door and was greeted by Bruce, who had already accepted her into his home. She picked up the fluff ball and lay on the bed. He curled up next to her head, and they both went to sleep.

Chapter 52

Hannah woke up about ten minutes before Ryan was due home. She hadn't intended on sleeping that afternoon, but exhaustion took over and felt an uncontrollable desire to lie down. She went to the bathroom to splash some water on her face and to inspect the new hairdo. She loved it. It was short and dark blonde with red highlights, and the way it was cut, her natural curl became the star. She flicked her head a few times to watch how it moved and how it just fell perfectly around her face when she was still. She decided against wearing her new dress as she wanted to wear it on the weekend as part of her surprise for Ryan. She applied some lip gloss and smiled again at her reflection. She still couldn't believe how much happier she was in the past few days compared to how the last few years of her life had been. She heard the click of the key in the door, and she stood in the hall doorway leaning on the wall, looking all casual like. Ryan came in and immediately stopped to pet Bruce and then hung his coat up. He hadn't seen her at first, but the look on his face when he turned to find her was priceless.

'Oh wow,' was all he repeated for a good two minutes. He came over to her and pulled her close. He kissed her like it was the first time, and she kissed him back like it was to be the last time. Ryan stepped back and did a twirling motion with his hand, and Hannah pirouetted like a dancer so he could see all of her.

'You look incredible. Amazing! I didn't recognise you!' He walked past her and into the bedroom, where he kicked off his shoes and searched a drawer for his trackpants. 'So I guess I don't need to ask what you did today.'

Hannah flopped on the bed and watched him change. 'I didn't want to feel afraid to go out, so I thought if I changed my look, then it would be less likely he will notice me. I figured the hair should be the first thing to change, and then on the weekend, I thought I could go clothes shopping and get rid of the pieces he would recognise. I want to get on with our new life together and put the past behind me. I hope you don't mind.'

Ryan lay on the bed next to her. 'You don't ever have to ask me for permission to do things. As long as you are happy and don't lose who you are, then I am happy to support you. Maybe we could go out Saturday night to celebrate?'

Hannah grinned at Ryan and nodded. She pushed him onto his back, sat on his stomach, and pinned his arms down. 'So I don't need to ask permission, hey?'

'Never.'

'That's good to know.' She kissed his forehead, jumped off, and walked out of the room; from the kitchen, Ryan could hear cupboards opening. 'You hungry? I will get dinner started if you are.'

'Yeah, I am!' he yelled back and then under his breath added, 'But it wasn't dinner I was hoping to eat!' He got off the bed and joined Hannah in the kitchen. Together they cooked, ate, and cleaned up.

The conversation revolved around Ryan's day and what he actually did. She had never really asked in detail before and was interested. She hesitated a few times as she wanted to ask him something, and finally, he stopped talking about work and asked straight out, 'What is it you want to know? You've had this look ever since we finished dinner like you want to say or ask something, but you just haven't, and now curiosity is getting the better of me.' He leaned back in the couch so as not to appear intimidating and let Hannah take her time to talk.

'I wanted to ask if you went to the café for lunch. And if you did, if Lucy said anything to you. I really hope that I haven't made trouble for her is all.' Hannah's face showed a look of sorrow and regret; she hated the thought of putting her friend in an awkward and potentially ugly position. Ryan leaned forward and took Hannah's hand; his expression had softened, and she could tell he was looking for the right words.

'Yes, I went there for lunch as I was concerned for her too. I sat at my usual table and waited for her to be free. She came and brought me a drink and indicated to a table at the back where a man sat on his own. He just sat there and stared at the door. She didn't say anything else at that time as she didn't want to alert him that she was talking to me about you. She told me when I had finished lunch to go out the side door and wait around the back, and she would come and find me. I ate my lunch and left by the side door as Lucy had asked. She came out a minute later and told me what happened when he got there. She said that she was there at eleven as normal to open up, and he got there about ten to twelve. He was calm and not aggressive in any way. He asked what time you were supposed to start, and she gave him the story about you quitting by text and showed him the messages. She then continued your cover by asking him questions like what happened, if you were OK, if he knew where you were. Then she said that he was almost in tears and said you were just gone, so this was the first place he would check, knowing how much you loved working there. Then he ordered a coffee and sat at the table and was just there. Not talking to anyone or being a nuisance, but he was checking his phone every couple of minutes and what appeared to be dialling your number. I rang her just before my meeting to check in, and she said he was there until two. He asked her to call him if she hears from you, and he wrote his number on a piece of paper, then left quietly.'

Hannah was relieved that he hadn't gone in there all guns blazing and causing trouble for Lucy, and at the same time, she felt really sad that he was hurting. She hadn't really thought about how he would really feel; she just assumed that he would be angry and violent. Her thought quickly went to Amy, and then she panicked that he would take this out on her. She needed to see her and see for herself that she was OK.

'How about Saturday we go see your sister? I felt bad cancelling on her today, but I know she will understand when she knows the full reason why.'

'That's a great idea. We could catch up with her in the afternoon and then go for dinner or a movie or something in the evening.'

Hannah was happy. She knew there would still be hard days, but with Ryan by her side, getting through them wouldn't be impossible.

Chapter 53

At three in the morning, Hannah was still awake. There was one thing still bugging her. She knew Sean would have been trying to contact her, and she had turned her phone off two days ago. She had to know what the messages said. She slipped out of bed quietly, closed the bedroom door behind her, and went to the kitchen. She put on the kettle and found some chocolate hiding in the back of the fridge. She made a cup of tea and sat on the couch, armed with chocolate for comfort. She looked at her phone and felt a lump forming in the back of her throat. She pushed all emotion deep down and turned the phone on. She knew it would take a few minutes to load; she flicked the button on the side to mute so there wouldn't be any beeping that might wake Ryan. She knew if she really needed him to hold her hand through this process, he would be up in an instant, but she needed to do this part on her own. This was the consequence of her actions, and she needed to go through this part alone. She needed to read the messages and hear the voicemail and feel Sean's pain and anger. She needed to come back to reality for a while as she had let herself live in a fairy tale of sorts for the past few days, and she wasn't that naïve not to understand that someone had been hurt by her choices.

The next couple of minutes took forever, and her impatience grew. Finally, the phone was on, and she could see numbers flickering on the phone and message symbols. This was it—the moment she could no longer avoid. Fifty-six messages, and 171 missed calls. Hannah started with the text messages; she wasn't ready to hear his voice yet.

The first message, calm but demanding to know why she wasn't home. The next was getting angrier, but still not realising that she had left, just not home. Number three, angry and bordering abusive. And so it went on for around two hours after the first text was sent. A new message approximately every ten minutes; then it changed. The next few messages were of confusion. He had discovered her things were gone. The messages were soft and almost full of fear. She figured he had come to realise that he was now on his own. The messages started to make reference to voicemail and her not answering her phone. After around twenty or so messages, the text started to become garble; this was when she knew he had been drinking for a while. They didn't make a lot of sense, and she had to start guessing the words he was attempting to type as autocorrect was taking over, and it was incoherent. Then she got to message forty; now he was going from drunk and sorry to angry and bitter. According to Sean, Hannah was all sorts of things: a bitch, a whore, useless, ugly, a loser who deserves to die. She understood he was angry, and lashing out at her was the norm for him. The names were nothing she hadn't heard a hundred times before, so it didn't really bother her; she would have been more worried if the name-calling didn't happen.

It was the last four texts that shook Hannah. They were long texts and in very graphic detail described how he was going to hunt her down and kill her. She read these messages several times and realised that they were timestamped to just over an hour ago. He was angry, and she felt an element of fear; if he ever did find her, she knew that there was a real chance he would attack her, and she really couldn't say for sure if he would try to take her life. That would all depend on the circumstance of when they crossed paths.

Hannah put the phone down; she needed some time before she listened to his voice. She was shaking and unsettled. She finished her tea and ate a few squares of chocolate. She had read somewhere that eating chocolate releases endorphins that make you feel happy. She looked at her phone again and stuffed three more squares of chocolate in her mouth; she needed all the help she could get for the next stage, voicemail. Although there were over a hundred missed calls, there was only eight voicemail messages, and she was grateful for such a small number. She dialled the voicemail number, put the phone to her ear, and waited for the messages to play. They started the same as the texts, confused and sad turning to anger and ended with a death threat. His voice was chilling. He was very articulate. His words were considered and deliberate, and she couldn't hear any signs of him drinking; he knew exactly what he was saying and wasn't saying anything just for scare tactics. He meant everything he said. Hannah hung up the phone and fumbled as she tried to turn the phone back off. The last message—the very calm and detailed message—was left only a short time ago, not long before she got up to work through the messages.

She stood up and picked up her cup to take back to the kitchen; she placed it on the sink, and without warning, she started crying uncontrollably. She slowly sank to the floor with her back against the cupboard and wrapped her arms around her knees. She found it hard to breathe as she cried; her ribs ached, and she felt her brain starting to burn. Her lower back was starting to ache sitting on the cold kitchen floor, but she couldn't muster the strength to get herself up from the floor. She must have sat there for an hour, her head leaning on her knees and her arms wrapped around her legs, thinking about what she needed to do next. She was confused whether or not she should let Ryan hear the message; one path was he needed to know what Sean was capable of and if he still wanted her here knowing that, and the other side was to delete the messages and protect Ryan from as much of the bad stuff as she could. He didn't need to hear what was said; in fact, no one ever needed to know.

The pain in her back was becoming too much, and she released her grip on her legs and stretched. It hurt all the way from her lumbar down through her knees and into her calves. Her left calf seized up, and Hannah all of a sudden had to find the strength to get up so she could put weight on it and walk it out. She winced as she walked, and eventually, the paid subsided. She massaged it for a minute and then decided that she needed to go back to bed. Her brain hurt, and she was exhausted, and now her leg kept twitching. She was cold and started feeling sorry for herself. Quietly, she climbed back into bed next to Ryan and closed her eyes; her body started feeling heavy, and she let herself drift off to sleep.

Chapter 54

Dear Diary,

I was speaking to a counsellor today who suggested that I talk to you every day. She is a gentle lady, the counsellor, and she said that if I put down in writing all of the things in my head, it would help me transition to the next stage in my life. She said I should start with everything that has happened in my life so far that has caused me to get to this point. So here goes.

My name is Hannah, and I am thirty-two years old. I met my husband Sean when we were in school, and we were married soon after leaving. He is all I have ever known up until earlier this year. He would never let me work as he said my place was at home, making sure that he had everything he needed. I cooked, cleaned, did the shopping, and everything else that he deemed to be woman's work. At first I didn't mind as I thought I had a pretty cushy life. The other girls I went to school with all had to get jobs and do all the other stuff, yet I was lucky I had a man to provide for me. We lived a fairly simple life. Nothing fancy, and that suited us. He would have his mates around every couple of weekends to watch whatever was the match of the week. They'd all sit around drinking and carrying on, and I would stay in the kitchen and bring out food when it was demanded. After a couple of years, I got bored. No job, no friends, and felt like I had no existence outside of the apartment. I guess if we had lived in a house rather than an apartment, we may have had kids, and I really think that is the reason we never left. I don't think Sean ever wanted kids. He never said those exact words but would never want to talk about it either. I think after the last year, not having kids was a blessing. So a few years into the marriage, I was bored, and then the boys would come over and start at me. They would swear and carry on at the TV, and when I entered the room, they would slap me on the arse or just grab at me, and I hated that. So I would tell Sean to control them, and he would defend them. Oh my god, that would infuriate me. I was his wife, and he would defend their bad and inappropriate behaviour, and somehow I was always in the wrong, and I would get yelled at. And God forbid if I ever stood up for myself to them, I would get smacked. At first he would just grab my arm and drag me into the kitchen to yell at me, and then he couldn't be bothered going to another room to yell, so he would do it there in front of them. And if he had way too much to drink, he would push me around. There was one time one of his friends said something along the lines of him thinking I was sexy, and he wanted to do me. Well, Sean thought this hilarious and offered me as a prize. That's right, a prize. So they did a best of three arm wrestle, and Sean won. So instead of letting it go, he dragged me kicking and screaming at him to the bedroom when he took his prize with the door open for them to watch. I was so humiliated and angry, and I think that is when I really started wanting to get out. That incident would have been a bit over five years ago, and I never forgave him for that. So then it just became normal. He drank, he yelled, I yelled back, he pushed me, I cried and went to bed. Now don't get me wrong. It didn't happen every day or anything, but it wasn't an unusual situation, and his friends just got used to the way he treated me, and I never got to go anywhere with him as his wife. When his friends had parties or BBQs, I was always left at home. If it wasn't for the once a month family dinner at my parents' house or the person at the register at the supermarket, I wouldn't have any contact with another person. I tried to make it to the markets as many Sunday mornings as I could. The markets would have to be my most favourite place in the entire world. There is something about the noise and chaos that excites me. And the smells, oh wow, how the different smells were and used to make everything all better. There is a small bakery towards the back that makes the most amazing breads, and I would always take my time and weave through the aisles to get there. The fish sellers make me laugh. They yell and pick on each other, and they are almost like a circus the way they try to get the customers to come over. I could stand and watch them all day if I could get away with it. Now where was I? Oh yeah, my miserable existence shut away from the world. So then life just happened. Every day was the same as the last and every weekend came and went with nothing new ever happening. So I would ask myself over and over why don't I just leave? And it's a valid question with so many different answers. Now to the outside world, Diary, my answer probably would look like excuses. And unless you have lived it, you would never understand. Now that I am out, I see so many things I could have done differently or in some cases should have done, but I didn't. So what were my reasons for staying? He is my husband, and I promised myself to him until the day I die or something to that effect in our vows, so leaving would be breaking a promise. Other days I was too scared to leave, too scared of the outside world I knew little about. Where would I go? How would I pay for things? Would I find a new purpose for being here? And in the weeks that were calm and almost civil, I wouldn't think about leaving at all. Every day that went by with no yelling gave me hope that our 'bad patch' was over. Then there was that day I went to the markets that changed everything. That was the day I saw Ryan for the first time, and I don't know why I, forgive me for the cliché, fell in love at first sight. We were on opposite sides of the market, but when he looked at me, I knew straight away that I needed to leave and get out of this dark place I was in and start a new life. And because I thought the universe had it in for me, I find out that Sean cheated on me. I guess I could have lived with a one off, but to find out that he was starting a relationship with her was devastating. I mean what was I doing wrong that he needed someone else? I always did everything that I was told to do. I wasn't allowed to leave except to go to the supermarket. If he was unhappy, then his own damn fault. He created this life and certainly was the one controlling it, so why did he need to have another life on the side? I mean what the hell, right? And that's when for the first time that I could ever remember I wanted to hurt him badly, and I don't mean physically. I mean crush him emotionally and her. Who was she, and why does she want my husband? It's not like he was a great catch or anything unless you are into cavemen who treat you like crap. So of course she was going to be part of my grand plan to destroy Sean. So I did what now look like stupid things. I stalked her, stole her mail, took photos of her, and tried to work out how I could use her. Oh, and I quickly realised I make a bad stalker. I had no real idea on how to stalk someone or that what seemed like a dramatic finale to end it all was really just ridiculous and never would have achieved anything. If I'm going to make a career out of creating evil plans, then I might want to do a bit more research. So anyway, on with the story. Don't think I mentioned yet that I got myself a part-time job. It was working in a little café, and it's only three or so hours a day, but I absolutely love it. My boss Lucy is like one of the most wonderful people that I think has ever existed. So now my life has gone from non-existent to very complicated. I have a home life I hate, complete with an abusive husband, a new job which is to be a secret from him, his affair and the woman I am attempting to stalk, and a mystery man who is always on my mind. Keeping up, Diary? Good. Now my secret job is going along well. I'm making friends for the first time since school, and I feel like I have a purpose. Home is OK at the moment, and I am still doing a piss poor attempt at revenge. Then just to rock the boat, my mystery man happens to be a regular customer at the café, and now I am seeing him several times a week. So this could be a problem I hear you say, and yes, you are correct. So now I am getting to know him, falling for him when we spent some time together while Sean was away, and the more I talk to him, the more I know he is the one meant for me. Only upside to all this is that I had some pretty hot and steamy dreams, and with this new found libido, I reconnected with Sean in a way that hadn't happened in years. So to recap where we are at, one cheating husband, one secret job, and one new man in my life I want to be with. Now this is where it gets really complicated. Sean finds out about my job, but I managed to convince him that it was a good thing. I met the 'other' woman who happens to be Ryan's sister, and to top it off, I started to get to know her, and now we are friends! Bet you didn't see that one coming, Diary. So I couldn't tell her who her new boyfriend was, and according to her, he's just super (sorry for the sarcasm, but he really isn't super at all), and she starts counselling me on why I should leave an abusive relationship, lol. So now do you see the irony? It's funny really, don't you think? Life can be unpredictable. You make just one different decision one day, and everything changes. I chose to take a part-time job to try to stop myself from going completely insane, and now look where I am just a few months later. I am out of the marriage from hell and living with the most amazing man. Oops, I skipped ahead then, sorry. So let's take just a few steps back to a week ago. Sean goes on a trip with his mates and takes Amy (the new girlfriend) with him. I try my hand at stalking again. This time, Ryan, and this time, it went my way. I 'bumped' into him at a bar he was going to, and then I spent the weekend with him, and on the Sunday, I went and collected my stuff and moved in with Ryan. Now I know what you are thinking, Diary, and you might be right. How can you move from one relationship to another like that? My counsellor talked to me about taking some time to grieve the end of my marriage. I thought this an odd thing to say, but as she explained, we should always take the time to grieve the end of something almost like it died, and that is what the end of a marriage is, a death of a relationship. But I figure that Ryan knew my situation before asking me to live with him, so he is aware I have some baggage, and there may be a time or two that I am going to need some alone time to sort things out in my head. And before you judge me, I didn't accept Ryan's offer lightly. If I had somewhere else to go or had a job that paid enough for me to rent my own place, I would have taken that option, but I didn't, so here I am. I think the hardest thing that I need to accept is Sean's anger about me leaving. He got home, and I just wasn't there. I didn't even leave a note offering an explanation. I was just, well, gone. I don't feel guilty about leaving as I believe I needed to for survival. Is that wrong that I don't feel bad at all? I don't know how I am supposed to feel, and I guess sometimes I overthink this stuff and try to force myself to feel the way I think other people think I should. I have cried a few times randomly, and it's not from sadness, but it's from relief and exhaustion. The feeling of being free is very overwhelming at times, so I let it come out in tears, and then I feel back in control, and I am hoping that the outbursts will become few and far between in the next few weeks. I guess I should tell you about the messages now. Last night at about three, I turned on my old phone to read and hear the messages from Sean. At first they were OK. Then they got angry. Then he got drunk, and they made little sense. But the ones at the end were scary, like straight from a horror movie except they were real, and his last voice message I can never unhear. He wasn't drunk. He had an eerie calm to his voice. He spoke slowly and was very articulate. His words were very deliberate and almost rehearsed, but I guess he had been saying them over and over in his head before he left the message. He went into great detail about how the next time he saw me, how he would end my life. Hearing it sent chills through my whole body, and now I have this paranoia which forces me to constantly look over my shoulder even inside the house. The thought of leaving the house makes me nauseous, and my hands shake. He doesn't know where I am now, and I am praying that he doesn't find me randomly as I believe everything he said in that message. And the most horrible thought I have is knowing he is capable of killing me, and I don't think he would hesitate if he got the chance. I've seen the look in his eyes when he is angry and been on the wrong end of his bad moods, and that is absolutely nothing compared to this message. This message is why I have to talk to Ryan about leaving the state. Knowing that Sean is out there and will always be looking for me, as he reiterated I belong to him, and he will hunt me down. So I can't stay, and while I am here in Ryan's house, he is not safe either. If Sean ever found me with Ryan, he will kill him too. This I am sure of. So, Diary, this is my story so far. Do you have any advice for me?

Chapter 55

Another night had passed, and Hannah hadn't left the house again. She woke early this Saturday morning; her body ached from the panic attacks and the relentless anxiety. She gently got out of the bed and showered. She made the water hotter than normal in hopes that it would relieve the aching. She didn't dress straight away after drying herself in a very fluffy oversized towel; she just put her robe back on and went to the kitchen for breakfast. She looked at the time, and it was a little after six. She was exhausted and seemed to wake more tired than when she went to sleep. She made a coffee, sat on the couch, and put the TV on. There was not much on at this time of the day, but she did manage to find some re-runs of some old Eighties sitcoms and settled in for some mindless watching. One coffee down and she was ready for another. She went back to the kitchen and made a second cup. Then she went back to the sofa.

This time, she thought about today; they were meeting Amy mid-afternoon at a new café that made hot chocolates with hot milk and melted chocolate. Ryan had heard about it from someone at work and just had to go and try it, and it wasn't far from home. She could feel another panic attack building as she thought about what to wear and how long she would be out, but she managed to control this one. Her counsellor had suggested she research some breathing techniques to help control the panic when she felt it coming on. Hannah was pleased with the result after this minor attack, and she was sure if she kept using the techniques she had learnt, she would be back to normal very soon. She was looking forward to returning to work on Monday; she missed the staff and especially Lucy, and she craved the social interactions. Ryan had given Lucy Hannah's new phone number, and they had been in contact every day. Lucy said she would start Hannah in the kitchen to start with until she was confident to work the floor again. Hannah checked her new phone for messages, and there was an unread text; curious, she opened her phone and saw a love note from Ryan around the same time they were getting ready for bed last night. She felt warm and safe again and so much in love.

It made her wonder if Sean had left any more message on her old phone. Using the strength she just gained from Ryan's text, she found the old phone and turned it on. She was confident that he would not be trying to ring her at this time on a Saturday morning. She hated the minute or so it took for the phone to start up and search for messages. And there was the familiar beep of messages loading. Four new messages and only six missed calls with no voicemail. Hannah checked the call log, and only four of the missed calls were Sean's, and there was one each night at around the same time. The other two were those of her mother, who never left voicemail. She opened the messages and immediately went to her mother's text just confirming Hannah was coming to see them on the weekend. Then to Sean's three messages. The first one was jumbled, so she figured he had been drinking, but she thought he was trying to say sorry but couldn't be certain. The second one was a simple question. 'Why?' And the third was weird; she wasn't sure what to make of it. It wasn't an apology or a threat, but almost sad. 'It's hurts to let go, but sometimes it hurts more to hold on.' Did this mean he was letting her go, and it was over? Surely, after the chilling threat a few days before, he wasn't just going to let her go that easy. She hoped that he would, but she knew him better than that. She powered the phone off again; she wouldn't risk having it turned on any longer than she needed to.

Hannah lay on the couch and turned her attention back to the TV, and Bruce came to join her. He curled up in front of her chest and purred so loudly she couldn't hear the people talking. She didn't want to wake Ryan, so she just watched them, only hearing a few words of each sentence. The sound of the cat purring was hypnotic, and without realising it, Hannah fell fast asleep.

'Hey, sleepyhead' was what Hannah woke to. She slowly opened her eyes and was disorientated for a moment. She lifted her head, and as her eyes focused, she realised that she had been sleeping on the couch.

'Hi,' she responded while stretching and yawning. 'What time is it?' Hannah sat herself up and rubbed her eyes and then the back of her neck. Bruce jumped down and also stretched; he looked at Ryan and yawned.

'It's midday. I thought you might be getting hungry, so I have made lunch.'

Hearing the time and that she had slept the entire morning away, Hannah panicked and stood up. 'Why didn't you wake me earlier?'

'Well, the two of you looked so cute sleeping together, I didn't have the heart to disturb you until now. And I also know that you haven't been sleeping well, so I wanted you to get some rest. I figured you needed it, but since it is now the afternoon and we are meeting Amy at three, I thought I had better wake you up.' Ryan walked to the kitchen and picked up a large plate. 'It's beautiful outside, so I thought we could eat out there, but you might want to get dressed first. It is a little on the cool side still.'

Hannah looked down at herself and saw the robe, so she nodded at Ryan and went to the bedroom to dress. She found some trackpants, a jumper, and slippers. She opened the back door and squinted as the bright sun hit her eyes. She shielded her eyes with her hand and went to join Ryan at the table and cast her eye over the platter he had prepared for lunch. It looked delicious, filled with cold meats and cut-up vegetables, cheese and crackers, and some fruit just to finish it off. Hannah hungrily picked from the platter, and with the warm sun on her neck, she felt like she was in paradise. They spent nearly two hours sitting and talking in the sun. Hannah could have spent all afternoon just doing this, but she knew when Ryan said they should get ready to go, he was right. She didn't want to be late to meet Amy, who was always on time.

At three o'clock exactly, Hannah and Ryan walked into the restaurant and scanned the tables for Amy. There she was at the counter, collecting menus. She turned around when Ryan called, and her smile was so big that it made several people stop and look at her. With menus in hand and a skip in her step, she came over to the two of them and hugged them tight.

'Oh, it's so good to see you again, Hannah!' Amy said while just about squeezing the life out of her. 'I'm so happy you are out of that bad place and with someone who worships the ground you walk on.' She said the last part a bit louder so Ryan would hear; he raised an eyebrow at her. 'Well, it's true.' Amy continued, 'You do and don't you ever try to deny it!' She let Hannah go and took her hand as they walked outside and found a table. Amy sat down and looked at Hannah and studied her. Hannah suddenly became self-conscious as she remembered Amy hadn't seen her new hairstyle yet. 'I like it,' Amy finally said. Hannah smiled and looked to Ryan for reassurance; he responded with a nod. 'Oh, and I thought today would be a good day for you to finally meet my boyfriend too.' Hannah froze; her heart beat so loud that she could hear it in her ears. Amy looked up and smiled again and waved. 'Here he is.'

Chapter 56

Ryan got up from his seat and turned around. He saw Sean come in and walk towards them. Ryan recognised his face but couldn't place where he knew him from. As Sean reached the table, Amy hugged and kissed him; she held his arm and then extended her other arm to Ryan.

'Ryan, this is Sean.' Her face beamed, and she introduced the two men in her life to each other. All of a sudden, it came to Ryan who he was and why Hannah sat as if she was glued to her chair. Sean put out his hand, ready to shake Ryan's; he reluctantly responded. Amy then turned to Hannah to keep the introductions going when she was stunned by the look on Hannah's face. It was of pure terror; she had never seen someone look so frightened. Sean finished his pleasantries with Ryan and looked over at Hannah; at first, he didn't recognise her, and then it hit him. His whole body language changed, and they just stared at each other. Hannah was still stuck to her chair, so afraid to move, and she was barely breathing.

Sean moved around the table behind Amy and stood in front of Hannah. Amy was confused as she watched this interaction; she put her hand on Sean's arm, and he shook it off. He leaned over close to Hannah, and in an eerily deep voice, he said, 'Hello, Hannah. I like the new look. I didn't recognise you at first, but I guess that was the point, huh?'

Sean grabbed Hannah by the arm and pulled her up out of her chair. 'I think we need to talk, don't you?' Then he yanked at her arm to get her to walk away from the table. Amy, who still hadn't put it all together, grabbed at Sean.

'What's going on, Sean? Would you let Hannah go please?' Amy turned back to Ryan, who wasn't sure what to do; he was weary not to antagonise Sean as he didn't want him to hurt Hannah, and knowing that Hannah left without even a note, Sean was going to want some answers. Ryan looked around and saw it was reasonably busy, so he felt OK that he wouldn't do anything in public; and as long as they stayed close by where Ryan could see them, he would let this conversation happen. Ryan came to Amy's side and sat her down; he needed to explain who Sean was to Hannah and why the sudden confrontation. Before Ryan could get Amy to sit back at the table, Amy started to follow Sean; and this time, she really grabbed at his arm to get him to stop and answer her. Sean spun suddenly and glared at Amy.

'I need to talk to my wife!' He still had hold of Hannah's arm in a vice-like grip. Amy couldn't believe what she had just heard as Hannah's husband used to beat her, and Sean was far too gentle to be like that. It just couldn't be true. Not wanting to accept that statement, Amy grabbed Sean's arm again.

'What do you mean your wife? I don't understand.' Amy's voice was shaky, and she was on the brink of crying. Sean turned back to Amy and shook her hand off him again, and this time, he pushed her backwards and raised his voice.

'This is my ungrateful whore of a wife who decided one day to just leave! She owes me an explanation, and I want it now!' He turned back to Hannah and jerked her forward again to make her walk away from the table. Amy fell backwards from being pushed and stumbled on a chair as she tried to balance herself, and she hit the ground hard on her bottom. She yelped in pain and grabbed at her stomach, and then the tears came. Ryan rushed to her aid and tried to lift her up, but Amy couldn't move. He could see her in pain, and the tears were streaming down her face.

In between gasping for air, she looked at her brother and whispered, 'I think he hurt the baby.'

Ryan panicked for the first time, stood over his sister, and moved the chair that had fallen back onto its legs. He put his arm under hers, gently lifted her to her feet, and slid the chair under her so she could sit. She was in so much pain, and he wasn't sure what to do next. He looked over his shoulder and saw Sean and Hannah a few tables away. They were standing up, and Sean held Hannah by both her shoulders and seemed to be shaking her; he could hear him yelling at her but couldn't make out what he was saying. And he couldn't really see Hannah as she was behind Sean, but Ryan was too focused on his little sister. He pulled his phone out of his pocket and started fumbling with it. A waitress came over to him and said she had called for an ambulance and the police. She handed Amy a glass of water and asked Ryan if he needed something. He was trying to take it all in but shook his head and kneeled in front of Amy. He looked so worried. Amy had stopped crying and assured him she was OK.

'I wanted to tell you all today about the baby, which is why I got him to come too. I didn't know he was married, Ryan. I didn't know he was Hannah's husband. You have to believe me.' She started crying again, and Ryan pulled a chair next to her and sat down. He put his arm around her in comfort when they heard a scream. The both looked in Hannah's direction and still could only see Sean's back. They could just see a bit of Hannah, and she was still standing with Sean. Ryan looked closer and saw one lady patron scramble away from her table in shock. Amy and Ryan looked at each other as neither could make out what the screaming was about. Amy looked at her brother and said, 'Go to her, Ryan. Make sure she is OK.'

Ryan stood up and walked around the few tables between him and Hannah. He stood to the side of the two of them, when Sean looked to side and met his eye.

'You want her? She's all yours!' And with a mighty effort, he pushed Hannah towards Ryan, and she fell in a slump to his feet. Ryan fell to his knees to help her, and in his peripheral vision, he saw Sean walk out of the restaurant.

Chapter 57

Hannah was frozen in the chair. Did she just hear Amy say Sean was here? She felt her heart beating in her ears, and her stomach was in her throat. Her skin went cold, and she found it difficult to breathe. She felt Ryan stand up and heard Amy introduce Ryan to Sean, but she didn't dare look up. She could hear some minor pleasantries, and she could see out of the corner of her eye Amy shuffle down the table to be standing directly in front of her, ready to introduce her to Sean. As she felt eyes watching her, she looked up to meet Sean's gaze. He initially went to offer his hand as you do when you meet someone new, and then she saw the change in his look and stance when he realised it was her. He held her eye contact and moved behind Amy to stand next to her. Hannah's body felt like cement, and she still couldn't move. Sean leaned in close, and she could smell coffee on his breath.

'Hello, Hannah. I like the new look. I didn't recognise you at first, but I guess that was the point, huh?' Sean grabbed Hannah by the arm and pulled her up out of her chair. 'I think we need to talk, don't you?' Then he yanked at her arm to get her to walk away from the table. Hannah stumbled a little as she forced her heavy legs to move. She could hear Amy behind her say something to Ryan, but the beating of her heart was still so loud in her ears that she couldn't make out what was said. Sean shoved her again, and the grip he had on her arm was stinging as her skin was twisting under his fingers. Again forced to stop as Amy spoke to Sean, and this time, he heard Sean yell at her, 'I need to talk to my wife!'

Hannah cringed at that statement, and she knew Amy would be confused. Hannah felt her heartbeat slowing down, and she stood there, and she turned back to look at Amy.

'What do you mean your wife? I don't understand.' Amy's voice was shaky, and she was on the brink of crying. Hannah's heart sank as she could hear the hurt in her friend's voice.

'This is my ungrateful whore of a wife who decided one day to just leave! She owes me an explanation, and I want it now!' He turned back to Hannah and jerked her forward again to make her walk away from the table. Hannah stepped forward and again turned over her shoulder when she saw Amy stumble and fall over a chair that was behind her. Hannah went to turn her body so she could go to her aid, but Sean's grip on her arm tightened, and he pulled her sharply away. After passing several tables, Sean stopped and twisted Hannah's arm to force her to face him. She tried to look past him to see if Amy was OK, so Sean grabbed her by the shoulders and stood in front of her to block her view.

'Stop looking at them and look at me!' His voice was angry and his grip tight. 'Who the hell do you think you are leaving me like that? I come home, and you are gone! Your phone turned off and you quit your job. But now I see the truth. You stupid little whore. You left me for him?' Sean pulled her close to him, and his face was barely an inch away from hers. 'So did you really think you would get away with this? I told you I would hunt you down and make you pay for this betrayal. And how easy did you make it? See, your plan just came undone, and you came to me.' He lowered his voice and stared deep into her eyes. 'Tell me, how long you have been planning this?'

Hannah struggled to get words out. Her throat was dry. 'You have some nerve accusing me of betrayal when you were just introduced to us as Amy's boyfriend.' Hannah surprised herself; the words just came out, and as she heard herself talk, she felt the fear leave her body. She felt strong and needed to stand up to him. 'I've known about you and Amy for months, so don't you dare try to come across as the victim here! I saw the texts, I saw you at her house taking her flowers, and I know you took her away with you last weekend!' Hannah straightened her posture and spoke with conviction; she was finally calling him out on his affair, and it felt good. For so long, she had wanted to yell at him, 'I know about you!' But she couldn't, and now after all these months, she found the strength within to confront him. She saw Sean's face turn red with anger, and she knew he had no idea that Hannah had so much knowledge about the intimacy of his affair.

Hannah continued, 'I decided to befriend Amy just so I could find out everything that had been going on, and you were so ignorant and self-absorbed you had no idea that I knew everything and was watching your every move. From the overtime at work, which never existed, to the Saturday afternoon where you were supposedly watching sport at Dave's.' Hannah smirked at Sean, who hadn't said a word in defence. 'So, Sean, who the hell do you think you are?' Hannah and Sean just stood there for a minute without a word being spoken. Then it happened. Then the whole game changed.

Hannah heard a lady scream. She could feel the breath leave her body; she gasped but couldn't get any air back in. Her vision was starting to blur. She put her hands to her throat and frantically tried to pry Sean's fingers loose, but his grip was so tight that she couldn't. The world around her started to fade to the background, like she was disappearing into the darkness. She could make out shapes moving around her and voices talking, but they seemed to be drifting off into the distance, and she just couldn't make them out anymore.

She moved her eyes to look to the right of her and could make out Ryan; his image was burned in her brain, and she knew he had come over to once again rescue her. There he was, her knight; the sun shone on him, and he glowed like an angel. She felt her body relax, and she smiled at him as the final breath inside her left her lungs, never to return. Her body was heavy, and she could no longer hold herself up. The light faded. She blinked slowly one last time, and then there was nothing.

Free preview:

Hannah married Sean right out of high school. They were childhood sweethearts, and she thought he was perfect. He was strong and smart; everyone liked him, and he liked her. They were great together, so it was no surprise when they married and moved into their own apartment. It wasn't too long into the marriage when life became boring. Sean still worked for the same construction company, and Hannah was still his housewife. She couldn't remember when exactly the arguing started. He was probably drunk on a Friday night after drinks with the boys at the local pub; she was bored and started nagging at him the moment he walked in the door, and now it was just part of their routine.

On the way to the library, Hannah passed a quaint little café. It was small on the inside and always smelled great; they had a nice garden down the side, where there were tables and chairs for diners to enjoy their meals outside. It was nothing fancy, but was always filled to the brim at lunchtime. As she walked by, something caught her eye—a sign in the window stating 'Help Wanted – Enquire Inside'. This got Hannah's attention, and for the first time, she wandered inside. Hannah waited patiently in line, all the time looking around and taking it all in. The floors were wooden, the walls exposed brick with various pieces of art hanging in no particular order, big windows in the front, and a side door leading out to the tables outside. There was music playing in the background; it seemed to be current music. *The radio perhaps*, she thought. The tables were wooden with matching chairs and in the centre had a small vase with a coloured flower. Although the place seemed full of people, it wasn't overly noisy. Hannah had a great feeling about this place, and when she got to the front of the line, she was just about bursting with excitement at the thought of working here.

'Hi, what can I get for you?' said a cheery young girl.

'I'm here about the "Help Wanted" sign in the window,' Hannah replied, trying to keep her enthusiasm in check.

'Hey, cool. Let me just go grab the manager for you. I'll just be a sec.' Then the young girl disappeared into the kitchen. A short moment later, an older lady—maybe in her mid-fifties—appeared with a welcoming smile.

'Hello, I'm Lucy. Thank you for coming in. Please come and take a seat over here, and let's have a chat.' Lucy gestured to a small table in the corner, and Hannah immediately felt relaxed. 'So . . .,' Lucy started and looked at Hannah with a questioning glance.

'Hannah.'

'So, Hannah, please tell me a bit about yourself and why you would like to work here.'

Hannah sat up straight, folded her hands together on the table, and smiled at Lucy. 'Well, I'm 32 and been a housewife all my life, and I really think now is the time I did something for myself. I don't have any qualifications or experience, but I can promise I will work really hard, and I won't let you down if you give me a chance.' Hannah blurted it all out in one breath. She didn't think about what she was going to say; it just sort of came out. Lucy sat back in the chair and smiled at Hannah.

'I like you. You have enthusiasm and a friendly face. The job is Monday to Friday for the lunch shift, three hours a day, maybe a little more, depending on the crowd. You would start by learning the till and getting orders to the kitchen, and when you have got the menu under control, you would rotate with the others waiting and clearing tables. How does that sound?'

'Just perfect! I can't wait! When do you want me to start?'

Lucy laughed. 'Come in a bit before opening on Monday, and we will show you what you need to do and get your training started.' Lucy stood up and extended her hand to Hannah. 'Welcome to the team, Hannah.' Lucy took Hannah's hand in both of hers and held it just for a second. 'You will need a plain white T-shirt, black pants or skirt, and comfy shoes. Think you can manage that?'

'Easy done, and I will see you Monday!'

Hannah left the café on top of the world. This was to be her secret; there was no need to cause trouble by telling Sean as she already knew what he would say. He would forbid it. In his mind, he was the man, and the man was the income earner. She, being the woman, should be home looking after him. Hannah didn't understand why his mindset was stuck in the Fifties, but it just was. She was convinced he needed to control her, and keeping her at home was his way of staying in control. With a skip in her step, she continued on her way.

Printed in the United States
By Bookmasters